Raine

Bekky Crandlemire

LOCAL AUTHOR

Copyright © 2011 Bekky Crandlemire

All rights reserved.

ISBN:1466349387
ISBN-13:9781466349384

I DEDICATE THIS BOOK TO MY FAMILY,

ELDON, MOLLY, JAKE AND ELLY
XOX

CONTENTS

Acknowledgments

BOOK ONE – UNAWARE

BOOK TWO - UNVEILED

ACKNOWLEDGMENTS

AS THIS IS MY FIRST NOVEL I HAVE SOME VERY SPECIAL PEOPLE TO THANK.

MOST IMPORTANTLY MY MOM, FOR BACKING ME EVERY STEP OF THE WAY AND HELPING WITH THE EDITING AND ANYTHING ELSE I ASKED OF HER.

MY SISTER KASSIE AND DAUGHTER MOLLY FOR THEIR FAST READING AND SUPPORTIVE CRITISIM.
MY DEAR FRIENDS TONYA AND SAM FOR LENDING ME THEIR EYES AND EARS DURING THE PROJECT.

AND FINALLY MY HUSBAND FOR TOTALLY UNDERSTANDING WHEN DINNER WASN'T MADE AND LAUNDRY WASN'T DONE.

BOOK ONE - UNAWARE

Chapter 1

Sleep pulls at me from the far corners of my mind. So tired that delirium has almost set in. I keep telling myself not to let go, don't let the darkness take me in. I know once I am there, the control is given over and I have no choice but to watch all that happens before me.

I can barely keep my eyes open; even 2 pots of coffee and caffeine pills don't seem to help. I have tried so very many things, exercise, prescription drugs, illegal drugs and still I can only manage at the most 72 hours before I must submit to the unconscious.

I have lost so many people over the years, some stuck it out with me longer than others but the end result is always the same. My "sickness" has driven them all away. To be perfectly honest, I can't even remember most of their names. My reality now is to just stay awake; awake and somewhat sane.

To pass me on the street you probably wouldn't guess that I am a walking zombie. Not really, but that's how I feel. I seem quite ordinary in every way. Nothing makes me stand out or apart from the thousands of people that make up this city. Average height, dark brown hair, kept short and green eyes. I remember in high school we were asked to tell our best feature to the class as some sort of self esteem building work shop. I said my eyes. At one time they were so alive and sparkled with life and anticipation of what life was going to bring my way.

I see myself in my pretty pale yellow bedroom I painted with my mom on my 14th birthday. I loved color and would change the color of my room and my hair as often as possible. The walls were decorated with posters of my favourite supernatural movies as I was obsessed with anything that was weird and unexplainable. The wall facing the window was full of pictures, all of my family and friends smiling and laughing and I, smack in the middle of the crowds enjoying every second of life. It was so simple then; my biggest worries were school finals and what dress to wear to prom. Wow, has time changed everything.

Now sitting on the edge of my old couch unable to stand any longer, I see what my life has become. Looking around my old crappy apartment with its ugly gray walls and cracking plaster. I long for those simpler times, for the life I used to have.

8:05 am the clock on the stove blinks. Tuesday I think. I should be getting ready for work at the bank, my first real job out of high school. I enjoyed working there, interacting with everyone and really being a part of society. I was good at it too; always polite and kind even to the most stubborn and rude customers. I thought I would work there until I met a great guy, got married and had a couple children. That's all I ever wanted to be, a mom and have what everyone else had. I don't think I was being greedy, just a plain and simple life. I still find myself daydreaming about that future, knowing now that it could never happen to someone as screwed up as me.

Now with my savings all gone and every credit card maxed out, I have no choice but to live in this dump and collect my disability cheque every month. Yes, I am technically considered disabled because I cannot work and be a contributing member of society. Let me tell you, that does a lot to ones self-esteem.

I should look up that teacher that gave us that exercise in high school and ask her what I should do next. I have no idea! Walk, that's what I will do next. Just make my body get up and out the door, which always keeps me awake for a while longer. Maybe someone on the street will catch my attention and get my brain motivated to be alert for an hour or two. See, I play this game with myself and make up stories for the strangers I cross paths with. Sometimes I follow them and see how close to reality I am. It ends up most people are pretty boring and really lack any sense of adventure. That is the life I once wanted.

Once I caught a man cheating on his wife. I watched him at the park say goodbye to his children and kiss his wife. I followed and saw him three blocks down grab a bleach blonde about half his age and start making out with her right on the street. I had a moment of moral dilemma as to whether I should go inform the wife but realized what could I possibly say to her?

"I was watching you and your family and then followed your husband and saw him kissing some tramp on the street." I don't think so.

I try very hard to not draw attention to myself and that definitely would. I do better in the shadows, where I am unnoticed. I thought often about committing myself to a mental institution but know they can't help me. I don't want to be analyzed and drugged beyond me knowing what is reality and what isn't. The things I see and hear in the "in-between" as I call it are as real as you and me. I feel them to the depths of my soul and ache to stay there. Don't get me wrong it scares me to death. That place is dark and so deep and seems to suck you in and not let you go. All but me of course, I am there, not ever to stay but never to really be apart either. It's like watching a movie for four years, one I cannot tell anyone about. I can't touch or move anything, they don't hear my cries. I have given myself a title in this other realm "ghost spectator"; that's what I feel like there.

In truth that's what I feel like here as well. The craziest part is that I feel more comfortable in that reality; I belong there in all the chaos. They don't know I am there, watching.

At first I would hide and be as quiet as humanly possible afraid they would find me and the creatures would torture me as they do to anything that gets in their way. I eventually figured out that I could do pretty much anything I wanted and they never even noticed me. I would scream and throw things and nothing. After this much time I have studied their every move, these creatures of the darkness. Their twisted misshapen forms, minimal brain power and unrelenting cruelness. I know their names and know who is aligned with whom in their great war.

Yes, war. It has been going for hundreds of years and continues to this day with no end in sight. I do not know what the battle is over just that both sides want something of great value and neither seems close to acquiring it.

When I had my first visit in the dark realm I thought it was just a nightmare, a terrifying crazy nightmare. I woke screaming and crying, the creatures terrified me so much. After a couple weeks of the bad dreams, my parents had enough and sent me to a shrink. The middle aged pudgy man put me on sleeping pills and analyzed every aspect of my life, week after week. After months of no rest and the pills not even touching my mind, the shrink came to a conclusion. I was severely abused as a child and should be heavily medicated because I should be considered dangerous. If I was to ever act on these twisted "fantasies" I would put myself and those around me in great danger.

That is when I moved out, so as not to frighten everyone around me. The funny thing is, these "nightmares" never made me feel violent or suicidal. I knew I wasn't dangerous but everyone else believed the expert and not me.

At first I managed okay, keeping my job and just letting myself go to this other world at night when sleep was needed. The thing is, it is not sleep. I know that now. My body does shut down but my mind is still wide awake. I don't get the REM sleep that is needed to get real rest. I have not felt real sleep in so very long. I know that makes little sense when we are taught you need REM to survive. I am here and somewhat sane, and not sure why.

The hallucinations began a few months after moving out on my own. The first time is still vividly clear to me. I was on my way to work one beautiful sunny morning and waiting to cross the street. The sky suddenly turned black as night and the earth began to heave under the pavement. The concrete broke away like a child breaking a Lego building. Cars careened every which way, people were screaming and running for their lives. And there I stood staring, unable to move or even breathe. That is when I realized I was once again a spectator but this time I know I was awake. I tried to scream or reach out to someone or something but couldn't. Around me was pure chaos and yet I stood unmoving.

I remember looking down at my hands and caught sight of my watch. I watched as the hands slowly moved and counted to myself 1, 2, 3... and when I got to the count of ten a flash of brilliant white light exploded all around me. I blinked and everything was back to normal. Again I was standing there waiting for the crosswalk sign to change. The same man stood beside me in his business suit completely oblivious to what had just happened.

These daytime hallucinations happened again and again. The same scene of chaos and destruction while at the bank or in the laundry mat. Each time I was completely immobile for the ten seconds and then the white light, I blink and everything put back in place as if nothing had happened. This is when I had to give up my job, my life; I was too terrified to even leave my apartment for weeks.

Now all I want is to sleep, go to the place where I am not seen or heard where I can watch my horror movie in peace. That is why I must keep moving and in this reality as much as possible.
Splitting my mind between here and there is just too much. There, is death and destruction and where I want to be but cannot stay. When I come back to this life I feel so totally devastated and disappointed. I feel as if I break into tiny pieces when the darkness releases me and it takes me too long to put myself back together. Why would I rather be a ghost than a living and breathing person? Because there I am in the shadows

learning and caring about what happens, here I care for nothing. I love no one and no one cares for me. Even though the creatures don't know of my existence I feel a complete sense of belonging.

"Raine, Raine !"

I hear from across the street, breaking me out of myself. God, I haven't heard my name spoke in so long. I almost forgot I had one. I automatically look in the direction of the person calling to me. I see a short bob of fire red hair and an arm waving at me enthusiastically. I recognize her but cannot place her face or remember her name. I quickly plaster on my best fake smile and give a little wave back.

As soon as I give the girl this recognition she comes bounding towards me, life and happiness exuding from her every move. I turn ever so slightly to make a run for it as I am suddenly frightened of the little redhead. What does she want with me? Is this a trap to take me away to the mental institution? Who would have sent her? Why does she look so familiar?

She gets to me then, I cannot run, that would be something a crazy person would do. I notice she is not as petite as I first thought; we stand about the same height and look to be about the same age. She is dressed in a fitted pretty blouse with tight designer looking jeans. Her beautiful red hair makes her stand apart and obviously get noticed. As I study her for some clue as to who she is her arms go around me in a tight bear hug. I have not been touched by anyone in a very long time, it jars me and I am not sure how to react. She starts to babble on as she releases me from her grasp; I catch a couple words here and there. Something about high school and how she barely recognized me. Ha, something is triggered in the back of my mind. Julie, her name is Julie and we were friends in high school. She looks the same, except in more expensive clothes. Her beautiful round face full of freckles open and friendly as ever. I take a quick glance down at my own clothes and realize I look more homeless than anything else. My ripped and worn blue jeans that fit like old jogging pants and my army jacket I bought at the thrift store for its warmth and plain look. Anything to blend in. Concern crosses Julie's face while she looks at me as if waiting for a reply. I take a wild guess and say,

"Fine, how are you?"

This must have been the appropriate response as the crease between her brown eyes fades away. We talk small talk for a couple more minutes and I find out she just moved back to town and is working in a law office downtown. She recently got engaged and is planning a summer wedding. When she asks what I have been up to I turn on the fake smile and make up a fascinating story about working for a non-profit organization helping youth get their act together and off the streets. Thus the explanation for my outfit.

I go on about how this fills my life with such purpose and can't imagine doing anything else. As the words pour freely from my mouth I can't believe what a good liar I have become. I guess when you have no one to answer to it gets pretty easy. Just as we are about to part ways I stop and grab her rather abruptly. I don't know what possessed me to do it. I heard the words coming out of my mouth before I could stop myself.

"How do I look different? You said you barely recognized me. What does that mean?"

Julie turns slowly to meet my gaze. This time when our eyes met she looks sad and a little guilty.

"I was just so far away and couldn't really see you and..."

"Please don't lie, I want the truth."

She sucks in her breath and says,

"Well Raine, you look very tired…"

(Yes I know that!)

" and well, your eyes they aren't the same. I don't know how else to put it, you just look empty".

We stand staring at each other in complete silence for a couple seconds and then I release her arm and turn without a word. I won't say I am hurt or angry even. I am surprised that someone who I barely know could see that in me. I think she's standing and watching as I walk away because I hear no noise behind me. I feel a little guilty for making Julie say those words to me. I know she didn't expect our conversation to take such a turn; exchanging pleasantries was probably the extent to most of her interactions. I remember she never had a bad word to say about or to anyone.

Empty. Well there you go! Am I really? I have been describing myself as a ghost and ghosts are empty, aren't they? Isn't that how I have been living my life? To hear it spoken to you is a little unnerving… thinking I was going thru this world as invisible and then the first person I speak to in months hits the nail on the head like that kinda screws with my already screwed up head.

As I walk, the exhaustion hits me again in a wave, this time almost knocking me to the ground. I catch myself on a bench along the sidewalk and quickly sit before I fall. I put my face in my hands and will myself awake.

As I sit and think about my latest encounter a feeling of unbelievable dread hits me like a Mac truck. Every part of my body is screaming for me to run and escape whatever is about to happen. My body won't cooperate as I sit, unmoving. My immediate thought is that I have fallen asleep on this bench and I have jumped into my darkness, my alternate reality, but it is not dark here. There are no screams or shadows of other world creatures, just the bench and the street as cars go by and everyone goes about their day. A second thought that comes to mind is this is one of my hallucinations, but I am not frozen just stuck and no one is running for their lives. I count to ten anyway, just in case and wait for the bright white light to save me. Nothing.

My skin begins to tingle with panic and my heart feels as though it is going to escape my chest at any moment. I start to pant and sweat and think for a fleeting second that maybe I am having a heart attack or stroke. Could something so typically ordinary and human be happening to me? It almost gives me a feeling of belonging to think these thoughts. Then just as I become adjusted to the idea of dying right here on this bench, it happens.

Everything stops. I mean everything. The cars rushing by come to a complete stop; the people walking their dog across the road stop, as does the dog. I hear no sound from the playground I know is just around the corner that should be full of small children this time of day. This is very strange. I am the one that stops and the world keeps going, this is not right. My heartbeat slows and I am again able to sit up. I stand and realize I feel good, I mean really good. Not tired, not hungry and not empty. I must be dead. I turn to the bench expecting to see my body still there slumped over, eyes lifeless and staring. Nobody on the bench, I am still complete in my body, soul and all.

I stand there for a moment not knowing what to do next when something catches at the corner of my vision. A movement. I turn quickly and catch sight of something darting behind a building just down the block. What could it be, everyone is frozen... or are they?

I hesitate, not knowing if I should follow. I should go back to my apartment and wait for the world to reboot or whatever. That is the logical and practical and sane thing to do. I turn to my right, ignoring the thing that was darting around and start to head home. I stare at all the people I pass in mid-stride or in mid-swing or laugh. Then I realize that there is no sound at all. No birds or car horns or stereos, nothing but quiet. The world seems to be on hold. What if this is the apocalypse? Why is everything affected but me? The irony is not lost on me that this is the best I have felt in 4 years and there is no one awake to share it with. I actually feel hopeful and almost happy. I feel like putting on some clean clothes and going to lunch with some friends, if I had any. I feel like living when everyone else is not. Can I ever get on the same page as the rest of the world?

As I round the corner to my crappy apartment something again catches my eye. Across the street, directly in front of me something flies by at lightning speed. Directly behind it is another shadow but this one hesitates when it sees me. The form has eyes and what looks like a human body in the shadow and light it is made out of. The look in those almost human eyes is one of great surprise and anger. I stand frozen, hoping it will leave and continue chasing the other flying object. The eyes move over my body slowly up and down as if trying to figure out what I am. They are looking at me as if I am the alien thing here, not it. I have not seen anything like it even in the darkness of my mind.

This is not one of the many creatures I have become familiar with in my other reality. There is something graceful and elegant about this shape. I can tell this is a creature not to be messed with and there is great danger behind its eyes. As we locked stares something comes flying out of nowhere and throws me to the ground. My head hits the sidewalk with a hard thwack and immediately stars are encircling my head. The pain is making me dizzy and weak. I feel as if I weigh a thousand pounds. I try to shake it off and focus. I stare at the ground that my face is plastered against.

Finally when things start to come into focus I try to stand. I can't. Something is keeping me on the ground. I try to turn my head and see as a hand grabs the side of my face and I feel the warmth of breath on my cheek. "Stay Down", is all he says, his voice soft and low. No anger or threat in his words but more concern. I figure my best bet is to do as told so that's what I do.

I lay as still as possible listening to the throbbing of my head getting worse and worse. Tears start to roll down my cheeks and hit the ground around me. I don't know the reason for the tears; fear or pain or both perhaps. It could be the fact that I am just feeling something, anything for the first time in forever.

"What do they call you?" the voice on top of me asks.

When I don't answer he repeats, harsher this time,

"What do they call you?"

"Raine"

I manage to squeak out.

At that, the heaviness on my back is gone. Sounds start up again; so very loud the world is, overpowering. Attempting to sit up I expect to see some crazy shadow man standing over me. I look around from my place on the ground and see nothing. Everything is alive again and moving and noisy but no man made of light.

Wow, my head hurts. I feel my forehead and realize I have a big goose egg right in the middle between my eyes. Tears are still streaming down my face. The overwhelming emotion totally catches me off guard and I feel as if I will never stop crying. Slowly I begin to rise to my feet, testing out my strength and ability to stand. Stumbling a bit, I begin the walk home, only about a block. I can make it.

I make my way into the apartment, grab a dish towel, go straight to the freezer and grab some ice. Sinking into the old gold velvet sofa that was here when I rented the place, I place my cold pack on the ever growing lump on my forehead. The throbbing is subsiding somewhat and I begin to try and process the events of the day.

As I think back on all the strangeness starting with running into Julie and ending with being saved or assaulted, not sure which, it is a lot to process.

My eyelids start to get heavier and heavier. I am pretty sure I have a concussion and everyone knows you shouldn't go to sleep after a head injury, especially alone. I think about this for a second and realize I don't really care what happens to me at this point. Sleep is pulling me under and I finally let go...

Thump, thump, thump. The sound vibrates thru the wall of my apartment, thump, thump, thump. The sound is familiar and bringing me back to reality. I realize it is the bass to my next door neighbors sons stereo system. He always cranks the music before his mom gets off work. I don't really mind, I have no sound system of my own, not even a radio. I rise to a sitting position and stretch out my arms and legs, feeling all the muscles pull and relax into position. As I do this I suddenly remember the day I had just lived thru and feel for the bump on my head. It is still there, the only reminder that what happened was real. As I get up I am totally overcome with thirst. I get myself a glass of water, a couple of pain killers for my headache and head to the bathroom for a well deserved shower.

After peeling off my jeans and shirt I rummage thru the small dresser that holds my few pieces of clothing. I decide on a clean black t-shirt and comfy yoga pants. I make my way to the bathroom and drop my clothes onto the small vanity. As I look up, my reflection makes me let out a little scream. I know, such a girl thing to do, but wow. I look like someone kicked the crap out of me; more Neanderthal than a 22 year old woman. Swelling and bruising have taken over my whole forehead. I glance down at the rest of my battered body. I take inventory of the damage. Both elbows scraped and bruising, one knee still bleeding a little and my hip black and swollen. I then take a closer look at my body underneath all the damage. I haven't looked at myself for so long and am a little surprised by what is there. My body has developed and changed over the last four years without me really noticing. I guess living in two different worlds and not ever resting makes you not notice some things.

I have hips and curves where there used to be none. My body is soft and womanly looking. I am shocked by how much I enjoy what is looking back at me. I then lock sights with myself in the mirror. My eyes are back, no longer dark and empty. They are light and alive with excitement. Maybe this is just a result of my head injury. Tomorrow I will go back to the plain unattractive woman I have always viewed myself as being. Giving my head a little shake and feeling self conscious about admiring myself, I get in the shower and let the hot water take me away and with it the craziness of the day.

I am beginning to feel calm and level headed and almost sane when a thought strikes me hard and fast. I grab at the shower railing to steady myself. I have slept. I mean really slept. I don't remember visiting the darkness or my creatures there. I always remember. What time is it? How long was I asleep for?

I jump out of the shower and throw on a towel. Racing for the kitchen where the only working clock is, I check the time, 4:35pm. I know when I grabbed the ice it was 11 or so in the morning. Could I really have gotten 5 hours of real sleep, like normal people? Maybe my concussion is worse than I think. I should probably go to the hospital and get checked out. I race back to the bathroom ready to throw on my clothes and head out when I hear it.

"What do they call you?"

I freeze in my tracks, the voice is back. It is him. Not sure what to do as I am standing in my towel at the door of the bathroom. Run? Where? Not knowing what awaits behind me, I turn slowly. I keep my eyes on the ground and slowly raise my head until I stop on a shadow in the corner of the living room. A moving, fluid shadow with light radiating from it and eyes staring at me. Clenching my towel I wonder if I should try and find some sort of weapon before it's too late. This thought is fleeting as the shadow shimmers and convulses until it becomes solid.

I feel as though my eyes may actually pop out of their sockets as I look at the man, a human looking man, coming towards me. He is tall and is wearing ordinary clothes. Don't know what I expected but it wasn't jeans and hiker boots. His long sleeve gray t-shirt looks a little too small as it clings to his visibly muscular body and his hair is black. The same color of the darkness that overtakes me night after night and curly hair covering his eyes that peer from behind the locks of black. I see they are light, a great contrast to the blackness of his hair. To my surprise he looks awkward and so very out of place here in my crappy apartment.

"What do they call you?"

Again with the same question. I look at him a little ticked that he can't seem to remember my name.

"Raine !" I reply.

I know this is the same one that tackled me just hours earlier. I recognize his voice so deep and pure. Not sure what to do next I stand and wait. I figure he has broken into my house and he is the one who tackled me to the ground so he should probably make the next move, right? He is looking me up and down just like the other one of his kind did. There is a difference; he does not feel as dangerous.

After a minute of complete silence I decide I have had enough and turn around go into the bathroom and shut the door. I do not want to be naked in front of him and if he has something to say he will have to wait. I smile a little to myself realizing that I have thrown logic completely out the window as most people would probably run for the door or pass out but not me, I am going to get decent for my materializing-out-of-nowhere, made-of-light-and-shadows guest. Crazy, yep that's me.

I slowly open the bathroom door and look into the living room, he is still there standing in the same spot.

"Why did you leave?" He speaks.

What kind of question is that I think to myself.

"I needed to get dressed."

"Why?"

"Because you don't stand around in a towel having conversations with people, that's why."

Again with the staring. Okay I guess it's up to me to figure out what he wants.

"What do they call you?" I ask almost mockingly.

I don't know why I am not scared of him. I should be, I know that but there is no fear.

"I am known as The Black Knight in the other realm but here I am Jack."

"You are human?"

"Yes."

"Why are you here?"

"You saw us. The world stood still and you did not. I was sent to find out what you are and if you are enemy or ally."

Okay, so how do you answer that? I don't know anything about anything and he wants to know if I am on his side or not. I decide to sit down as my knees are getting weak and I don't want to pass out in front of my guest; that would be awkward.

I decide to tell him the truth.

"I don't know why I didn't stop like everyone else; I was just trying to get home when I saw your friend fly by. Why did you knock me to the ground?"

"We were checking to see if the world was truly still and we could conduct our business in peace. I am a scout for my people and must make sure all is safe before the others arrive."

That really didn't answer my question so I try again.

"Why did you tackle me?"

"I feared that the darkness might get to you if you remained moving and in plain sight, they come for those who they sense they can capture and turn into one of them."

Darkness, that's where I spend half of my life. Those creatures are like family to me, I feel as if I better keep this to myself for now.

"So you were saving me from bad guys?"

At that Jack actually shows a sign that he is human and lets out a little laugh, relaxing his shoulders he moves a little closer to the couch where I was sitting. I move over thinking he might want to sit but he makes no effort to.

"Yes I guess I did save you from the bad guys. You are very different from the others we run into. They scream and run and beg us to leave and never come back. Why are you not frightened?"

I think for a moment, not wanting to sound insane.

"I guess I have always known there is more in this world than we can see or explain. I mean I hoped there was, because fitting in here has been very hard for me, so to think that maybe I belong somewhere else has made life a little easier."

Why was I telling him all this. It had been so long since I had a conversation with anyone and now here I was on my second one of the day. Look at me being social.

"Are you in pain?"

I look up at him a little surprised by the question. He is staring at my forehead and I remember I look like a cave man. I now decide it is a good time to blush, something that used to happen to me all the time when I was normal. I feel the heat hit my cheeks and am not sure what to do. A smirk twitches at the corners of his mouth and all of a sudden I feel mad. I mean really angry. How dare he embarrass me like this?

I scream at him,

"Yes I am in pain. You smashed my face into the pavement and gave me a concussion. I have scrapes and bruises all over my body!"

"I am sorry, I did not mean to hurt you. That is the other reason I am here. I am here to take the pain away as well as the memory of today. You will wake up tomorrow without any recollection of me or your injuries. Your life can go back to normal."

I almost laugh at this, normal. I am anything but normal.

"I don't want you to take away today" was all I could think of saying.

It's true, I want to remember the day I felt alive and the day I slept. If I have to live with the injuries so be it I want to remember.

Jack cocked his head to one side and looked at me as if I were out of my mind.

"No one has ever said no before. They always beg for us to relieve them of the burden. I must complete this task Raine, I am sorry."

For the first time Jack sounds human and I like the way he says my name, it makes me sound more important than I am. I want to remember him. So I tell myself to fight him; not to let him take this from me. I know my mind is screwed up but somewhere I know I can fight it. So I will try.

He grabs my hand gently and places it between both of his. He feels so warm and strong. I look into his eyes and can feel something like an electric current passing between us. I know my injuries are healing; I can feel the headache give way and can see clearly again. My body starts to heat up and everything feels good and whole and new. As I look into his eyes I see they are blue and so very deep. He is the most beautiful thing I have seen. Then I feel it, the pressure in my head. I can feel him trying to get inside and erase today. I keep staring at him looking for signs that he is struggling but he just sits there with a calm and knowing stare. I push against him with my mind and don't let him enter. I know I am winning when I see his expression change. He starts to frown the littlest bit and a bead of sweat is forming on his brow. I push harder until he is completely gone from my mind. It is as if I have physically pushed him as he lands on the far side of the couch with a thud.

"What the hell was that?" He looks at me shocked.

"I told you I didn't want you in my head, so I didn't let you."

"You can't do that, no one can do that!"

He stands up then, visibly shaken. I remain calm, not sure why but I knew what I was doing was right.

"You lied to me, you are not human, what are you?"

Panic is in his voice. I didn't mean to scare him. I just wanted my head to belong to me that's all.

"Don't know. I know I am pretty screwed up and have crazy dreams and haven't slept in four years and have really awful hallucinations but other than that I am your average girl next door."

I stand then and decide I have had enough for one day.

"Please leave" I say and to my surprise with those two little words he was gone. As if I ordered him away and he had no choice but to obey. I feel guilty for being so mean but I am done. I need time to process everything and figure out how I did the mind blocking thing and why. Why am I not freaked out and how did I know he couldn't get into my head?

I have a lot to contemplate and I am a little worried about going back to the darkness now... will it be different and can I still get there? Things have changed, I can feel it. I'm not sure what to expect which is strange for me as I have lived the same day over and over for four years. I don't think I am a ghost any more, the question is... what am I?

Chapter 2

I know I have only been a knight of the light realm for two years but I am really beginning to embrace my new life. I love that I now belong somewhere and feel what I am doing is of great importance to the world. I protect those I love even though they do not know it. I am good. That's all I ever wanted to be.

Growing up I was always held to such a high standard and was never quite good enough. Highly educated parents, who expected nothing less than perfect, were always very hard to please. I grew up always beating myself up for my imperfections. Once I graduated high school I picked a university as far away from my life as possible. I wanted space and room to breathe and figure out who I was. I now feel I am getting to know that person and actually liking him.

They came to me one night in my sleep. A shadow figure with intense eyes that seemed to look right thru me. They asked if I was ready. I said no. Every night they would come and ask the same question and always I would reply the same. I thought it to be a strange dream, they did not scare me but I was not willing to let go of the little control I was gaining in my new life. I wanted freedom and I knew they were asking for my compliance and servitude. Finally after months of the same question night after night I had enough and wanted the dream to end. I said yes, yes I was ready and that's when my new life began. The next morning I woke up and thought I had finally defeated the dream, I had given a different answer so the cycle was broken. I heard a knock at my dorm room door. There stood a man dressed in a business suit and hat. I thought he looked very old fashioned. As he raised his head I saw his eyes. They were the ones from my dream. I backed away scared that my dream had come to life.

"Are you Jack?"

"Yes."

"It is time."

I followed him out of the room and out of that life. My family really hasn't spent much time looking for me. I checked the papers and news at first but nothing. I wonder what reason they gave their high society friends for my disappearance. Maybe I am abroad studying in some very expensive school or I ran away and am enjoying my trust fund and will be back when I am broke. I guess I hold a little bitterness towards them, I am their only son and they don't seem to care what happened to me.

Life has been a whirlwind since then, everything I was taught that was make believe is real and I mean everything, plus so much more. That is my purpose, make sure people still believe in the supernatural as stories not reality. Most could not deal with reality, it would drive them insane. I am trained as a scout sent ahead of my brothers to render the world still so we can go about it freely when hunting the enemy. Yes, there are creatures out there that are fighting to become part of the human world to overtake it. The human mind is one easy to control, they seek to find a way in because of our numbers. We are the most populated creatures to ever live and to control us, is to control everything! So the light has been seeking out knights to aid in the fight against the darkness. We were picked for our openness to the unbelievable and our pure hearts. That is what we are told anyway. They say we cannot be gripped by the darkness because we are so good that they cannot penetrate our psyches. I don't know if this is true but it does give me the confidence to fight without worry that I could be changed into one of them. The problem is we are beginning to lose. Our numbers have drastically decreased since the first battle four years ago. Our numbers sliced in half so they had to begin recruiting, something they hadn't done in a hundred years. It is a slow process, delving into the minds of each and every human. Only in the dream state can they enter and search for clues as to whether you are one of the chosen few. Of course there are those they do not bother looking at; those that are very obviously dark down to the core and children. Children cannot be chosen because they are all pure of heart and need time to test the boundaries and see which side they land on. Also anyone with unbreakable family bonds, for there is nothing stronger than love for our kind and that bond cannot be broken, not even by them.

I live now to serve and protect our kind, to keep the monsters away so others can live in peace. I know my purpose and am fully accepting of that responsibility. I am also very good at it. I am one of the few that has mastered the art of erasing memories, until today.

What happened? I am trying to make sense of the day. My fellow knight Aaron and myself were on a scouting mission to retrieve a valuable object that helps to harness our power. The problem is we do not know what it looks like so we have been searching for a very long time. We were in the process of searching the streets feeling it might be close when we spotted movement. It looked like a homeless woman, which we run into occasionally… that and drug addicts. Anyone under the influence of certain drugs or with certain mental conditions cannot be frozen. Their minds are not working like the masses. I took my place behind the individual in case this was a trap by the dark creatures. I then spotted the darkness heading towards the woman and knowing it only needs seconds to infiltrate her body, I dove to protect her from the creature. I know she hit the ground hard but I had no time for gentleness. The darkness disappeared in an instant and then I heard her begin to weep. Not sure if I was dealing with a druggie or someone that is mentally ill, I decided to keep her down for both our sakes. She tried to look up at me but I stopped her, she did not need to see me or what I am. I told her to stay down and she obeyed. I then asked her to identify herself. She did not respond, I spoke again louder in case drugs had hazed her ability to think. I need her name and for her to speak so I can track her and find her later to erase all this from her mind. She then answered in a soft voice. "Raine." At that our time was up and the world began again I was sucked back into the void, the in-between, to protect myself and my kind. I can return as soon as the okay is given that all of us are out safe and sound. It usually only takes a small amount of time for the roll call to take place and get back to our missions. I find the others and give my report, I say that I must go back and erase the mind of a homeless woman that is of really no significance.

The others show little interest and are off to either clean up others that were found, train or rest. I step back into the world of humans as easily as I left it. No one notices me as I step out from behind a large tree in the park I was near when I was here last. I check to make sure I am dressed appropriately and look ordinary before I proceed. Yes, quite ordinary. I then close my eyes and focus. I need to be still and listen for her. She does not sound very far away so I start to walk following the sound of her inner self. I know it sounds weird but I have been trained to sense people and once I have made a connection with them they are really quite easy to track. I walk about a block and discover I am standing in front of an old apartment building. So, she is not homeless. That leaves one other option, mentally ill. It is very hard to predict the reception I will receive from these people. Some think I am an angel, others the devil. Some even think I am god coming to forgive them their sins; sometimes entertaining but always quite draining. I proceed up the steps and feel her pulling me towards her. She is calm and happy and seems perfectly competent. This is unusual, I sense no drugs in her system and she seems quite stable. I get to her door, knocking is out of the question I must come to her as before so she believes what I say. I concentrate for half a second and am in her living room, in the shadows. My form is not full yet, this is when I must draw attention to myself so she sees who I am.

"What do they call you?" I say in my most non threatening tone.

She stops dead in her tracks. I then notice she has on only a towel and wish I would have noticed that before I made myself heard. Waiting for her reaction I begin to turn into my solid state, as I do this she turns and watches. Now is the part when they either run away or faint. I wait but all she says is "Raine!" in a annoyed voice. Is she not surprised to see me. I am sure she has never seen anything like this before but yet she stands there looking a little pissed. I am trying to figure out how to proceed when she turns from me and goes into the bathroom and slams the door. What? She has something of more importance than to talk to me. When she comes out she is dressed and still looks ticked. I have to say I have never dealt with this before. I ask her why she left and she proceeds to tell me I have no manners and she does not have guests over when she is naked. Mentally ill… she is definitely in that category. She wants to know my name and if I am human. I answer, becoming entertained by this situation. It doesn't really matter what I tell her soon enough it will all be gone from her memory. She asks some more questions which I answer in complete honesty. She tells me she has no idea why she didn't stop and makes me laugh when she asks about me saving her from "bad guys". I am actually having fun with this strange woman with the bruised and painful looking forehead. Crap, I should tell her why I am really here and get on with it before I get too involved. We are not supposed to get involved with ordinaries, it distracts from our mission. I tell her I can take the pain away and her memories of her, what must be, horrific day. She looks at me as if I am the nutty one and says no. NO. You can't say no, you have no choice in this situation. I must do my job. I sit beside her ready to make it all go away. I look into her eyes and see how much intelligence and sorrow is deep within them. I will take away some of that pain. I begin my process of sending her all my energy to heal her wounds. She looks expectantly at me and her face begins to change and transform. I then notice she is quite pretty and has to be about my age. I begin to delve into her mind and erase me from it when I hit a wall. I cannot get in. I try harder, with all my power to break down the barricade, she is not letting me. I guess she can say no. I am getting worried, then she pushes me completely out of her head with such a force that I am actually thrown backwards. She has lied to me, she is not human. I don't know what she is but she is not normal. I scream at her and demand the truth. She tells me she has bad dreams and hallucinations and hasn't slept in four years. Then she does something that I have never even heard of before, she demands I leave and I have no choice. In a blink I am back on the street in front of her apartment. What just happened? I can't make sense of it. She has the power to block me and she can move people at will. I leave for home where I can think in peace. I did not sense danger from her or darkness in her heart. She seemed as though she didn't know what she was doing just that she wanted to do it.

Who has such power?

Chapter 3

How did I send him away like that? I am pretty sure I did it, I mean he looked shocked so he couldn't have done it. I have been sitting for hours looking out the window trying to sort things out in my mind. I feel so good physically and even mentally. I feel like me, but better. Memories are flooding back to me from my childhood and teenage years. I remember everyone's names and places I use to love to go as a child. I see my parents and long to be near them. I have not longed for, or thought of such things for years. So far from my mind are the creatures of the darkness all I see is him and the light. I feel deep down that all this must be tied together, this can't be a coincidence. I have been dreaming of dark places and scary things for so long I forgot that there must be light and goodness in the world. Am I good? What side do I fall on. I so longed to be part of the shadows but now maybe I can be part of the light. I feel vindicated somehow that I am not crazy, there are other things in this world, unexplainable wonderful things that others do not see. I glance at the time flashing on the stove and see it is now 3am. For the first time in years I am not afraid to face sleep, I know I am doing exactly what I was meant to do. Observe the dark realm for some reason I am yet to understand. Maybe this is my mission, my little part in the bigger picture so I will do my best to perform the tasks set before me. With a little excitement I get ready for bed. I have not slept in my bed for quite some time, so I decide to change the bedding and make sure all my pillows are fully fluffed. I jump in at about 4am, ready for what awaits me. My eyes close and I feel myself drift, slowly, to sleep. I dream, for the first time, I dream.

I dream of Jack. He steps out from behind a tree and starts towards me. Children are laughing and running all around. The day is full of happiness and fun. I start walking towards him, he does not see me as he turns down the street in the direction of my apartment. I notice that he is wearing the same clothes he had on in our first meeting and start to wonder if this is a dream or a vision. He keeps going until he is in front of my building and looks up to my living room window. It is suddenly dark and I am sitting there looking out just as I had done that evening. I do not see him but he is staring at me. Jack looks worried, like he is afraid. I don't want him to be afraid of me, I want to talk to him.

I call out but he only stares at the other me on the window sill. I am again a ghost spectator, but I know I am asleep this time not in the in-between. A knocking at my door jars me out of my deep sleep. For a moment I can't remember where I am. As I look around my room I remember I am home and safe. Knock, Knock, Knock, it comes again this time louder and with more force. I jump out of bed and head to the door. I know that knock, the only person I ever speak to is behind the door, my landlord. I am late on rent again and am prepared for the yelling that is about to begin. I open the door and flash one of my brightest and best smiles at the grumpy old man on the other side.

"Good morning Frank!." I say in my happiest voice. "How are you today?"

A look of shock crosses his face as he sneaks a look past me into the apartment.

"Raine, is that you?" he asks in a quiet, hesitating voice.

"Of course, you see me all the time how can you not recognize me?" I reply.

"You look different, younger and kinda glowy."

Glowy, what does that mean? I have never heard anyone say someone looks glowy. I know not to push Frank as his mood can snap at any second.

"Can I help you with something Frank?"

"Oh, yeah your rent is late but I can give you a little more time if you need it."

He looks flushed like he is almost blushing. I quickly looked down to make sure I have clothes on. Yep, fully dressed in my t-shirt and yoga pants.

"Thanks Frank, that would be great."

I give him another smile and gently close the door. I am starting to feel a little uncomfortable with how he was staring at me. I didn't hear him move from behind the door for a couple minutes then he mumbled something and scuffled down the hall to his place. As I search the fridge for something to eat I wonder what that dream meant. I feel as if it wasn't a dream but me watching what really happened last night from another point of view. And where were my dark creatures? I have not seen them in so long I am beginning to wonder if I will ever visit them again. They are a part of me, they will not mourn me or miss me but I want to know what happens next. Which side will win and what have they been fighting for all these years. So many questions and no one to ask, or is there? Jack, he must know. He is of another place, not the darkness but he will know, of that I am sure. He spoke of it when he was here... he saved me from it.

I must find him, but how? I can't exactly wait for the world to stop again, who knows how often they do that. Something suddenly becomes clear to me. If the lightness can stop time maybe the darkness can as well. Perhaps it affects me in a different way; my hallucinations? Could it be? They are always so terrifying and the exact opposite of what occurred to me yesterday. They have happened too many times to even recall. Maybe the knights have just arrived and the darkness has been present here for a very long time. I must get some answers. Think Raine think. If I was a knight of the light where would I live? Probably not in the welfare district. Probably not in this dimension at all. As I stuff a piece of toast into my mouth I ponder the thought. How to get in touch with someone that is made of shadows and light and can fly and materialize out of thin air? Hmmmm, I take a chance and yell his name, "Jack!" Nothing happens. I try again "Jack!", again no response. I begin to feel a little stupid and decide to get dressed and out of the house. I walk the streets of my neighborhood and find myself back at the bench where everything began yesterday. I sit for a moment soaking in the sunshine enjoying the warmth as it tickles my bare arms and face. I have missed so much in this world. The simple pleasures I have given up so I could be somewhere else. I am glad to be here now on this bench feeling alive and almost normal. I listen to all the sounds around me and find myself drifting in a daydream of warmth and light. That's how I feel, light. I feel in control and powerful. Like I have a say now as to what happens to me instead of letting everything else lead me wherever they see fit. The dark creatures, society and even the light knights. I have control for the first time in my life and it feels pretty damn good.

I contemplate getting up and on with my day when a hand comes down on my shoulder and his voice whispers in my ear,

"Please don't send me away again, I just want to talk."

I open my eyes and see Jack standing over me, hands up in a please don't poof me into another dimension sort of way. I smile at him, I am so glad to see him. I guess this totally catches him off guard because he looks confused with my silent reply.

"Do you think I look glowy?"

I know out of all the questions I should be asking, this one really shouldn't have even made the list, but I am a girl and want to know if I look glowy! He just looks down at me with a confused expression on his face.

"I don't have a clue what you are asking me. You look fine."

Well thanks for that, every girl wants a extremely good looking guy to tell them they look fine.

I move over on the bench and offer him a seat. He reluctantly sits beside me in the sunshine. He really is something to look at. Tall, dark and handsome doesn't even come close to describing Jack. I turn and face him with one leg up on the bench. He seems very on edge.

"Is everything okay?" I ask.

"Yeah, I guess so. I have many questions for you about yesterday."

"So do I. Did I make you disappear, or was that you?"

I sit waiting for his response.

"That wasn't me. I have never seen anything like it, one minute I am trying to erase your memory the next you order me out of your head and then out of your place. How?"

He looks at me as if I have some answers for him. I give a little shrug as if to say I don't know. I feel safe with him knowing he cannot control me and also knowing he is more frightened of me than I am of him.

"I just knew I didn't want you in my head and then I was pissed off so I wanted you out of my place all together. Where did you end up?"

"On the street in front of your building, I haven't told the knights that I didn't succeed in wiping your mind. I don't know what to tell them."

He then looks at me with those gorgeous blues of his and I feel as if I can tell him everything and anything.

"I don't want to get you in trouble but I really don't know any more than you. Before yesterday I was just a crazy person who was minding her own business and today I feel alive and completely sane for the first time in years."

"Why do you say that? Crazy people have an illness and I can sense those, I can also sense addicts and you are neither. Have you witnessed anything like yesterday before?"

I reply, "No, but I do have dreams; dreams of dark creatures that live in the shadows who are at war and have been for years.

I don't know what the war is about but I know they are relentless. They fight amongst themselves for control of the dark realm."

I look up at him and think he is actually listening to me. Not judging me or trying to figure out what hospital to send me to.

"I know it sounds crazy but this is my reality, I visit them night after night."

Jack says nothing. I am starting to feel alone and a little vulnerable at letting him know my crazy secrets when he suddenly grabs my arm.

"You must come with me right now."

He looks completely freaked. Standing with one hand outstretched towards me.

"Where? Why?"

"You are not crazy Raine; you are describing the war; the one we are fighting right now. I don't know how but you have seen our enemy and know more about them than we ever could. We need your help."

He looks at me pleading. I believe him. This only makes sense. I know my creatures are bad so if he is fighting them then he must be good. I will go with him.

"Okay." Was all I said.

I am scared of the unknown but I am more scared of not going with him and going back to the way things were only a few short hours ago. I take his hand and give him a little smile. He pulls me up and I wait for the some sort of magic thing to happen. A black hole to jump into or a flash of light and we will be gone to another dimension. Instead he starts to walk down the street. I stumble behind him wondering what kind of angel-like knight of the light walks home.

"Where are we going?" I ask.

"I am taking you to my house where I can summon my brothers and you can tell us everything you know about the darkness." He says very seriously.

"You live in a house?"

He comes to a complete stop and I almost run smack into his back.

"Where did you think I live? In a hole in the ground or perhaps on a cloud?"

Sarcasm really isn't a very attractive quality in a guy.

"You are a knight of the light realm aren't you? Call me crazy but I didn't think you lived in a split level duplex down the street."

I can throw sarcastic remarks with the best of them. He looks at me a little shocked.

"How do you know that?"

"What?"

"That I live in a duplex down the street."

This time I am the one shocked.

"I didn't know, I just was guessing."

I feel a little embarrassed, like I have invaded his privacy. He starts walking again still holding my hand and shaking his head like he can't believe what I just told him.

"Any other secret powers you would like to share before you meet the others?" This time, no sarcasm.

"Powers, I don't have powers. I would say I am observant and my dreams or whatever you want to call them are just my whacked out brain that lets me see things others can't. I wouldn't call that powers."

I know deep down this isn't exactly the truth but I am not ready to admit that I am that different. I am obviously not like anything Jack has seen before so that means again I am an outcast, not like others in this world or any other. That thought makes me sad down to my core, I want to fit in somewhere and now find out that may not be possible anywhere. I feel very alone again.

We walk in silence for a bit longer until we reach his street. All the duplexes look the same but I know which one is his. I do not share this information and let him guide me. I know where he keeps the key and the exact layout of his home as if it were my own. He opens the door to his very typical small suburban home. It is neat and tidy and very homey feeling. We go up the flight of stairs to his kitchen and living room. I know where he keeps his pots and pans and exactly what he has for food in his fridge. I feel a little light headed; this is all getting a bit overwhelming. I ask if I can have a glass of water and he goes into the small kitchen to get it for me. I take the second to breathe and try and block the flow of information to my mind. I am being bombarded with images of all his stuff. Everything from his shampoo to every book that lines the bookshelf. Even what channels he gets on his tv and what numbers are programmed into his telephone. Why the hell do I need to know all this? Who cares about what brand of toothpaste he uses. He comes back and hands me the glass of water. I just miss it as it crashes to the floor and me along with it. I feel my body hit the ground and then nothing.

I wake up laying on something soft and cushy. I feel disoriented but good. The information flow has stopped. I can think again. Jack is above me looking down with great concern.

"I'm okay," I say to try and make him feel better.

I am embarrassed that I again needed him to look after me.

"Are you sure, you took quite the fall, what happened?"

"I was feeling a little sick and then the room started spinning and that was it."

I try and sit up but realize my head is still a little jumbled and decide to stay where I am for the moment.

"When was the last time you have eaten anything?"

"I had toast this morning, why?"

"I will make you something to eat; I need you in good condition when the other knights arrive."

With that he is off to the kitchen. I figure I am going to get bacon and eggs as that is pretty much all he has. I slowly sit up and when I feel that I can stand without fainting again, I head into the kitchen to join him. I was right! I can hear the bacon sizzling in the pan and see the egg carton on the counter. I smell the food and realize I am hungry. He doesn't notice me at first and I decide to watch him in silence as he cooks for me. I have never had a guy cook for me before. It's nice having someone look after me for a change. Jack then looks up and catches me staring at him. I blush, oh no… last time I blushed he got tossed out on the street. I wait for something to happen but it doesn't, he looks away at the pan of eggs and asks how I like mine. I tell him I don't care and ask if he would like some help. He politely declines and motions for me to go and sit at the counter. I oblige. This moment seems very ordinary to me, something people do every day and yet he is a knight trying to save the world and I have a direct line to the bad guys and he is waiting for the rest of the good guys to come so they can poke and prod at my brain for information. Even for me this seems weird. Jack brings over two plates of food and it looks really good. I dig right in without a word. I see him smile out of the corner of my eye, I guess I don't eat like a lady, but I am starving and don't really care.

"Is it good?" he asks.

"Yes, thank you. You are a good cook. When are your buddies coming?"

"They should be here shortly, I notified them when we got here."

He then grabbed the cleaned off plates and took them to the sink. I got up and took them out of his hands.

"I will wash, you can dry." I say to him.

He looks as if he is going to refuse but I don't give him a chance I start the water and get out the dish soap from under the sink. I find a clean rag in the bottom drawer and begin washing.

"How did you know where everything is?" Oops, I screwed up.

He doesn't miss much does he.

"Lucky guess, isn't that where everyone keeps their cleaning supplies?"

I try and laugh off what I have just done. He seems to be okay with my reasoning and begins to dry. We finish the dishes up in silence, comfortable silence.

I then begin to feel the hairs on the back of my neck stand up and that tingly feeling come over my body. It is not as intense as yesterday but it is the same type of thing. I look up at Jack and see his focus has changed to the living room.

"They have arrived."

He says to me and gives my arm a gentle squeeze as he leaves me alone in the kitchen to greet his guests.

I guess this is it, I tell myself. Time to meet some good guys.

Chapter 4

As I leave Raine in the kitchen I take a deep breath and silently pray they have sent Aaron along with the rest of the group. I know Charles will be coming as he is the leader of us all, but Aaron has always been there for me and I know he will stand up for me if they decide me keeping this from them is a punishable offence. I don't know why I didn't run to them right away and tell them of her. That is what we are trained to do. We work as a team; no secrets, equal trust. But for some reason I feel protective of Raine even against the rest of the knights and have no idea why. I know she feels lost right now and is just trying to figure everything out but I also know she is hiding something from me. One moment she seems so fragile and weak and the next I feel power exuding from her like a tidal wave. I don't think she knows she is doing it. She is a strange and wonderful creature that I don't understand, perhaps that is why I feel drawn to her. There is little in this world or the other that I cannot read and figure out.

I step into my small living room that all of a sudden is crowded with six grown men. Yes, I feel relief that Aaron has come along. I smile at Charles and greet the others. I ask them to sit as I explain some of what has been happening the past 24 hours. They all remain quiet never interrupting as I finish by telling them that she is in the kitchen. Two of my colleagues jump up at that news and look as if they are going to change to their knight form. I stand ready to get between them and the girl if need be. Why am I protecting her? Against my brothers? I am not right, maybe she has done something to me. The thought crosses my mind and I immediately dismiss it. I know she is not controlling me or the situation and it is me who feels the need to save her and keep her safe. Charles steps in and calms the room. He agrees to meet her and tells my brothers I have done the right thing by investigating further before involving the whole. I am relieved to hear this and go to get Raine.

She is leaning against the stove looking off into space, nervously biting her nails. I always thought that to be a gross habit but I guess she has good reason to be a little on edge. She looks up at me and I can tell she is thinking of running. It's not as if we could stop her. I rest my hands gently on her shoulders and tell her I will be right by her side the whole time. I don't know if this is going to give her any comfort but I want to be by her side. She smiles a little and gives me a nod.

"I am ready." She says.

I feel a wave of strength pour over her and I know she is. As we enter the other room I see her square her shoulders and let out a deep breath. I make polite introductions and ask everyone to take a seat. She looks from face to face. I see a little smile touch her eyes and wonder what she is finding so entertaining. Charles is the first to mention her abilities and gets right down to it.

"How many creatures of the dark realm are there?"

She replies in a soft but firm voice, "About a hundred or so. Their numbers are hard to keep tabs on as they kill each other on a regular basis and then must go and get more. I don't know where they get the new monsters but it seems rather easy to acquire them."

Looking around the room I can tell they are starting to believe her.

I tell her something she probably doesn't want to know but feel that she deserves the truth.

"They get them here. The new creatures of the dark are human, when they decide to live in the shadows instead of the light they start to resemble what they look like on the inside."

"Is that why you all look the way you do?"

She asks looking around the room at each of the men sitting here.

"What do you mean by that?"

Charles asks as if she insulted him.

"Well if you hadn't noticed you are all pretty good looking guys. I mean I don't see one flaw on any of you. So I gather that you all chose the light so your inside self is, well, beautiful."

Raine blushes a little, I guess she realizes calling a room full of grown men beautiful is kind of awkward. I see Smith smile to my left, I have never seen him crack a smile, he shows no emotion as he has always felt emotions were for the weak. But here he is in my living room smiling at her. She doesn't seem to notice.

"Thank you for the compliment Raine, can we continue with our discussion please?"

Raine just nods and seems to be getting a little ticked. I guess I should have warned my comrades what happens when she gets mad. She explains details of the shadow creatures dwellings and how they train to fight us, she tells what they eat and who are their leaders. She knows so many details of their lives it's hard to believe they never sensed her there. I can see she is getting drained and think it is time to stop for the night. She has been talking for hours. I interrupt Charles and ask if we can stop. Raine looks at me gratefully and I see I was right, she looks as if she is about to faint again. Charles is surprised by my request but knows I am good at reading people and trusts I know what I am doing. As the group of men, my family, stands and readies themselves to leave I notice that Smith is whispering something to Raine. I immediately feel jealousy rise within me. Jealous?... I have not felt that emotion since high school when a new guy at school was flirting with my then girlfriend. Even then it was not like this, I actually want to strike out at Smith but he is my brother and she is just a girl we are using for information on our enemy. Why do I care if someone is speaking to her. We are not supposed to get involved, our lives are devoted to a higher purpose. Smith knows this as well. I interrupt anyway and shake Smiths hand and thank him for coming. I can tell Raine thinks that I was rude by the look she shoots me. Oh well, at least they aren't talking anymore. Aaron gives me a punch on the arm as he walks by and bids farewell to Raine in a very gentlemanly fashion. He has always been so good with words and people. I envy him, I never learned the graces of society very well. I have a tough time telling people how I feel and what I want without sounding like a stuck up phony. I am given a look by Charles which tells me they are ready to depart. I know he would like me to ask Raine to leave and go in the other room as he does not want to divulge any more information about us than absolutely necessary. Just a precaution.

I ask Raine to join me in the other room so the others can leave. She follows me out and back into the kitchen. I turn to her and see she can feel the others leaving, her eyes go wide for a split second and then she relaxes. I smile at her and want to tell she did a great job. I want to thank her and let her know I really appreciate everything she has done for us. I want to know what Smith said to her. Instead she speaks first.

"Are there no women knights?"

"What?"

"You heard me, are there no women worthy enough to help save the world?"

She crosses her arms and leans against the counter waiting for my response.

"Um, yes there are women knights. Of course they are allowed to be one of us. There are not many because most women have children or want children and that keeps them a part of this world. You have to let go of your human bonds and fully embrace the light and most women find more importance in being a mother. This is not a bad thing for if we did not have them to guide and help the young our kind would not even be here."

Satisfied with my answer I lean opposite her and wait for her to say something.

"Okay then, that answers that doesn't it."

She looks tired. I should take her home.

"Are you ready to go home?"

"I guess so, I feel pretty worn out. How do you think that went?"

I reply "Very good. You answered everything and gave us tons of information we have never had before. Hopefully it will give us the upper hand. We really need it."

"I don't think Charles likes me very much, he seems very suspicious of me, like I have some sort of agenda. Do you trust me?"

I want to.

"Yes, I trust all that you have told us is the truth and you are not trying to sabotage us in anyway."

"Thanks I guess."

She looks disappointed in my answer, what did I say wrong?

"I am going to head out. I need to get some sleep. Can I borrow a jacket or something, it's a long walk home and I only have on this t-shirt. I didn't expect to be here this long."

"Oh, yeah sure. I will get you something."

I head to my bedroom and find her my brown leather jacket. It will be big on her but it is warm.

"Is this okay?"

She kind of looks at me sideways and accepts the coat.

"Thanks."

She turns and heads down the stairs and out the door. And me, I just stand there and let her go... should I do something different?

Chapter 5

I don't know why I am so pissed, I am a grown woman and have always looked out for myself. It's not like I need him to walk me home or anything. I head down the steps of Jacks place and off towards home. I am totally drained; these last couple of days have been so crazy. The night sky is so dark tonight, more so than usual. I look around and realize the streets are deserted.

That's odd, there should be someone out and about, walking their dog or coming home from the local movie theatre. But nothing. Feeling like one of those stupid girls in the horror movies, knowing they are next because they are alone and it's dark and no one is around to hear them scream, I decide to pick up the pace. Just a few more blocks and I am home, back to my crappy apartment, safe. I pass one dark alley and then another I take a peek down each one as I fly by and then start to feel a little silly. Paranoid much?

I round the last corner before my street and wham! Something picks me up and I feel as if I am flying. I come crashing down in the alley beside my building. It is very dark here, no street lights or even the moon to give way to any shadows. Just blackness. I then feel it, a cool breath on my neck, whatever it is it is very close. I stand frozen, not like in my hallucinations but out of fear. I don't scream, I don't even dare to breathe. What am I supposed to do? I am about to try and move when the slimy fingers encircle my throat. The hand is bony and I can feel every knuckle pressing into my neck, it is so cold. Then I see the eyes, they are only and inch from my face looking down at me from above. Words begin to drip from its misshapen mouth.

"You have chosen the wrong side little one."

It then begins to stroke the side of my face with its other hand. I cannot speak or move, I recognize the voice from the in-between, it is their leader.

Questions start flying thru my mind: how did he find me? Has he always known I was there watching? What is he going to do with me?

I stand staring, pressed against the wall and gripped with fear. I need to do something or I will be killed. He is not a merciful creature, he kills anything in his path and now that is me. The fingers around my neck start to tighten. He is staring at my throat. I have watched him kill before and know he likes to rip out the jugular of his prey with his razor sharp teeth. Still stroking my cheek, I begin to cry. I then feel an overwhelming sense of calm come over me. I have power!. I did it to Jack in my apartment and I can do it again. I wish this creature in front of me away, over and over in my head. I imagine him gone. I close my eyes and pray with all my heart for him to disappear but still I feel the breath on my skin and the fingers tightening slowly around my throat. Jack, I think of him and how easily I made him leave and all of a sudden the fingers are gone and I hear a mournful cry that is not of this world. I fall to my knees and gasp for breath. Choking and coughing and crying I look into the darkness and see a light. Bright and shimmering, it is fluid and almost dancing around the now wounded creature of darkness. The creature turns its eyes to me and says in a low steady voice,

"See you in your dreams little one."

With that he is gone. The darkness of night takes him away. I close my eyes and fall against the building behind me. I lay there for a moment and remember I am not alone. My eyes fly open and I see him, Jack runs over and crouches beside me.

"Are you alright?"

I just look up at him and shake my head no. I am not alright. I did not sign up for this. I want my insanity back. I want to only observe and not be a part of any big picture. I want to go home and lock the door and never come out. He then gently raises me to my feet and sweeps me up into his arms. I wrap my arms around his neck and press my face into his chest. His heartbeat is strong and sure and makes me feel safe. Then a strange sensation takes over my body and I open my eyes to see the purest white glow all around us and in the next second we are in his living room. He releases me and as I stand, I look up at him.

I know this isn't the time, but I start to laugh. My rescuer is wearing only pyjama pants, plaid pyjama pants. This sends me into hysterics. Jack is staring at me like I have completely lost my mind. I think I have. Who almost gets killed by the head monster of the dark realm and has a laughing fit afterwards? I try and gain my composure so he will stop looking at me like that.

"I am alright, I just need a minute,"

I manage to choke out. My throat is really sore. My hands go up to touch my neck and wow does it hurt. Jack comes closer and ever so gently lays his hands on my neck.

"I can take the pain away."

I nod yes and let him do his thing. We lock eyes and I feel my neck start to heal and again feel warm and fuzzy inside just like the first time he healed my wounds.

"Thank you."

I feel completely healed, physically that is.

His hands linger on my neck for a moment more before he pulls them away and turns to go to the kitchen. He returns quickly with a glass of water for me. I drink it and sit down on the couch. He takes a seat beside me and I start to tell him what happened when I left just a little while ago. I describe in detail the creature and what he said to me and how I thought I was going to die.

"How did you know where I was and that I was in trouble?" I ask.

"I didn't, you called me there. I was lying in bed and all of a sudden I was in the alley and saw him on you. I panicked and threw my light at him. I know this will not kill these creatures but it was enough to get him away from you."

"So you think I made you come to me?"

"Yes, I felt you pull me there."

"I was thinking about how I got you to leave my place yesterday and was trying to do the same thing to it. I wasn't trying to bring you to me."

Jack then gets to his feet and starts to pace.

"Maybe your power doesn't work on dark creatures only my kind. And don't argue with me and tell me you don't have any powers, I know you do and I am pretty sure you haven't told me the extent of them either."

Jack sounds frustrated with me. I don't want to keep secrets from him any longer. He is right I need to accept that I do have abilities. It's hard to grasp. People don't wake up one day and become superheroes do they?

"You're right, but I don't know what I can do and it's all really confusing right now. Thank you for coming and rescuing me, I would be dead right now if you hadn't been there."

His face softens and again looks at me with concern not frustration.

"Do you think you can do it again?"

"What?"

"I was thinking you could try and summon one of our kind and we can test our theory. Can you try?"

"I guess so, but you are the only one so far that I can summon or make disappear. Maybe it's just you my powers work on."

"I doubt that. I am a knight of the light realm so I think you should be able to do the same with any of us. Try summoning Aaron, he is my closest brother and I trust him the most."

"Okay, I really have no idea how I did it though. I just thought about you and you came."

I am getting a little worried that Jack has a lot more faith in my abilities than I do. I stand and motion for Jack to take a step back and make room, for what I am not sure. I close my eyes and concentrate, I think of Aaron. I picture his sandy blonde hair and brown eyes. He is a little shorter that Jack but just as muscular. I try and picture his clothes and his smile but all I see is Jacks smile. I feel something and open my eyes, Jack has moved to right in front of me, my nose touching his chest. I look up and am about to ask him what the hell he is doing when he loses his balance and starts to fall, he grabs my shoulders and we land on the couch.

"Why did you do that?"

I ask a little ticked off and sick of being thrown around.

"Were you thinking of Aaron or me?"

He says smiling. Why I have no idea.

"Aaron, why?"

"Because you moved me to practically on top of you that's why. I was standing watching you and the next second I was across the room right in front of you."

I begin to blush and push him so I can sit up. I turn away from him so he can't see my face. This is embarrassing, I started out thinking of Aaron but found myself comparing him to Jack.

"We can try again tomorrow, you could probably use some rest."

I can tell he is trying to get me to relax, but if my only super power is to make Jack go where I want I don't know how that's going to help out much.

"I can't go to sleep."

I say, remembering what the dark creature said before he disappeared.

"Why?"

"Because they are waiting for me. They know I will have to come there eventually and I am scared. I can't face him again and you can't protect me in the darkness."

I feel my face change with panic... what can I do?

"Do you remember how you blocked me from your mind and wouldn't let me erase your thoughts? Well maybe you can do that in your dreams too. Maybe that's why they haven't been able to get to you until now and only in this reality. You are so much stronger than you think Raine."

With that he grabs my hand and gives it a squeeze. I turn to him and look into his eyes. How can he believe in me this much? We have known each other for a day and yet here he sits giving me pep talks and making me feel competent and strong.

"I will try."

With that I get up and start heading for the door. A strong arm grabs my arm. I look up and see Jack staring at me again like I am a crazy person.

"Where are you going?"

"Home."

"No you're not, they could attack you again, you need to stay here at least till morning. I am not letting you out of my sight."

I guess that was kind of stupid of me. I must not be thinking right.

"Where do I sleep?" was all I had the energy to say.

"You can have my bed, I will take the couch. It's down the hall to the left."

"I know where it is."

Oops, shouldn't know that should I, but I am too drained to care.

"Goodnight."

And with that I turn and head down the hall.

"Goodnight."

I hear him say softly as I close the bedroom door.

I go to his closet and grab the extra blanket and pillow he has neatly placed on the shelf. I am about to go and give them to him when there is a soft knock on the bedroom door. I open it and hand him the bedding.

"How did you know I kept these in the closet?"

This time I could tell he isn't leaving without an explanation.

"I know where everything is in your house. I don't know why or how but I do."

"What?"

"It's hard to explain, I will try tomorrow. Right now I need to lie down."

I give him a gentle push on the chest so he will back up and I can close the door. I hear him walk back down the hall and start making his bed on the couch. I guess I could have taken the couch and let him have his bed but I am almost delirious and need sleep. I will apologize in the morning.

I remove his leather jacket and hang it on the back of the door where I know he keeps it. I then take off my runners and jeans and hop into bed. The sheets are soft and warm on my skin and it takes only seconds before I am gone. I am walking in this dream, walking a tight rope it seems with light on one side and dark on the other. I see Jack and the other knights looking at me expectantly and waving me over. They all look friendly and kind and beautiful. I give them a smile and a wave but something keeps me moving forward. I then turn my attention to the other side. Here are more faces also looking at me expectantly, mangled and deformed. They wave at me to join them as well. I see the leader who attacked me come up between the crowd and as he walks closer and closer I stop, unable to move any further on my rope. I feel him almost on me but this time I can scream and I do.

"Raine, Raine wake up!"

Someone is shaking me and I open my eyes to see Jack holding me. I look around the room now light with day. I am so glad to be awake and here. I grab and hug him tightly to me. I don't want to let go of him and he does not seem to be pushing me away.

"Was I screaming?"

I say into his chest.

"Yes and yelling for him to leave you alone. I am gathering he is the creature that attacked you last night. Did he get to you?"

He begins to stroke my hair and I feel a chill run up my spine.

"He tried. And then you woke me up."

I start to release my hold on him realizing I am practically on his lap in just my thin t-shirt and panties. I haven't been this close to another human being in almost five years and it feels very foreign to me to have someone touch me. This is probably not something Jack should be doing either. He said he had to give up all human bonds when he chose his life and I would think that means girlfriends as well. God, my brain works differently. Here I am wondering if he is allowed to have a girlfriend and he is just making sure I haven't been attacked by a crazy monster in my dream.

"What time is it?"

I ask as I move a little farther away on the bed.

"It's almost noon, you were out for a good ten hours."

"What, I haven't slept that long in years! My dream was only a few minutes long. I am usually there from the moment I close my eyes until it decides to release me hours later. I must have blocked it like you said. I think I did it."

This is very exciting to me, probably the best news of all. I smile at Jack so happy with myself. I mean I obviously don't have total control yet but this is very good news. He smiles back and gets off the bed.

"Let's get something to eat."

He says over his shoulder at me as he rummages through his drawers looking for something.

"If you're looking for your jeans they are on the dryer in the laundry room."

I might as well help him out; he knows I can do this now anyway.

With a smirk he shakes his head and goes to get his pants. I quickly pull on my jeans and shoes and wish I had a toothbrush as I look in his bedroom mirror at my dishevelled appearance. Oh well, maybe we can swing by my place so I can change.

He comes back fully dressed and looking like a million bucks. I feel self conscious and a little inferior to be going out in public with this man.

"Can we stop by my place so I can get cleaned up?"

"Of course are you ready to go?"

"Yeah, let's go."

Chapter 6

What a weird night. For me that's saying a lot. I have seen so much in the last two years but nothing like the last 24 hours. The fact that she can call for me at will and dismiss me just the same is a little unnerving. I am used to being in total control of myself and my actions. It's not that I don't want to be there for her and

I am very happy I was there to save her last night, but giving up that control is a tough one for me. I wonder if she can turn it off. We will have to train and see what her limits are. If there was any doubt before I am sure she is good and on our side. The darkness would not want her dead otherwise. I am waiting by the door for her when she comes down the stairs towards me. I catch her eye and she smiles. I wonder if she knows the effects of her smile. It radiates from within her and makes you feel like you are basking in the sunlight. I shake my head and try to get out from under her spell. I politely open the door for her and we head out. As we walk down the street I feel almost like an ordinary, headed for breakfast with a pretty girl. I need to bring myself back to reality and ask her about her ability to know so much about me and my stuff. She explains about being overloaded with information the first time she entered my place. She says it was like someone turned on a switch and she then knew everything about my home. I ponder this for a moment and wonder why the universe would need her to have this information. I am sure that where I keep my keys and what kind of coffee I drink is of no real significance to the universe. We reach her apartment and head up to her place. As we reach her door I see an old man heading towards us. I can spot the darkness and no, he is just an ordinary so I let him approach.

"Raine, I need to talk to you!"

He bellows. She stops and turns towards him.

"Yes, Frank."

"I know I told you yesterday that I can wait on the rent but the owners stopped by and I need it now."

She glances in my direction obviously a little embarrassed. I tell her I will wait inside so she can have some privacy. I go and leave her to deal with her landlord. As I look around her place I realize that this is a pretty crappy place. She must be destitute. I guess this makes sense, how could hold down a job when she has spent the last four years watching the darkness? I will have to bring this up to the brothers and see if we can help her out. We have contacts in this world and can supply her with what she needs. I hear the voices outside the door get louder and realize things are turning ugly. It is probably better if she doesn't lose control, who knows what she can do to this old man. I decide to go and diffuse the situation. I open the door and she looks up at me a little shocked.

"What seems to be the issue sir?"

I turn my attention to the elderly man.

"I need rent, now!"

Raine looks ready to explode, I grab her arm and whisper for her to calm down. She seems to understand what I am saying and takes a deep breath.

"Sir, I will pay whatever she owes. Let's go down to your place and figure this out."

The old guy nods once and glares at Raine. He then turns slowly and starts heading back down the hall.

"I don't want you bailing me out, I can take care of myself."

She has now focused her anger on me.

"Listen Raine, I can pay your rent it is no problem. If you want, think of it as payment for helping us out."

She stares at me and her look starts to soften.

"Okay, but I will pay you back. I am not a charity case."

"Whatever you say, let's just get him off your back for now."

I turn and go in the direction of the landlord and Raine goes inside the apartment and shuts the door.

Once I settle up her debt I head back to her place. I knock once and she yells for me to come in. She is already changed and looks as if she is ready to go.

I like what she is wearing, she no longer has that homeless look about her. She has on nice jeans and a pretty green sweater that brings out the color of her eyes. Her short hair is spiked up a bit and her lips are a glossy pink color. I should stop staring but I can't.

"Are you ready?" I ask.

"Yes I just want to try one thing first, if you don't mind. Will you try and get in my head again."

"Now?"

"Yeah, there is something I have been wondering about and I want to see if it works."

She goes and takes a seat at her small dining room set and kicks the chair out on the other side for me to sit in. I am a little weary of trying this again since last time she physically kicked me out as well. I go and sit opposite her and grab her hands, she smiles at me and we lock eyes. I begin to enter her mind slowly and cautiously... she is not blocking me yet. I feel some resistance but she is letting me in. Then I feel what she is trying to do, she is letting me in but only where she will allow me to go. It is as if I am in a maze but there is only one direction I can take. Usually minds are wide open to me and I can easily get to where I want and extract whatever I need to. She leads me to the farthest corner of her mind, here it is dark and the shadows are everywhere. I can see the in-between and she shows me a dream, I think. The one from last night. I see her walking the rope and the two sides fighting for her attention. I see me looking up at her wanting desperately for her to pick us and I see the darkness also calling to her. She then pushes me back and out of her head. We are still holding hands and staring at each other. I blink and come back to reality. She looks at me with great anticipation.

"Did you see it? My dream, did you see what I was trying to show you?"

"Yes I did. Why did you want me to see that?"

"Because I want to prove to you I have no secrets, I want you to trust me as much as I trust you."

I realize she would like a response but I am overcome with emotion and don't know what to say. I grab hers hands tightly in mine,

"I trust you with my life."

I am falling for this girl, I feel it in every inch of my body and can't resist it any longer. I know it is not right and I know I will be breaking the rules, I don't care.

"Move in with me." I blurt out.

I see the look of shock in her eyes and realize this sounds crazy.

"I mean, I think you should stay with me until we are sure you are safe. I have plenty of room and the darkness cannot reach you there, it is protected. Besides you know where everything is."

There, that sounds better. She tilts her head to the side and slowly removes her hands from mine.

"You are probably right, and was that a joke? I can't believe you actually made a joke!"

She gets up from the table laughing and tells me she is going to go and pack a few things. I take a few deep breaths and wonder if I am doing the right thing. I am not impulsive, I am safe and controlled but ever since meeting Raine all my personal rules have flown out the window. She returns with a backpack slung over her shoulder.

"I'm starving!"

She says and heads for the door. I follow silently behind and out into the sun.

"I know a great little diner just down the street, how about it?"

She looks at me and I nod approval. I don't care where we go or what we do I just want to be near her.

"What did Smith say to you last night before they left?"

I can't help myself, I have to know. She looks sideways at me and I wonder if she can see the reason I ask this question.

"I was just wondering because he is not a big talker, especially not to ones that are not brothers."

"He just told me that he is willing to help if I need it and gave me his number."

She says like this is no big deal. I don't even have Smiths number, if I want to get a hold of him I must contact the brothers in the light and they summon him. What does he want with Raine? I try and keep the shock off my face and answer simply "Oh."

"Why, is that not allowed? I don't have your number but I guess I don't need it since I can just think of you and you have no choice but to answer."

She laughs at this not waiting for me to respond.

We walk for a short while and then we are in front of the very ordinary looking diner. I open the door for her and she shoots me a look that says she can do that. I am not trying to offend her, just being polite. We take a seat in a booth and the waitress is there within seconds.

"What will it be?"

She asks us as she pours us each a cup of coffee.

Raine answers quickly with her selection; obviously she knows the menu off by heart. I don't really care so I just say I will have the same.

"What is the war about?"

She asks as I take a sip of my coffee.

"We are fighting over ordinaries, humans. The darkness wants control of this world and we are trying to stop them. This has been going on for hundreds of years but they started to win after a great battle four years ago. There is much more darkness in the world now than before and that makes their job all the easier. We are trying to find an object that will help our side out. Tip the scales in our favour if you will."

"What is it?"

"We don't know, but the stories have been passed down through the knights for generations and there was never need for it until now. We always had the upper hand because good ruled this world so they had little chance to take it. All we know is that it will help in the final battle, it can only be used once and then the decision will be made. Only one side will remain."

"Wow, that's some heavy stuff. Do you know when this final battle will take place?"

"No, the knights have been preparing for it for a very long time. We cannot win though. Not without the weapon."

"How do you know it's a weapon?"

"I guess we don't but we have always assumed it to be, if it can help to destroy the darkness doesn't it have to be?"

"I don't know, here comes our food."

She looks over my shoulder smiling at the waitress I assume. She digs right in as the food is set before us. I watch her, she eats as if this is her last meal, I imagine bringing her home to my parents; they would be appalled. I am simply entertained. I like that she doesn't care what others think. She is right about the food, it is very good. We finish up and are ready to leave when someone taps me on the shoulder. I tense instantly and am ready to fight when I hear the familiar chuckle.

"Hey bro, mind if I join you guys?" It is Aaron.

I look up at him and smile.

"We are all done, what are you doing here?"

I ask a little confused as to why the social call. He ignores the fact that we look ready to leave and pushes in next to Raine. She happily moves over and makes room for him. The waitress is back with a cup of coffee for Aaron and a menu. He refuses the menu but accepts the coffee.

"So what are you two up to?"

He asks Raine directly.

"Oh, I was starving so I brought Jack here for a bite."

She shoots me a sideways glance as he takes a sip of his coffee. I can tell she is not sure what she should say. I repeat my previous question.

"What are you doing here?"

"I stopped by your place and you weren't there so I tracked you."

Aaron is an excellent tracker, one of our best. This means he knows that Raine left my place this morning and not last night and where she lives. He is my brother, I can trust him right?

"You are only supposed to track if there is an emergency, you know the rules."

I state a little ticked.

"Yes I do, so do you or do you need a refresher?"

Aaron stares me down and I can tell he knows I have broken the laws of our kind so I might as well come clean, partially at least. I explain that Raine was attacked last night and the darkness now knows where to find her. I tell him that she is going to be staying with me for awhile so she can be protected because we owe her for all her help. Raine sits quietly as does Aaron until I am finished. My friend looks relieved when I am done and his whole demeanour softens and changes into my best friend again.

My suspicions were right, he was here because he was told to check up on me, something I know he would have hated doing. The waitress brings the check and as I reach for it Raine snatches it out of my hand.

"It's on me boys."

She says with her radiating grin. She motions for Aaron to let her out and she goes to the counter to pay. I am left alone with Aaron.

"Why did they send you? Do they no longer trust me?"

"Of course they trust you, they wanted to make sure you were safe. Charles does not have complete faith in the girl and wanted to make sure you had back up if need be."

"Do you think she is dangerous?"

I ask, hoping he does not share Charles point of view. He takes his time thinking as I wait.

"No, I think she is confused and needs our help."

With that she returns to the table.

"Ready to go?" she says.

"Yeah let's get out of here, where are we off to next?"

Aaron asks looking from Raine to me.

"I think we should take Raine to the training field, she has some unexplored abilities that we need to get under control."

I say this with a smirk knowing she knows what I am talking about. She shoots me a look and then gives a little smile. Aaron just nods and follows along.

I feel optimistic about the day, the sun is shining, I have my best friend by my side and this creature unlike any I have ever encountered smiling brightly at me.

Chapter 7

Not sure what to expect... I find myself a little anxious at the thought of going to the knights "training field". I am not a warrior, I have never been in a fight in my life. And when faced with danger what do I do? I call Jack to come save me. I am turning out to be some bad ass superhero.

As we walk down the street, the boys a pace in front of me, I study them. Jack walks with great confidence and poise and a little cockiness as well. Aaron on the other hand almost slouches when he walks making him look even shorter that he is. He is dressed like Jack but seems almost uncomfortable in his skin. I can't imagine why, he is a knight too, so that makes him pretty damn special. He is just as good looking as Jack but doesn't seem to have the faintest idea he is. I think I like Aaron. He is real and regular and does not intimidate me. Jack on the other hand intimidates the heck out of me, I feel inferior to him in every way.

We arrive at the end of a suburban street. All that is in front of us is a broken down apartment building. I am trying to figure out how this could be a field of some sort when Jack grabs my hand. I tingle from his touch and almost let go in case he notices my reaction.

"Are you ready?" He asks me.

"For what?"

"Just don't let go of my hand."

I look at him and nod. I trust him. Aaron walks in front of us and suddenly disappears. The front wall of the building seems to have absorbed him. I gather it is our turn so I grab hold of Jacks hand a little tighter. He notices my hesitation.

"Don't worry, I won't let anything happen to you. This is a place only for us but I have a feeling you won't have any problem entering."

"So you don't know for sure? You are just guessing? What if I can't get in, what will happen to me?"

I start to feel panic working its way to the surface. I am not a knight! The next thing I know Jack wraps his arms around me and jumps into the wall. I let out a little scream as we land on the other side. Aaron is standing with his arms crossed looking annoyed at Jack.

"You knew she could come in, why the dramatics?"

"I thought it would be fun!"

Jack replies and lets me go. I smack him on the shoulder but have to laugh; he really is starting to loosen up.

I stop and take in the surroundings. It looks so very plain and ordinary. It really is a field. I guess I keep expecting mythical places like in story books. A little disappointing I must admit.

"So what does she need to work on, Jack?"

Aaron asks, ready to get started.

"Well, she can summon our kind but has only managed to do it to me so far. She can also make us disappear from her presence. I want to see if she can learn to control these abilities. As of now she has not meant to do it either time."

Jack leaves out the try last night in his living room.

"I think it would work best if she tried on you. I will watch her and see if I can help out in anyway."

Jack then turns to me.

"Try to focus all your attention towards Aaron. I think your feelings are definitely attached to your ability, so let yourself feel a strong emotion. The first time you did it you were mad and the second you were scared." He added in a softer voice so only I can hear "last night I don't know what you were feeling, but maybe avoid that one. I don't want to knock you over again."

I blush, knowing exactly what I was feeling, I wanted Jack closer to me and then he was. I must block him from my mind... Aaron... concentrate on him.

"Okay, Aaron I am going to try and move you out of my sight. It might take awhile so please be patient."

Aaron gives me a thumbs up and I smile back. Okay let's try this. I close my eyes and imagine him on the other side of the trees that line the field. I peek and see he is still here. I clench my eyes closed and start to feel embarrassed. I have two men staring at me waiting for me to do something I don't know how to do. I think they should cut me a little slack as I am not a trained anything. Until a couple days ago, I was the crazy woman who wandered the streets. I feel anger start to build in my gut. Why are they putting so much pressure on me? I am not one of them. I need time to get this; give me some goddamn time!

"You did it!"

Jack grabs me and picks me up in a big bear hug. I open my eyes and look immediately to where Aaron was standing. He is gone. I did it. I smile at Jack and he quickly puts me down. He looks as if he is blushing. I shake it off and realize he is just excited that I can somewhat control this new power.

"What did you think about?"

"I was actually thinking about how you guys are putting too much pressure on me and I can't handle it. I guess you were right, my emotions control it. Should I try and bring him back?"

"Yeah, go for it."

He takes a step back and waits for me to begin. This time I decide to try with my eyes open, I didn't have them closed the last times I did it. I concentrate on Aarons face and will him to me. I try and fool myself into thinking I need him. I want him beside me, I can't live without him. I am starting to sound like a sappy romance novel, but I can't seem to get angry again so I may as well try this. I am about to give up and then standing before me is Aaron. He looks a little shocked, staring at me as if I have three heads.

"That was you? You did that to me? I had no control, I went wherever you sent me."

He looks at Jack and they exchange a glance I can only call caution. I think I freak them out a bit.

Jack makes me try again and again, all afternoon taking turns on each of them. They try everything they can to block me or protect themselves against my calls but nothing works. They go where I want and when I want. I then try both at once, this is tougher for me because I have to concentrate on two images at once. After some practice I can do this also. I am learning the stronger the emotion the farther and quicker I can move them. I finally need to take a break and sit myself down on the ground. I lay my back against the cold earth and close my eyes. The boys are discussing strategies on how they might be able to use my abilities and going on and on about why they think I was given this gift. I start to fade, I feel my eyes getting heavy and begin to head into the shadows.

I feel comfort wash over me. I am in the in-between, the place I have lived for so many years. I look around and the dark and shadows are all around me, but I feel safe. I am hoping it is as before and I am just a spectator. I duck behind a boulder to be safe. It doesn't take long for one of the dark creatures to scurry by. He is mumbling something to himself, I catch a few words "she is screwing everything up, he is going to be so upset." He then stops dead in his tracks. Sniffing at the air he turns in my direction. I don't make a sound and wait for him to continue on his way. He doesn't, he comes over to the boulder and again sniffs at it. They have never made any notice of me before but he seems to be smelling me. I try and will myself awake, it's not working. I see his big head start to come around to my side of the rock when someone calls to him. His attention is distracted for just a split second but that's all the time I need to head back into the shadows. I walk for a minute in the darkness wondering what to do next. I want to leave, I know I don't belong here anymore. They know I am here and I am getting the sinking feeling I am the one the monster was talking about. As I walk alone in the darkness, I start thinking about the light and the knights and I want to be there, with them. I feel too vulnerable here. In the next instance I see light up ahead like looking down a long tunnel. I pick up my pace trying to reach the light, I hear voices coming from behind me. When I turn I see a group of the creatures quickly coming up on me. I turn back to the light and run. They can see me, there is no doubt and they are chasing after me. I let out a scream as the creatures are so much faster than me, they will be on me any second. I run with all my strength and as soon as I reach the light, I awake. I open my eyes and see the two boys looking down at me. They scare the crap out of me and I scream again. I jump to my feet and take a second to get my bearings. Aaron apologizes for scaring me but Jack just looks at me with concern written all over his face. I want to go to him and be held by him. He makes me feel safe and I want his arms around me. Instead I give them both a little smile and tell them I am fine. I ask if we can leave and go back to Jacks house. I am done. Jack does not push me for any information, I figure he is waiting until we are alone. I don't know why he does not want to share everything with his brother knights but he seems to want to keep some of my weirdness between us for now. I start heading the way we came and the boys follow. I don't stop and wait for Jacks hand I just keep walking when I see the wall, and pop I am out the other side. I turn and wait for them to come through. When they do they both look surprised.

"When I said you could go thru the wall I meant with one of us, not on your own. How did you know you could?" Aaron asks.

"I don't know, I just knew after I went thru the first time I could do it on my own."

I begin to walk away and the guys don't follow this time. I am starting to get a little agitated. I turn back to them.

"What's up guys? What aren't you telling me?"

I look from one to the other. Jack finally answers.

"You don't understand the way our magic works. The field is protected. If you are not one of us or with one of us you cannot enter. You should have been killed on the spot. I mean dead."

Okay that explains their shocked expressions. I feel my legs get weak and start shaking, I need to sit down. I do, right there in the middle of the sidewalk. Jack and Aaron come over. Looking down at me they each grab under my arms and lift me to my feet. They look around as if I am embarrassing them. I could have just died and they are worried about me drawing too much attention. I let them drag me up the street and down an alley. I wonder what we could possibly be doing in the alley when the light hits my eyes and the next second we are again in Jacks house. Now that's a power! They sit me on the coach gently and go into the kitchen together. I just sit there, not moving. I guess this is what you call shock. Everything is hitting me at once. What the hell is going on? I discovered I am not crazy... but now

I am supposed to participate somehow in the battle between good and evil. I've been close to death more than once in the last 48 hours and now I am sitting in a practically strangers living room waiting to see what they want to do to me next; let alone that the dark creatures can now attack me in my dreams, great!

Chapter 8

I lead my friend into the kitchen where I know she won't be able to hear us. She has more power than I ever imagined. We cannot control her. She can barely control herself. We do her bidding and she is immune to our defences. Maybe Charles is right in being cautious.

"Jack, what are we going to do? Are you sure she is good? Are you sure she is on our side?"

Aaron fires these questions at me with a scared tone to his voice.

"I don't know." I answer honestly. "I do know that she has let me into her head and I do not sense any darkness in her. She sees the darkness but it has not entered her soul."

"Well that's good. What do we do now? We have to tell the others."

I know he is right, this is getting to be too much for me to handle. I still feel the need to protect her but now also feel the need to protect my brothers and myself.

"You go and report to Charles; tell him of everything that happened today and I will talk to Raine and see if she is okay."

Aaron nods and with that is gone. I know he is freaked by this and I want him away from Raine. She trusts me but I need to keep the others away until we get some more answers. I grab a bag of pretzels off the shelf and head back to Raine. As I enter the room I see her sitting right where we placed her, she hasn't moved an inch. She still looks really freaked. I move closer and take a seat next to her. She doesn't even glance in my direction.

"Raine here, I brought you a snack; you should eat something."
She doesn't move.

"Raine can you hear me?"

Maybe she is gone into the other realm. I didn't know she could do it awake but there is a lot I don't know about her. She then seems to snap out of it and looks around the room. She takes a second to get her bearings and then smiles a cautious smile at me.

"Sorry, I was zoned out there wasn't I?"

Grabbing the bag of pretzels out of my hand and shoving some in her mouth. I can tell she is on edge and not wanting to talk.

"Did my backpack make it here?"

She asks looking around the room.

"Yeah, it is by the door."

I get up and go retrieve it for her. I hand her the bag and she makes no move to accept it.

"Raine what happened in your dream?"

She sits there with a blank look on her face. I see her eyes start to moist up and am scared she is going to lose it. I need to keep my distance from her. I am already way too involved but I can't watch her cry and not do anything about it. She is a living thing and I am supposed to be a knight that protects all living things. I am searching for a loop hole.

"They know."

She says and then bursts into tears. She wraps her arms around her legs and tries to comfort herself by slowly rocking back and forth. I reach out to her and then pull back.

"What do they know Raine?

"The darkness... they know when I am there now. I can't go back, they will kill me or capture me which is worse, way worse. I can never go to sleep again. How am I going to never sleep again?"

Her eyes are pleading with me for answers, answers I don't have.

I don't know what to do. I don't like not knowing what to do.

There is only one thing I can think of. She must come with me, into the light. I stand and offer her my hand. She gazes up at me and puts her hand in mine, the tears subside for the moment. I say nothing to her and wrap her in my embrace. She stands still looking at me waiting for me to make the next move, I do. I let my light sweep over us and we are gone into my world.

She lets out a small gasp and I worry that maybe my intuition was wrong, maybe she can't enter the light. Only our kind can, but after what she did at the training field I assumed she could. I look down and pray I have not done the wrong thing. She is still looking at me and seems fine.

"Why did you bring me here, into the light?" Raine asks.

"Because I don't know how to help you and I want you to be alright." I answer honestly.

I then feel the presence of one of my brothers. I release Raine from my embrace and take a step back. When I turn I see Smith standing with his arms folded looking on with disapproval. I begin to tell him why I brought Raine and that I take full responsibility for my actions when Raine interrupts.

"You said you would help me Smith, well I need help. I am sorry I am invading your home but I have nowhere else to go, please."

She looks at him pleading. Smith softens as she speaks and I can tell he is taken with her just as I am. I want to be jealous but I have no time for that, she needs our help, all of us. Smith just nods and leads us to the temple. I know the others will be there waiting. I hope she can smooth talk them as well. We have never had an outsider here, ever. As we reach our sacred ground I turn to tell her the rules.

"You must abide by our rules when in the temple." She nods and I go on. "You can only enter if you are pure of thought, no ill intentions towards our brothers and no secrets can be kept. They will know everything."

She looks a little scared at this information but again squares her shoulders and I feel her confidence build. I want to grab her hand and support her in what she is about to do but cannot. I am now on the sidelines and whatever is decided behind those doors I must obey. I have no say in what happens next but they will look after her, I hope.

We enter the hall and I see she is looking up at the grand paintings that are overhead. They tell of our history, the battles we have faced and the heroes we have lost. They remind us of what needs to be done to keep the light and dark in balance.

In the main hall is a group of knights waiting. They would have been alerted as soon as we came into the light. They would have felt the invasion of their home by an outsider. In my two years here I have never broken a rule. I have been the model student and knight; they will not expect this from me. I don't expect this from me.

The knights turn and look as we enter the loosely formed circle of my brothers. I know them all, some are hard with years of battles and loss under their belts. Others like me are new and open to all this world holds. One thing we all share is our love of the light and the ordinaries we protect.

Raine is looking from face to face searching for something, I have no idea what. She then turns to me gives me a little wink and walks into the centre. What is she doing?

"Hey everyone, I am Raine. I know you are all probably wondering why I am here, well I need your help. The darkness is after me, I don't know why but they want me and I am not sure how to escape them. Jack here has told me very little about you and I know I am an outsider but I want to help you. I will do anything I can to help the light succeed in their war with the darkness."

She takes a breath and waits for someone to say something. I hold my breath in anticipation.

"How the hell did you get in here?" It's Lila.

She is one of the few women in our group. She is a fierce fighter and totally loyal to us. She has been around for a lot longer than me.

"Hi, it's so nice meet you. I got here with Jack; he brought me into the light."

Raine is smiling at Lila warmly, she looks really happy to see another girl.

"You should be dead, how are you not?"

Lila replies in a rude tone. Raine looks taken aback by Lila's demeanour.

"I don't know, I have powers and don't quite understand them.
There are a couple different things I can do and I guess this is one of them."

"And what are the others?" Lila asks.

"I can move knights of the light with my mind and..."

She hesitates and gives me a quick glance. She cannot keep anything from them in this place. She will have to tell them that she can block her mind off from us and that she knows everything about me and where I live.

"...and that's all."

What? How could she possibly do that. No one can stop themselves from divulging everything in the temple. Why did she not tell them the rest.

"We will have to discuss this situation amongst our kind. You will wait and see what our verdict is. Smith can show you where you can rest while we meet."

"I can't rest, if I relax in any way they will enter my mind and get me. I must stay awake."

Lila gives Raine a look of confusion and finally replies,

"Fine then just go and sit there until we figure out what to do with you."

Raine looks at the ground as if she is being scolded by her superior. Smith silently goes to her and grabs her arm. She looks up, a little startled and lets him lead her out of the temple. I must stay and lend any information they need. I hope they do not ask me about Raine's abilities; she did not want to tell them and she must have a reason. I may not have a choice though; I cannot defy the rules of the temple as she can. I will do my best to keep her secrets safe as well as honor my code and convince the knights to help her, the outsider.

Chapter 9

I feel as if I am in a dream, being lead out of this great hall of the knights. I watch the figures on the ceiling as we pass, they look so magical all dancing the dance of war. Some of the images look almost godlike in their poses over their enemy, the dark creatures. In every frame they are winning even with their brothers laying amongst the dead the light wins, every time.

Smith still has a hold of my arm and is leading me into the light. I can't see his face so instead focus on his bulk. He is a huge man. I can see why he is a knight. I don't think he is that old, perhaps in his early thirties and just as beautiful as all the others. Smith seems harder though, like he has faced more and has a great chip on his shoulder about it. He doesn't want anyone to see him inside or out, just his amour.

As we continue on I begin to realize that this place we are in, the light, is in every way the opposite of the dark. There are no corners where shadows can live, or ugly boulders protruding from the earth. It does not smell of rot and death. Here is the smell of love and life. There are trees and grass; the ground is soft, you want to lie in the light and bask in the joy of it. This makes me wonder why I was always sent into the dark, was I that awful of a person that I did not deserve to be here instead?

We come to a clearing with a bench in the middle of it. Smith motions for me to take a seat. I do as told. To my surprise he sits beside me. He looks at me and offers a warm smile.

"They will decide to help you, you need not worry."

Why is this man so fully on my side? He does not know me; he seems like one of their most fierce warriors. Why would he not be suspicious like the rest?

"Why are you so kind to me Smith? The others are all very cautious and they have good reason to be."

"I knew from the first moment I saw you that you were sent to help us not harm us."

"How do you know that?"

"It's just a feeling I have, it has always served me well in wars, I know who is on my side and who is not. And you are on our side."

"Maybe you should go back to the others and tell them this, I don't think I did a very good job at convincing them."

I mean it, if Smith is truly behind me he should be in there with Jack.

"They don't listen to me, I am here for my strength in battles nothing more. There are others in charge of decisions for the brothers. I do as told and protect. This is my duty."

Smith sounds very noble but what kind of life is it if you are never heard, your opinion does not matter. I know the knights of the light are meant to be pure of heart; I guess that doesn't mean you also need to be kind. Like that Lila, she is not a kind person, I can see it in her face. She does not want me here. She is beautiful like all the men but she uses it. I could see her working the room as soon as we entered. She is in control of them and she knows it. I am sure she was at one time pure of heart but I see a hole in her where love used to be. Why do they not see it? I was able to hold back in the temple and not tell of all my powers but she also does not have to divulge all she is thinking. I could tell she was keeping something from the others. Jack said this was not possible. I must let him know right away. Jack, I hope they are not too hard on him, he has only been trying to help me.

I realize I have again zoned out and see Smith staring at me intently.

"You remind me of someone I knew a long time ago."

I am surprised at this, he doesn't seem like the sharing type. I smile and reply,

"Who?"

"My wife."

I am completely taken back by this, I assumed they all became knights when they were young and unattached.

"You are married?"

"I was, before I became a knight. I was given the choice to give up all my ties to that world and become a soldier for good or stay and live as an ordinary."

"And you chose this life over one with your wife?"

I know I am sounding judgmental but if you have someone that loves you why would you ever leave that.

Smith turns and looks at me, I see such pain and regret in his eyes.

"Not at first no, they come to you in your dreams and ask if you will join them. I said no, I had a great life. I was a newlywed with a wonderful woman that loved me completely. We had our future all worked out and were planning on having children. Then she was taken from me. She was killed in a car accident. I was a mess, couldn't eat or sleep. All I wanted was her and knew I couldn't go on without her. They came to me again a few weeks later and I said yes. I didn't really care, I just needed a way out of that life and all that reminded me of her."

"I am so sorry Smith. I can't imagine what you have been through. I have never had someone like that in my life. You were lucky you did, even if it was just for a while."

I am not sure if this is appropriate to say but he needs to know that he had something some of us never get to experience and should remember that.

He looks at me with tears teasing at the corners of his eyes. Smith reaches out to me and pulls me into a big hug. He is almost suffocating me but I don't pull away, he needs this. I feel like he has been holding this in for so long never letting anyone know the real him.

He whispers in my ear, "Thank you." and continues to hold me tight.

Someone then clears their throat from behind us. Smith immediately lets go of me and stands. He looks shocked at me like I did something to him. I don't understand the look and go to say something when he turns and walks away. I turn and see Jack behind me at the edge of the clearing. He looks pissed. I guess things didn't go well. I stand and walk towards him preparing myself for the bad news. As I approach he takes a step back like I am a stranger.

"Jack, what's wrong?"

I ask. I go to grab his hand and he pulls it away.

"What was going on here? Is there something going on between you and Smith?"

I am completely caught off guard by the tone of his voice, he sounds almost angry.

"I don't know what you mean! Smith was just telling me about his wife and got upset, and I was comforting him."

I again reach for Jack and he pulls away. Okay buddy, I don't understand what your problem is but I am about to give up.

"What are you talking about, Smith isn't married. You can't be if you are one of us. Also, Smith doesn't have any deep feelings about anything so that is not what I walked in on. Why are you lying to me?"

He looks about ready to explode, what the hell? I feel like reaching up and smacking him upside the head but think better of it. I turn on my heal instead and march back towards the bench but I keep walking until I reach the edge of the clearing. I hesitate not having a clue where I am going, suddenly I want out of this place away from these people and to be alone. They are all totally screwed up and to have them as the ones that are going to save the world makes me want to laugh, or cry I haven't decided which. I take a deep breath and think of what to do now. Keep walking, just like in the past; that has always been my answer. So I head into the forest, it is not dark or scary it is in the light so it is peaceful and touched with magic. I walk and walk until I feel as if I might fall over from fatigue. Why did Jack have to be such an ass? I just want to know if they will help me and instead I am lost in the woods alone and wanting desperately to sit and close my eyes. I can't, they will find me and that will be it. I find a small path and decide to follow it. It weaves in and out of trees and finally ends abruptly at the edge of the woods. I cannot see past the edge ahead; it is dark. I feel the hair rise on my arms, I should not be here. I turn and start to head back the way I have come when I see a figure blocking the path. It is
Jack. He must have followed me. I don't want to talk to him. As I get closer I decide to just walk right past him without a word. I know I am acting like a juvenile, but I don't want to talk to him. I will go find someone else, maybe Aaron.

"Raine, please."

He reaches for me as I pass, I pull away just as he did and keep walking. Two can play that game.

"Raine wait, I am sorry, I shouldn't have reacted like that. I just..."

He calls after me, I don't turn or stop. He is now jogging to catch up to me, I feel a tingle go up my spine. This is fun, having a man chase after me.

When he reaches me he grabs my arm and spins me to face him. I go to protest but before I can move or speak he presses his lips to mine. Jack is kissing me and I am kissing him back. His lips are so warm and soft as they gently press against mine. This I definitely did not expect. My head is spinning trying to make sense of what is happening. One minute he is screaming at me and calling me a liar and the next he is kissing me. Mood swings much. Just then he releases me and takes a step back. I look into his eyes and wonder what to expect now. I don't dare speak.

"I am sorry Raine, that was totally inappropriate. I don't know what came over me."

Okay, so we are going to lie and pretend that didn't just happen.

"That's okay, I enjoyed it."

He is very tense and I want to lighten the mood. He gives me a little smile and takes a step closer. I know he will not kiss me again, it is written all over his face. This is really disappointing to me. I am surprised how disappointed actually.

"What did they say in the temple?"

Might as well get down to business. He clears his throat and says softly,

"Some are scared of you, they think you were sent here by the darkness to spy or sabotage us. I argued in your defence but the majority fears you are too powerful for us to defeat if you turn against us."

He looks to the ground, like he is ashamed that he did not help me. I lift his head in my hands until he is looking directly at me only inches from my face. I appreciate all he has done for me, I would not be alive right now if it wasn't for him.

"It's not your fault, you did all you could."

I smile and try and show him I am fine. This is not true of course inside all I can think is that I am totally screwed. I lean in closer and gently sweep my lips over his, not a kiss just a caress.

"Watch out for Lila, she is hiding something. Goodbye Jack."

With that I wish him away. I stand for a moment wondering if I have done the right thing. I do not want Jack in anymore trouble with his kind and I know if I told him what I am about to do he would come with me. It is my turn to save him.

I know what I must do; I must face my fear, alone. I again change directions and quickly head back to the edge of the light. This time when I reach it I do not stop, I continue on into the shadows. Every muscle in my body wants to flee but I will not. This is the place where good and evil meet, where light and dark blend together. I am again on the tight rope, good on one side and bad on the other. This time I am choosing bad, I will face them and do any damage to them I can so Jack and the others will be spared. I am not coming back from this, I know I will die but taking down any of the dark creatures with me may help aid in the war and maybe I can finally find peace. After years of constant turmoil to think that it is almost over is a relief, even if the relief is death.

Chapter 10

I have failed her. And now I stand again in my living room alone. My mind is spinning out of control. She is going to them and I cannot stop her. My kind cannot enter the dark realm; we fight between our two worlds or in the ordinaries world. She is going to try and defeat them on her own. She will lose. I fall to my knees as the tears fall down my cheeks. I have never felt so hopeless, I have failed her and now she will die.

I was so blinded by jealousy when I saw Smith with her in that embrace that I called her a liar. I never got the chance to let her know I would help her; I would always be there for her. I don't care what my brothers think; I believe in her and want nothing more than to protect her from the dark.

What can I do?

Just then a burst of white light fills the room, they have come for me. I will be punished for helping her escape. The knights had decided to keep her in the light as a prisoner until the battle was over. And now that she is gone they will think I warned her. Which is exactly what I was going to do.

I look up as the light recedes and see Aaron and Smith standing there looking down at me. I have nothing left in me and do not feel like pretending to be strong. It is rather cruel of them to send Aaron for me, they know we are close. Smith I can understand he feels nothing and follows every rule set before him. I used to be like that.

Aaron bends down and touches my shoulder.

"Are you hurt Jack?"

What to say to this, yes my heart has been ripped out, the girl I love is committing suicide as we speak.

I decide to say nothing. I will not make this easy for them.

"Jack where is Raine, they are saying you helped her to leave the light, that you have turned against us."

I remain still on the ground. I owe them nothing.

Smith then comes closer and grabs me roughly by the arm throwing me to the couch.

"She left didn't she? But you had nothing to do with it, that's why you are here, she made you come here."

Smith really is more perceptive than we give him credit for.

"Yes, I told her they were not willing to help, she told me goodbye and sent me home. She is gone into the darkness and there is nothing I can do to help her."

Another wave of pain flows through my body. Smith and Aaron exchange looks and Aaron sits down beside me.

"You know it is forbidden for you to care so deeply for someone."

I simply nod, of course I know that is why I have been trying so hard to fight it. Now there is no use, Raine will never know. Smith then speaks,

"If she has gone into the darkness there is no way a knight can help her. But..."

At this I raise my head to look at Smith. He starts to pace back and forth looking very intently at the ground.

"Were you not sent here to bring me in for punishment? You almost sound as if you are trying to help me."

"Yes I was sent here to bring you back but I requested Aaron come along as to keep you calm and under control. They will not suspect anything for a little while longer but we don't have much time."

So Smith is trying to help? He brought Aaron because he knows he is my closest ally.

I jump to my feet,

"What is it Smith, what do you know? Is there a way to help her?"

Maybe Smith knows something the others don't.

"It is just an idea I have been toying with. I have always wondered if we could get into the darkness, we would then have the upper hand. They would never expect an attack in their own world."

He has always been an excellent strategist.

"I have come up with only one way. You cannot enter as a being of the light, that we know is impossible, but if someone was to become a human once again, an ordinary then there is the possibility to enter the dark."

I let this sink in and realize he is right. The dark has no issues with ordinaries; they want them, as many as possible, they will not turn away a volunteer. But how? How do I forsake my brothers and turn away from all I know. They are my home and where I feel a part of something. I love my place among the light.

"Are you willing Jack? You have to ask yourself if she is worth it. If the answer is yes we must begin right away before our brothers realize what you are doing."

"Why are you helping me Smith? What's in it for you? And Aaron you should not be here. They will punish you both when they find out."

My friend cannot take the fall for me. I will not let this happen.

Aaron comes over to me,

"You are my friend Jack the first one I have ever had. I don't want you to do this but I know you will never be happy again if you don't. I can see the way you look at her, I have never seen you care so much about anything before her. I hope one day to feel that way about something."

He takes a step back and stands patiently waiting for me to decide. I then look over to Smith waiting for him to respond.

"I am here because I care for Raine. She is full of life and innocence and does not deserve this as her fate. I have felt love once and to turn your back on that is a tragedy. She deserves more, as do you."

I don't know what to say, Smith is not who I thought he was. I was wrong and owe him so much. All I can manage to say is

"Thank you." and shake his hand. He is a man of honor and strength like no one I have ever seen and now I know where it comes from. Love and human ties don't make you weak as the knights think, it makes you strong and the best of all the knights of the light realm.

I have made my decision, although there never really was one to make.

"How do we begin?"

Chapter 11

As I walk I can feel when I have crossed over into the darkness. I know they can sense me and will come to me soon enough. What to do now, wait for them to come or seek them out? I have never been one to stand my ground and fight, I don't really know what to do. I keep moving forward willing myself to continue. I will face these monsters, the ones I have known for years. I will do anything I can to stop them. This feels right, like a fitting end to a very long and horrible story. They have taken so much life from me, it is right I am here in the end.

I start to look back at my life and suddenly think of Julie, the girl I ran into the other day. Her life will be one full of love and joy. She will be married soon and have children. She will grow old with her husband and play with her grandchildren. Julie is going to have a beautifully perfect life and never know anything about what lurks behind the curtain. Blissful ignorance.

I approach a fork in the road, how appropriate. Which way to go, road one to doom or road two to the same doom. Decisions, decisions. I take the one that is darker, might as well get this over with.

I think of my parents and how they tried to fix me and my friends. I hope they all live long and happy lives. They deserve it.
I don't long to see any of them again; they are all better off never knowing what happened to me. Besides they would never believe it anyway.

I hear something coming from behind me. The voices are low and mumbled. I turn ready to face them. They stop dead in their tracks and look at me. They all have contorted and disfigured faces and bodies. They slowly approach with their crude weapons raised. I have nothing, nothing to make me look dangerous. I can see two of them used to be women by their forms. It's nice to see the dark doesn't discriminate either. Why do I think of such things at the weirdest times?

As they inch closer to me I feel this strange sensation build within me. I feel calm, eerily calm. I turn my head slightly and see more of them approaching from behind me. I need to do something; I didn't come here to let them slaughter me this easily.

"I demand to see your leader."

I say in an authoritative voice. This stops them all dead in their tracks. They look at each other and I see a small creature emerge from behind the one pack. He clumsily comes over to me. His head is too large for his body and one shoulder is humped, he is dragging one leg behind him, pretty!

"What did you say girl? It would be better for you to let us deal with you, he will not be as quick as we intend to be."

"I want to speak to him, he is expecting me."

With that I face down the nasty thing in front of me. I stare him in the eyes and do not give into any fear. As I look into those glazed over almost inhuman eyes something begins to change. I see him, the real him in his human form. I blink and rub my eyes. This can't be happening. He is changing. I take a quick glance around to see if the other monsters notice. They all look the same, not seeing what I see. The bombardment of information begins then; his name once was Douglas and he had a family. He got into drugs and lost everything, his wife left him and he never saw his kids again; then jail where he ended up killing another inmate and finally here. I feel light headed. Why is this something I need to know? Obviously he is a bad person that's why he became what he is, who cares about his sad story?

I close my eyes tight and when I open them he is back to normal, his monster self. He looks at me and shrugs his shoulders. I guess he thinks I am the weird one.

"Follow me."

He turns his back and starts to walk away. I follow silently behind. I notice only one other creature has decided to come with us. I must not pose a very big threat. As we walk we pass camps of creatures on both sides. They live in makeshift tents made out of old canvases. It reminds me of the refugee camps I have seen on TV. I start to realize their numbers are a lot greater than before. There must be at least three or four hundred. How did they increase in size so quickly? I told the knights there were only one hundred, they will not be prepared for so many. Jack, I wish I could warn him. He will be my one regret when I leave this life. I wish we could have met before. Before the dreams began and before he became a being of the light. Things would have been much different for us. I guess that is not necessarily true. I have no idea if he would have liked the normal me.

My train of thought is broken when Douglas stops and pushes open big metal doors that have suddenly appeared in our path. Things here are so different they appear and disappear, nothing is constant everything is always changing. The dark shadows behind the walls are even more menacing if that is possible. The air is thinner and colder and I know he is here. I take a step forward past Douglas and look around. I am still calm, which is freaking me out a bit. Am I that ready to die? The voice comes from the darkness and sweeps over me,

"I am so glad you came little one. I have been waiting."

I shoot my pal Doug a look as if to say, told you so.

"Yeah, I'm here. So what now?"

"What do you mean? You have come to die haven't you?"

"I don't get why it is so important for you that I die, I am just a girl who dreams of this place, I have never interfered or tried to stop you or anything."

He comes into view then and he is just as I remember him, scary! He has no concern for personal boundaries as he walks right up to me. He stands only an inch from me with his boney, twisted hands again caressing my face. For a big scary monster he is very touchy feely. I stand rigid not wanting to give him the satisfaction of seeing my repulsion. He runs his fingers down my face and on to my neck. He lets them linger there for a second and then down my shoulder. I want so badly to knock them away but find the strength not to. He is looking into my eyes and it happens again. He starts to morph into what he was. I am amazed at what I see. His name was James and he was an accomplished business man. I see him in a suit at a business meeting. He is tall and distinguished looking. His face is open and friendly. This does not make sense. I feel no darkness in this man. I blink and it is gone. He is again the monster. I want to know more but cannot seem to get back to him. The dark leader is studying me, watching every expression that crosses my face. I feel as if I am an insect under a microscope. He is looking for something in me and I have no idea what. As if breaking out of a spell he takes a step back from me. He looks to his followers who have been waiting silently in the shadow.

"Take her to the pit."

He then turns his back to me and looks as if he is leaving.

"What are you doing? You are keeping me prisoner? I thought you wanted to kill me?"

I fire the questions at him as his subjects grab at me and are pulling me away.

"I have had what you might call a change of heart. You will not die, not yet."

And with that he is gone back to the shadows.

Chapter 12

Smith is leading Aaron and me towards a building I am very familiar with. This is the training field I was at with Raine just a short time ago. He has not yet revealed his plan. I have been racking my brain trying to figure out how to do it. No one has ever tried to become an ordinary again after being in the light. Why would you? I will be giving up all my power, my magic.

Smith is still in deep concentration and has said little since we left my place. Aaron is trying to make small talk, without much success. All I know is we need to hurry; Raine has been there for too long, it might even be too late. I stop myself from thinking like this, I will make it in time and if I cannot stop her death I will be with her at the end.

I look up and see we are now in the field. I didn't even notice passing through. Smith looks over and motions for me to come closer. Aaron remains behind looking more and more miserable at each passing minute.

Smith takes a deep cleansing breath and tells me he knows what I must do. I am eager to hear and ready for anything.

"Jack, in order to leave the light you must do something to break the pureness of your heart."

He looks at me with sad but determined eyes.

"You are a soldier of the light and what you do needs to have grave repercussions. You have proven yourself too many times to make this an easy task."

"I know Smith, what do you think it will take?"

"I know the reason I was made a knight Jack, I was meant to help you so you can help Raine. She is an important part of this story and needs your help to fulfill her role. I have dreams also and they have shown me my path and I have fully accepted it.
You need feel no guilt over what you are going to do."

I have no idea what he is saying to me. Why would I feel guilt for Smith, he is a grown man and is in full control of his actions? I don't understand what he means.

"What are you saying? What is your role other than helping me figure out how to become ordinary?"

As the words fall from my lips a realization hits me. NO! I will not do what he is suggesting. How could I possibly do that? I stumble backwards as if he has hit me. I want to run away, this can't be happening. He sees that I understand and gives me a short nod. I shake my head back and forth and start walking towards the building. Aaron catches up with me and asks what is going on. I turn to him.

"Smith thinks the only way I can succeed is to kill him."

"Jack you can't!"

Aaron says as he grabs my arm and stops me.

"I know that!"

Smith comes up behind us and speaks quietly to our backs.

"You have no choice Jack, she is running out of time and as I said she needs to survive. This is bigger than you. The knights don't understand, she is the key, she is the weapon we have been searching for. Raine will end the war once and for all."

Could he be right? Is Raine the key? Of course, it all makes sense now. We have been searching for something so powerful it will help defeat the darkness not just keep it at bay. We have searched the entire world for it. We felt its presence a few days ago and that is when we started our search here. And we found Raine.

She has no idea what she is. If they kill her now we will never be able to defeat them and this world will come to an end. Darkness will take over and humans will be the prisoners of the shadows forever. I can't let that happen. I thought this was all about me and what I was willing to sacrifice for my love of this girl. Now I know it is about the survival of the human race and what we must do to stop the dark creatures. Smith is right.

I slowly rotate to face Smith.

"Why must it be you?"

"Because they came to me in my dreams. I am the most powerful of the knights and have defeated the most dark creatures. Your offence will make you so hated by the light that you will be sent to the dark realm instantly. And that is where you need to be."

Aaron looks from me to Smith and goes very pale.

"You can't be serious! You are willing to murder an innocent man, your brother, for some girl?"

I look at my dear friend and put my hand on his shoulder.

"No, but I am willing to do it to save this place."

I look around as does Aaron.

"We are supposedly so pure of heart we cannot fully live here in this realm. But do we really live? Ordinaries live to the fullest and leave their bodies knowing they have truly experienced life. We protect it but are not allowed to feel it. I have always been okay with it because I had no reason to want more. Raine gives me that reason and if she is the key to keeping this world safe and able to go on living, I don't think I have a choice. Please Aaron go back to the others and tell them of this. They need to know about Raine and that she is the key. They deserve to know why this is going to happen and about Smith and his great sacrifice."

I turn my back on my friend and feel him leave. He is doing as I ask and I am glad he will not witness what is about to happen. I see Smith readying himself. Every fibre of my soul is screaming at me not to do this. I am a being of the light and am about to do the worst thing imaginable. I am going to kill a brother.

As we stand in the middle of the training field, a place I have always found great comfort and peace, I look at Smith. He does not look sad or scared, he looks at peace. I guess this really is his role and he is willing to sacrifice himself without question. I walk over until we have but a few inches between us. I offer my hand to this giant of a man and he accepts. There is nothing more to say, this is how our lives are supposed to play out and we have both come to accept it. As we look intently at each other I whisper to him,

"I am so sorry."

He replies as only a knight of the light would.

"You are much braver than I will ever be," and then I do it.

As fast and as painless as I possibly can. I throw my light at him with more force than ever before. This is a punishing blow that no one can live thru. In an instant I see the life drain from his face. He is but an empty vessel now; he has moved on, and has hopefully found peace.

"I am so sorry."

I am now alone with the lifeless body of my brother in my arms.

I feel the darkness begin in the pit of my stomach. Agony then spreads to the rest of me. I sense that my light is slowly being sucked out of me and in its place the spread of shadows. I scream in pain and must release Smith as I convulse on the ground. The very depths of who I am is being twisted and reshaped. I hold on to one thought, Raine. She is there at the end of this, she is waiting for me. The pain begins to subside, I am no longer in the training field, it is cold and dark. I am in the dark realm.

Raine.

Chapter 13

I seem to be in an actual pit. I get to my feet and inspect the damage done from the toss into the hole. My pants are ripped at the knees and underneath I see blood starting to seep. My hands are a little marked up but nothing serious. My eyes begin to adjust to the darkness, I take in my surroundings. The space is only about ten feet wide and ten feet deep. I can see the dark creatures walking back and forth over my head. Not sure what to do now. I do what any normal girl would, I start to yell.

"Let me out of here! I don't belong here!"

I keep this up for a while all the time being ignored by everyone. Finally my throat is starting to get sore so I give up. I sit on the cold ground with a thump. When I began this journey to the dark realm I did not expect this, I don't want to be a prisoner, I want to get it over with. What use am I as a captive?

I lean against the side of my dirt box and close my eyes. I might as well get some rest, I am here in the dark so I am assuming I will not have my nightmares. I am already in the nightmare. This brings me some satisfaction; real rest would be wonderful even in a pit. I start to drift into the unconscious. I block out everything else and let myself go.

I wake up to the sounds of fighting. I have no idea how long I was out. I did not dream at all, but I think I did sleep. I rub at my eyes and look up there must be six or seven creatures above me all punching and kicking at each other. I watch for awhile and decide I will try sleep again. I find my spot and get comfortable. Just then what feels like a boulder hits me on the head. I am knocked over and lay there for a minute. What hit me? I then hear its voice.

"You are dead! I will rip you to pieces!"

Oh great, they threw one of them down here and now it"s going to kill me. I was looking forward to a bit more sleep first. I get to my knees and see the creature. He is not looking at me as he spouts his words, he is looking up at the other monsters staring down at us. I stay very still wondering if he even knows I am here. No luck, he then turns towards me and gives a gruesome smile.

"I guess it's not so bad, I have something to play with."

He comes over to me and raises me to my feet. He is just as deformed and stinky as the rest of them. I look into his eyes and wait to see if it happens. It does. His name is Austin and can"t be more than sixteen. He was a gang banger and killed three people in a drive by shooting. He has a mom and sister that loved him dearly. I decide to try something.

"Austin, your mom and sister really miss you."

He drops me to the ground and stumbles backwards as if I struck him. He is shaking his head back and forth vigorously.

"Why would you say that to me?"

He looks at me enraged.

"Because I know who you are and you need to remember."

"No I don't, I am a dark creature and I serve to rid the world of all that is light. No little girl is going to change that."

He spits the words at me. He has made up his mind and comes at me again. I back away but have nowhere to go.

"Austin, please don't do this. The shootings weren't totally your fault. You were looking out for your friends and they had killed your little brother right?"

Again he releases me and shakes his head.

"Stop it! You cannot know such things. What are you?"

"Just a girl who I think was sent here to help you."

That's a crazy thought. Am I supposed to help these monsters? Maybe. He begins to laugh then, a hysterical cackle more like it.

"You cannot help us. We are the damned, we live in the shadows and are what all nightmares are made of and we will bring our kind to the world so all will suffer at our hands."

Okay maybe not to help them. As he is just about to grab me for the third time a rope is lowered down and one of his buddies hauls him up. He gives me a little wave on the way up. I am alone again in my prison. I have no idea how long I have been down here. There is no day and night in this place, it is always dark. I pace back and forth in my cage of dirt wondering what will happen next, how long will they keep me here? And why are they keeping me? Their leader must have something planned. It turns quiet above my head and I feel the cold rush of air as he passes by. They must all be bowing or kissing his feet or something. The rope is then sent down again with a command for me to grab it. I do as told and they haul me up to the surface. Their leader, James is standing before me.

"Come with me little one."

He motions for the others to stay. This scares me even more, the last time I was alone with him he was squeezing the life out of me. He grabs my elbow and guides me out of the makeshift camp. His touch is so cold my arm feels as if it will fall off. We walk for awhile in complete silence. I have no idea what to expect, is this it? Is he taking me somewhere where he can take his time in killing me?

We come to an abrupt stop in the middle of nowhere. He releases my arm and turns to look at me.

"Are you scared?"

Just a little. I say nothing and turn my eyes to the ground. He lets out a ominous laugh and takes a few steps away from me.

"Do you recognize this place from your dreams Raine?"

This is the first time he has said my name. It throws me a bit but I still do not look at him. I know he is waiting to read my face and just as I saw inside him, I have a suspicion he can do the same. I will not let him in. I have secrets about the knights he cannot know and about Jack. I don't want to piss him off so I decide it is better to play along.

"No, I don't."

"You should, this is where you first visited us, four years ago wasn't it?"

He knew all along I was here. That is why I was never caught, they wanted me here. I wasn't invisible they were told to ignore me. At this I feel my temper beginning to lose control, I hate games and this one ruined my life.

"Why, why did I have to come here night after night and watch you and your monsters? Was this all part of your plan? Why am I involved? You could at least tell me that much before you kill me."

He looks at me then and we lock eyes. He is again James in his suit. He is happy. This image is so disturbing to me, how can he be the leader of all that is bad and have been this person? I am drawn closer to him. He seems a little thrown off by my approach. I must touch him to get a stronger connection, he is blocking me with such force but I think I can get around it. I touch his cheek, it is bumpy and icy cold but I don't pull away. It is if he has no choice but to let me. The wall is coming down brick by brick. I see behind it. He is again in his suit, this time covered with blood. Around him are bodies, women and children. He is sitting amongst them weeping. I have never seen such carnage. I pull away from him and have to put my hands to my knees to steady myself. I am then sick; I throw up until there is nothing left in me. I get to an upright position and see him staring at me.

"You saw didn't you?"

He looks almost proud. All I can do is nod.

"I knew you could do that, you know. I was told that one day someone would come and be able to see us as we once were. They said she would hold great power but was not sure what side she wanted to be on. That is why Raine, that is why we let you watch and we never harmed you. You are the key to our salvation. You will help us take over the ordinaries and rule. You will be my partner in the battle and for eternity."

I am speechless. What the hell is going on? I am not a key to any one's salvation, especially the dark creatures. I am here to help the good guys. I am one of the good guys. And by the way... gross, he is crazy if he thinks I am going to be his "partner".

"Why did you kill them all? I saw you, you were good once."

"I had no choice. I was good but all that changed when the dreams started, they pulled me in. Night after night I was told I could rule the world. I would have more power than any living thing. The darkness convinced me to join them but because I was pure of heart, as the light likes to call it. I had to prove myself without question. I did not want to kill all those people but I wanted power more. So I did. I saw the light leave every one of their eyes and with each death I became stronger and better."

"This is better? You are a monster; you rule a bunch of rejects in the shadows. You know nothing of love or joy only fear and hate. How is this better than your life before?"

"Enough! You may not speak to me like that! I am your king and you will do as told!"

He reaches for my arm and throws me to the ground. I crawl away from him as he grabs my ankle and stops me. He rolls me over and holds me down. I try and scream but nothing comes out. He bends his head in close to mine and looks as if he might kiss me. His breath reeks of death and decay. I struggle to get out from under him. He leans in closer and I turn my head from his. I try and go to my happy place but am brought back to reality by what he does next. With his sandpaper like tongue he starts at my chin and licks all the way up the side of my cheek. I have never been so grossed out in all my life. I lay there waiting for whatever he is going to do next.

"You taste of light. You are special Raine."

He then gets off me, leaving me to wipe his saliva from my face. Gross, gross, gross.

"You are free to go as you please. You are now my queen so the others will not bother you. There is one thing you should know, you cannot leave. If you do everyone you have ever loved will be killed. I have creatures posted near each and everyone, it will take but minutes for your parents and friends to die. I need insurance until you decide to fully embrace the darkness. And when you do, they will be safe."

And with that he is gone into the shadows.

Chapter 14

I come to, lying on the cold ground. I see shadows and darkness all around me. I must have passed out. I get my legs under me and notice my feet have morphed into grey and twisted stumps. The rest of my body also feels strange and different. I am a dark creature. The thing is, I still feel like me. I remember my life as a knight and what I did to become this. Smith! I killed him. The pain at thinking about this is still too great, so I push it from my mind. I must find her, she needs my help. I don't know how or what to do or if she will even trust that it is me but I have to try. This place is just as I had imagined it. It is the opposite of the light, dark and stank and hallow. I wander through the shadows looking for someone or something. After hours of nothing I come across dark creatures at the edge of what looks like a village. My immediate reaction is to fight and throw my light at them. I no longer have that ability; my light is gone. They pay me little attention as I pass; I wander into the camp and take in my surroundings. There are tons of them, they are everywhere. Many more than Raine had told us about. Maybe she didn't know.

I find a spot next to a fire and sit. My body is aching and I am totally exhausted. I try and make myself invisible amongst the chaos. Creatures are training and fighting all around me. It is loud and out of control. They are like wild dogs all waiting to be released from their cages.

I am then noticed. A large almost canine-like creature approaches.

"When did you arrive? Who brought you in?"

He growls at me.

"Why the hell should I tell you?"

I figure they won't respond to politeness. I wait for the response. Instead he just hits me on the back and walks away. Okay, that's how we deal with each other, good to know. I listen intently for any information that will help me find Raine. My patience is wearing thin, I must find her. I get up from my stump and decide to take a look around. I walk in-between different creatures of all shapes and sizes. There are men and women, some look quite young and others old. They all look very dangerous and none have even a hint of light within them.

I meander through the crowds and look for some clue as to where she might be. They must have discovered her by now, she has been here a very long time.

All of a sudden the crowd begins to part and I see him, their leader, walking towards me. I move to get back into the crowd and hopefully be unnoticed. He is something to look at, taller than the rest of them and he brings with him the air of death. The ground gets colder as he walks past. He carries himself with such arrogance and all the creatures seem scared into silence. No one dares move until he is gone from our sight. Slowly the noise level increases and the monsters go back to their fighting. I again begin to move through the crowd, this time in the direction of the leader. Someone picks me up from behind and tosses me to the ground. A group starts to laugh and wait for me to retaliate. When I simply stand and start to walk away they begin to yell and draw attention to our little circle. The one who threw me is egging me on. He has an axe in one hand and a claw makes up his other.

"You are a new one aren't you? Let us see what you bring to the darkness. You must fight me or we will kill you!"

I do not need much more encouragement; my temper seems to be somewhat unruly since I became one of them. I release my hold on it now and attack him. I have no weapons but I know how to fight. I throw myself on top of him and we hit the ground hard. We struggle and roll around for a few minutes and then I get the upper hand. I knock the axe away from him and manage to dive for it before he has a chance. They stand around us in a circle not letting either one of us escape. I get to my feet and stand over the clawed man. Without hesitation I swing the axe over my head and cut his clean off. I then turn to the crowd around me and raise the weapon over my head.

"Who is next?"

I yell waiting for any takers. No one seems to care in the least that I just killed their comrade. I don't either. He was a creature of the dark and he deserved to die. I wipe my brow and realize I have his blood all over my face. I leave it, thinking it will make me fit in more. No one steps up to fight me so I push my way through the crowd that has gathered. I guess I no longer look like a newbie, maybe they will leave me alone now.

I decide to get some space and maybe come up with a plan. I find a boulder protruding from the ground, it is away from the hoards of creatures but I can still see and hear what is happening. I take a seat at the base of it and lay the axe on my lap. I am completely done, emotionally and physically. There has been no sign of Raine anywhere. I begin to think maybe I am too late, maybe they have already disposed of her and are on to other things. Or maybe she never came here. No, I know that is not true. She told me goodbye as if that was our last and there is nowhere else she could go that I couldn't follow. I wonder how betrayed she feels by me? I kiss her and then tell her we are not going to help her. She never gave me the chance to tell her that I was still going to no matter what Lila and the others decided; I would be there for her.

I feel the earth turn even colder below me and look up to see the leader standing in front of me. He moves in silence. I recognize him from the alley; that was the first time I ever came face to face with him. He usually avoids battles with the knights and sends his minions to do his dirty work. For a split second I am scared he may recognize me. Then I remember... I am a dark creature now, which would be impossible.

"You are a competent fighter. You did well against one of my best. I need you to come with me."

I rise and follow. There isn't even a hint of remorse or anything in his voice. This is very unnerving, he feels nothing. We head back to the others and they again go silent and part for him to pass. I walk a step behind still gripping the axe. I should do it right now, he would never suspect and it would be over. I would be most definitely killed instantly but their leader would be gone. No wait, Raine said they would just find another one. That they were always fighting for position and then I would never find her. I will bide my time and wait for a better moment. I relax my grip on the axe just slightly. He motions to a few others in the crowd as we pass, he is collecting us together. By the time we are through the mass of bodies there are a dozen of us. We then pass through heavy metal doors that weren't there a second ago. This doesn't seem to faze the group so I go along trying to look stern and cold like the rest. He moves to the side and motions for us to enter. We proceed into the strange room that has no ceiling. The walls also look as if they are made of metal and it has a circular curve to it. Looking around I am not sure what to expect. Are we here to fight each other? Is this how the fearless leader gets his kicks?

"You few have proven to me that you are worthy of a very important assignment. You will be protecting my queen. She is new to this land and has yet come to accept our ways. You must protect her against all others of our kind and herself. She is unpredictable and needs our special attention. Do you understand?"

A few grumbles go through the crowd of monsters. One speaks out.

"We are made for fighting and killing, not babysitting!"

And with that he is struck down by the dark leader, nothing left but some ash on the ground.

"Any other complaints?"

He sweeps his arm around the circle looking each of us in the eye. We proceed one by one to bow our heads in compliance. I am spinning. A queen? I have never heard that there is a queen of the dark realm. If there is a queen does that mean the leader has now declared himself king?

"For the rest of you a note of caution, she has great power and I am not responsible for you if you do something to upset her."

He begins to walk away and then as an after-thought adds,

"She will be easy enough for you to find, she looks like an ordinary. Go now and do your job."

He then fades into the side wall and is gone. I feel my heart leap from my chest. It's Raine, she is alive. Alive and a queen?

Chapter 15

I feel dizzy and sick. I am a prisoner of the dark leader and he thinks I am his queen. He is going to kill my family if I don't obey.

He is a big scary ugly monster and thinks I am into that.
Why me?

I stagger around trying to make sense of it all. I need to leave, to warn the light that the dark is much more dangerous than thought. They have plans, big ones and they include me. I am a good person yet this race thinks I am willing to help them. I think James is drunk with power. He has no idea that I will never embrace this life, I will not become a dark creature. I know what will happen if I do, the human race will be obliterated, my family and friends along with it. Using them to keep me subservient won't work. But I will stay, for a while anyway to try and figure out what and when their next move is and how it involves me.

I decide to head back to the camp. I don't have to be afraid of the creatures any longer; I guess they are my subjects now. I start heading the way we came, trying to figure out what my part in all this is. I feel the presence of someone behind me. I can tell they are pacing themselves so as to follow, not catch up. My bodyguards I am guessing, the dark leader doesn't trust me, what a shame. I keep up the same pace and don't turn. They can keep following me for all I care. I walk and walk and walk. I go past the camp realizing I don't really want to hang out with monsters right now. I need space and time to wrap my head around all this, and food. I am starving. I can't remember the last time I ate. Hmm… I wonder if my bodyguards have to do anything I say. So I stop and decide to see. I turn and see six large monsters stopping abruptly. They look somewhat frightened. This is good. I motion for them to come closer and as

I do this I notice a few more of them come out from either side of me. I need a lot of protecting it seems.

"I am hungry. One of you must go and get me something to eat. And not here, I want real food from the human world."

They all just stand there and keep staring at me. What good is it being queen if your followers don't listen to you.

"Are you all deaf? Get me some food!"

They continue to stare at me. Finally one of them takes a step closer to me. He says nothing but stares into my eyes. The others take a step back as if afraid of what I am about to do.

"Good, I want..."

As I am about to tell him my order I see him. It can't be! I look into his eyes and see Jack staring back at me. My knees go weak and I am falling when he grabs a hold of me. He then shouts over his shoulder,

"The queen is ill, go inform the king and get her some food. Hurry!"

I see them scramble and take off. There is only two left and they have taken position a ways away. Jack still has a hold of me and lowers me to the ground. As he does this he whispers,

"You know it's me don't you?" I nod in reply.

"Don't say anything just listen. I am here to help you escape."

"You can't, I must stay. Jack, why do you look like them?"

I sit up then and notice the others looking at us. I put distance between myself and Jack as to not draw any suspicion. He lets me move away. He looks sad. I want to comfort him but this is not the time or place. The air then turns cold and he has arrived.

"What is going on here?" he bellows.

I must play my part and not give Jack away.

"I am not one of you, I need food to survive. I was about to pass out when one of your bodyguards caught me."

I turn to Jack and give a small nod of approval. James then turns his attention to Jack and also seems to approve.

"You have proven yourself once again, you will stay with my queen at all times make sure she gets everything she needs."

He then turns his attention to me.

"You will have food right away my dear."

He comes close then and strokes the side of my face, I do not move away but see Jack tense at my side. We must play our parts.

"And sleep, where can I do that?"

I need to speak to Jack and if he must be with me at all times we need someplace private to talk.

"I have made a place for you in my chambers of course."

I see Jack's hand go to his axe.

I respond quickly before Jack does anything stupid. I put on my best flirty girl voice.

"My king, you know that is not appropriate. I am not ready to share your bed."

I stroke the side of his face just as he does mine and try not to look completely disgusted. I can feel Jack ready to attack at my side, I plead with him silently to keep control. Let this play out and then we will have time to talk.

"Very well, I will have my subjects make you up a bed in the gallery. You will be close to me that way if you need anything."

Great.

I nod and take a step back. He turns his attention to Jack then,

"I am putting you in charge; make sure she has all she needs, if you don't you will end up like all the others that have failed me."

Jack just nods and steps closer to me. The dark leader leaves us then but we are still not alone. I give Jack a quick glance and address the troops.

"Please show me where I can rest."

The others still looked completely afraid every time I speak. I wonder what James has told them to make them look at me like that.

"Let's go!"

Jack commands and the others begrudgingly comply.

We walk, with Jack at my side and the other two leading the way. I can't bring myself to look at him. I prefer to just feel him by my side, this way I can imagine him as before. Of course when I look in his eyes I see the real him but I can't exactly stare at him without drawing suspicion. Why did he come? He should not be here, if they find him out he will be dead in an instant. We must be careful.

We arrive back at the camp and pass by my pit. Again the giant metal doors appear before us. The two creatures open them up and Jack and I pass through. The space inside has changed, it now is a chamber. It is a small area still with a dirt floor but there is a cot in one corner and a wash basin placed on a rock. The blankets on the cot are torn and old but actually look clean. I turn then to tell the others I want some privacy. As I do I see the two creatures leaving, Jack turns back to me as the doors close.

"What did you say to them?" I ask.

"I told them that you wanted time to rest; that I would stay and watch over you. They did not argue, they are really scared of you."

Jack does not raise his head as he speaks and seems to be hiding his face from me. I go to him and touch his chin to raise his face to meet mine. He does not repulse me like the king; I don't even really see the monster when I look at him. I make him look into my eyes. He is there and I see something I never wish to see again. Smith and Jack are in the training field and Jack is killing him. He is striking him with his light and Smith is dying. I back away from Jack and don't stop until I hit the far wall. How could he? He is a knight of the light and he murdered Smith. Smith was a noble knight that only wished good on the world. What has Jack become? I start to cry and feel as if the tears will never stop. I curl in on myself and wish him away, I want him gone. I look up and see he is still here. I guess he really is a dark creature otherwise I could make him leave. He looks sad and not sure what to do.

"Raine, I know I don't look the same. Please don't be scared, I would never hurt you."

I lose it then.

"Hurt me? What about Smith, why did you do it?"

"How do you know?"

He bows his head and turns away from me to face the wall.

"I can see it, I see what dark creatures used to be and why they are here. You are a murderer. You deserve to be here!"

"Yes I do. I did as you say and killed my brother. But, you have to know it was his plan. He told me this was the only way I could save you and you need to be saved Raine."

His voice is sad and full of remorse. He still is facing the wall. I am a mess, crying and in shock he did this. I can't wrap my mind around it.

Knock, knock. Two quick taps on the door and I jump up and wipe my face. Jack does not move.

"What is it?" I call out.

"I have food for you. May I enter?"

I think they have taken manner classes since they left.

"Yes."

A monster enters the room with a bag of fast food under his arm. He looks from me to Jack and shrugs his shoulders. I don't think he cares what is going on in here. He places the food on the cot and leaves. What a strange thing to see, a big gruesome creature of the dark being my delivery boy. I wonder if he went thru the drive thru?

I go to the cot and sit, not knowing what to say to Jack or if I even want to speak to him again, I decide to eat. The burger tastes a bit cold but unbelievably good. I gobble it down in silence while Jack never moves from his post against the wall. Once I have finished every bit of food in the bag I feel a little bit better. I still have no interest in talking to this monster before me. He betrayed his kind and killed one of his own, why would I trust anything he has to say. The silence is so very quiet. Finally I break it.

"Why do you think I need saving? Don't you see I am the queen of the dark realm?"

I don't mean it but I want to hurt him and this is a good way to do it.

"How do you know this wasn't my plan all along?"

He finally turns to me and I see how much pain he is actually in.

"Because I know you Raine. You are good, better than anyone I have ever met, human or knight. You need to leave this place and help my brothers, you are their only hope."

So he thinks I am the salvation of the light and James thinks I am the salvation of the dark. What if I am no one's salvation? I hope I am not the answer; it's a little too much pressure.

"Was this really Smith's plan? Why would he sacrifice himself to save me?"

I am not as angry as before but still don't totally trust this monster. I want Jack, my Jack.

"He believed in you and knew you are what the knights have been searching for. That day I first met you, remember, we were searching for a weapon, one that would give us the advantage in the war."

"And you think I am that weapon?"

"I know it sounds crazy but..."

I interrupt, "That is what the dark leader thinks also. That is why he has not killed me, he wants me by his side at the battle to use for the darkness."

"You can't Raine. He will take over the world. It will be the end."

His eyes are pleading with me and I am starting to believe his story.

"I know but he has my family and friends. If I don't do as told he will kill them all. I don't plan on helping him but need some time to figure out what to do."

Jack moves closer to me but not so close as to touch.

"I will help you, I will give my life to make sure your family is safe and you get out of here."

"We must do it together Jack and then you can tell the others and they will make you a knight again."

He gives me a heartbreaking smile and turns his face away from me.

"Jack, we are leaving here together!"

I am starting to get the idea that he has something else in mind.

"Raine, I preformed the most appalling of crimes. I killed my brother knight and not just any knight; he was the best of our kind. I will not be leaving this place."

Jack walks over to the door and leaves without another word. I fall on to my tiny bed and weep. I cry myself to sleep and do not dream. I am alone, again.

Chapter 16

Closing that door behind me was one of the hardest things I have ever done. She is behind that door and I want to be there with her and hold her and tell her everything is going to be alright.

She is going to be safe and so is everyone else. I don't know this to be fact. I am a monster, a murderer and she is a queen. I never imagined this to be the outcome when I literally ran into her just a few short days ago. I can't face her right now, she has lost faith in me and who can blame her. She saw me kill Smith and knows I will never again be the man she once knew. I stand outside the doors not daring to take another step; I will protect her for as long as I can. The other creatures are sitting around looking bored and paying me no attention. I must think.

The dark leader wants Raine as well. So he knows of her power but I wonder if he knows what that power is? I have no idea and neither does Raine. If we knew maybe we could figure out what to do next. I must get more information. Just then the dark leader approaches. He pays little attention to the others laying about and comes directly over to me.

"Is she resting?"

He is sure an arrogant S.O.B.

"Yes sir, she ate and is now sleeping. I stepped out to give her some privacy."

He cocks his head to the side and looks at me as if I am wacko.

"You have very good manners for a creature of the dark. When did you arrive?"

He is getting suspicious; I need to be more monster like.

"Not long ago sir, but I was told by the queen that if I did not show more respect and manners she would do something even worse to me than you could. And I saw what you did to that creature before so I am not taking any chances."

He laughs then and strikes me on the shoulder.

"You are right to do as she says, she is a powerful creature."

I see an opening and decide to take it.

"What is she my king? She scares us all so, maybe if we knew what she is we could better handle her."

He looks at me again as if deciding whether or not to answer.

"She is like nothing this world has ever seen before. She has more power than either the dark or light. She will decide our fate and I am going to make sure it is the right decision."

With that he pushes past me to enter the chamber. I cannot let him be alone with her, he is a dark creature but he is also a man and I saw how he looked at her before; he wants more of her than just a weapon.

"Sir, she said she did not want to be disturbed for any reason, that if any one entered her chamber she would not be responsible for her actions. Maybe you should let her rest and I will send for you once she is awake."

I hope this works. He lets out a sigh and closes the door.

"Fine, make sure someone gets me as soon as she wakes."

I nod and give him a small bow. Might as well make him feel he really is the king, this can only help me get more information in the long run. As he leaves I start to relax a bit. I want him as far from Raine as possible. I look around and see the others relax as well.

I decide to give Raine time to rest so I do the same; I take a seat leaning against the doors to her room. No one will be able to enter without me noticing, especially the dark leader. It doesn't take me long to drift off to sleep.

In my dream I see Smith; he is standing in the training field and waving to me. He looks happy and at peace. I start to walk towards him and see I am my old self, I also look happy. From behind Smith comes a woman, she is wearing a dress that makes her look as if she is floating towards him. She grabs his hand and they are beaming at each other. As I approach they turn to face me. The lady takes a step forward and stops right in front of me, Smith behind her still staring at the woman. She leans into me and whispers in my ear,

"You did the right thing, you are forgiven."

Then she gently places a kiss on my cheek. I look at her and tears begin to flow down my face. She flashes a brilliant smile at me and turns to go back to Smith. When she reaches him she jumps into his arms and they spin and laugh with each other. Smith looks in my direction and gives another wave. Then they are gone, they fade into the sun together.

I awake with a start. For a moment I don't remember where I am.

I look down and see my deformed hands and remember, this makes me want to cry again. Why would Smith come to me in my dreams and get his wife to tell me I am forgiven. I do not deserve it.

Just then Raine opens the door behind me. She looks around at all the creatures and then notices me at her feet. She looks bad, as if she has been crying for hours. I get up and look from her to the crowd of creatures that have come over to wait for her orders, I guess.

She sees the crowd of them and puts on her authoritative face.

"I need some clean water so I can wash up."

She passes the basin to one of the creatures and waves him away. He does as told and the others wait for instruction.

"The rest of you can go back to what you were doing. You there, I need you inside to help me move my bed, I do not like where it is located."

She motions for me to follow her. I close the door behind me and stay by the door. Raine goes over to her bed and sits. She rubs at her face and looks totally exhausted. I wish I could make it better for her.

"You are not staying here. I will make sure that when I leave this place you are with me. I know you came to rescue me but I think I need to rescue you instead."

I almost laugh at her, she sounds like her old self. She is so determined. I will go along with what she says, if she needs to believe we are leaving together then I will let her think that. I know this is impossible, but if this is what she needs to fight for the light so be it.

"Whatever you say. I will not let you down again Raine."

She looks up at me and gives a sad smile.

"You have never let me down Jack. You are still my knight and I will always see you that way, even if you don't."

She is breaking my heart. I don't want her to think of me like that anymore. She deserves better than this, this monster before her.

The doors then open and in he comes. He is staring at Raine and does not even seem to notice I am in the room. She pays him little attention and keeps her eyes locked on mine.

"You are awake my dear. I hope you are well rested."

She turns to him and tries to hide her disgust. I see it there though just for a split second before she gains her composure.

"Yes, thank you. Why are you here?"

Raine does not seem scared of the dark leader at all. She treats him as if he is a annoying acquaintance and nothing more. This makes me happy. He turns to me then and looks taken aback at her response.

"You may leave us. I need some time alone with my queen."

I reach for my axe and am ready to fight; he will not be alone with her, ever. Raine stands then and motions for me to stop. The king does not see her do this. She again motions for me to leave, I must trust she knows what she is doing but I do not think she knows what he wants from her.

"My queen, do you wish to be left alone with the king?"

He looks furious. How dare I question him? The thing is I don't really care what he thinks. I look at Raine and wait for her response.

"Of course you can leave me with the king, he will do nothing to harm me, will you?"

The dark leader looks confused and pissed.

"Why am I being questioned by a servant? You have no right to address me like this. Of course I will not harm the queen, now leave!"

Raine again motions for me to leave; I guess she knows what she is doing.

"I will be right outside if you need anything my queen."

I give the king a nod, hoping he has some sort of respect for women. If not, he will be dead very soon.

Chapter 17

I watch as Jack leaves my small chambers. I don't want him to go but if he stays he is sure to get found out. The dark leader is very touchy feely and I don't think Jack could handle watching that. I go back to sitting on my cot, waiting to see what James wants now. I know he will not hurt me, I am too valuable to him and the rest of the world it would seem. I don't like it but guess I had better come to terms with it. Everyone wants me but not because they like me or think I am a good person or they think I am interesting because I am the "key" to it all. I have no idea what that means. Am I an actually key, do I unlock something? This is an interesting thought, one I should think on more when not in the presence of the dark king. I decide to try and be somewhat hospitable to this creature in front of me. The more he trusts me the better.

"Thank you for the food and letting me get some rest. I appreciate the privacy as well.

He walks over and takes a seat beside me on the small bed. It looks strange, I have never seen him sit before. He looks awkward.

"You are welcome. I want you to be happy here. I know you are not used to it here but you will be, with time."

Yeah right.

"If I accept your offer, will I turn into one of you?"

This is something I have been wondering and decide it is best to keep the conversation moving just in case he wants to lick me again.

"I don't know, but I don't think so. You have done nothing to make you transform into this, you deserve no punishment."

I am glad to hear this, even though I will not be on their side I didn't like the possibility of looking like them, like Jack.

"So my dear, does this mean you are ready to give yourself over to us, to the dark realm?"

"I don't know. What am I supposed to do exactly in the battle? You say I have all this power but what does that mean?"

I hope he gives me some clue; I need to know what is expected of me from either side.

"All I know is that you will be the deciding factor in the battle, whichever side you choose is sure to come out as the victor.

Other than that I don't know exactly what power you hold. But remember, I hold power also and your family is at great risk if you defy me."

"I know."

I don't know actually, if I am the most powerful why can't I just wave my hand and make him disappear. Make the whole dark realm disappear; now that would be the ultimate power wouldn't it?

James turn to face me and grabs my hand. I don't pull away.

"I don't want to threaten you Raine, I would like nothing more than to make you happy and have you be by my side willingly. I am the most powerful of all dark creatures but with that comes great loneliness."

I have to try and keep my feelings in check. This thing beside me is a mass murderer and wants to end the world but also wants to have someone to share it all with. How touching. I sit very still unable to think of a single thing to say. I will not comfort him. He grabs me then and pulls me towards him, I have no choice but to be in the embrace; he is much too strong for me. I try desperately not to scream; if I do Jack will come and get himself killed. The monster paws at me, holding me close; he must think my lack of response means I am enjoying it. I struggle to pull back a bit but he just takes it as a sign to get rougher with me. He brings his hard and calloused face in to mine and tries to find my lips. I can't help it, I cry out. In an instant he has released me and he is across the room lying on his back. I look up and see Jack standing over me putting himself between James and me. The dark leader jumps to his feet and gives Jack a lethal stare. Jack glances back at me quickly and asks if I am all right. I nod and let out a scream as the dark leader lunges at Jack and knocks him to the ground. He sits on top of him and grabs around his throat.

"You will now die servant! I will watch the light leave your eyes and then feed you to the others!"

Jack is stuck underneath this monster… what should I do?

"James please don't kill him! He must have heard me scream and thought I was in danger. Please my king, I will do whatever you want, just don't kill him!"

As the words left my mouth I knew this was true, I will do anything to save Jack. I see his grip slightly loosen around Jacks neck. He does not move from on top of him but turns his head towards me.

"You will become my queen in every way if I do not kill this one insignificant creature?"

I nod yes.

"Why? Why is he the reason you will join me and not your family? There is more going on here isn't there?"

I look away and stare into Jacks eyes. I have tears running down my cheeks as I see him, the old him, the man I love.

With that the dark leader seems to get what is going on. Rage surges through his body as he stands and grabs Jack up from the ground. He throws him across the room at me and I catch Jack before he hits the ground again. I put my arms around him and hold him close. Jack does the same, he holds me tight for only an instant and then starts to release me. I look up into his eyes and tell him. This might be it for us and he has to know.

"I love you Jack."

And I place my hand on his chest right where his heart is. Suddenly there is a tingling sensation in my palm. I feel heat radiating from my hand. Jack continues to look into my eyes. I don't know if he can feel it but something is happening. I must release my eyes from his and look down. The heat has turned into light, bright white light dancing between my palm and Jacks chest.

I hear the dark leader suck in his breath. I pay him no attention though something is happening and I sense it is a good thing. Jack and I watch and the light gets bigger and brighter it is penetrating thru his clothes and into his body as if I am shocking him with electricity. His eyes widen and he looks back up at me.

"What is happening?"

"I don't know. Does it hurt?"

He shakes his head no. I leave my hand where it is and turn my attention for a split second to the monster in the room. I see he is also staring at what is happening with wide eyes. I see him reach for something under his long robe; it looks like a weapon, a knife. Everything becomes slow motion. I know what the king is about to do but I can't stop it. I am connected to Jack and cannot break it. We are one for the moment. I watch as the dark leader takes the knife and raises it above his head and then he releases it. I try and move Jack out of the way but it is too late. It strikes Jack in the neck, he looks at me with complete horror. Blood is spurting everywhere and he falls to the ground. Our connection is broken. I fall to his side and try to stop the bleeding; his deformed face is in complete agony. My hand is still tingling and out of nowhere I feel something rise within me. I feel power, like nothing I have ever felt before; and hate; pure rage. I turn to the dark king and slowly let go of Jack, who is grabbing for me but I have something to do before I can help him. The fury within me is building by the second and I want to rip this monster apart, I want to watch him die. I take a step towards him and another, he has nowhere to go. We are in a small room and the only door is behind me. Jack cries out in pain, this distracts me for but a second but long enough for the dark leader to fade into the shadows. I am furious but I know I will kill him, and that has to be enough for now.

I hear Jack gagging and choking on the ground. I run to him and pick him up in my arms. The wound on his neck is deep; he is losing too much blood. He cannot speak but seems to be trying to say something. I soothe him the best I can and try and figure out what to do next.

"Jack, it's okay. I am here."

I stroke his hair. I feel helpless. I have discovered my power but what good is it if I can't help Jack? He is getting quieter and quieter; I fear the end is near. I hold him tight to my chest and rock him gently back and forth. My hand begins to tingle again and I look down, Jacks chest is also glowing with the light I placed there. I have an idea. I look into Jacks eyes and see him as he used to be, the knight of the light realm. I see us practising in the training field and remember how I could move him at will. I see us moving then, together in his light. We are going into the light, to his home. I bend and gently kiss his lips and wish with everything I have that we are doing just that, moving to the light.

I feel his body go limp in my arms, my eyes open and he is barely there but he is Jack. He no longer looks like a monster. His beautiful eyes are looking at me but the light is leaving them. I then notice it is no longer dark around us. We are somewhere light and familiar.

"Hold on Jack, please. I have brought you somewhere for help. You have to hold on."

His eyes seem to focus again and he gives me a very slight smile. I stroke his dark curly hair and try and memorize his face. I love this face and want to remember it always. As we sit in silence staring at each other I hear a voice coming towards us. I look up to see knights, bunches of them running towards us. I scream at them to hurry and help. As they approach I recognize Aaron, Jack's best friend. He reaches us and falls to his knees. He looks at me searching for answers.

"I am so sorry Aaron, please help him."

"You did this to him?"

"It is my fault, don't let him die!"

Someone comes up behind me and pulls me away. I fight them and scream. I want to stay with Jack. Whoever it is, is much stronger than me and I fight in vain. I am being dragged away, my body finally gives up and I let them. I see more knights surround Jack and light ascends into the air. I send out a silent prayer.

Please save him, please.

I am then dropped onto the ground with a thump. I just lay there and sob. I have killed the most important thing in my life, I want to die, but not before I kill the dark leader, the king, James.

I hear a voice come from behind me.

"You really need to calm down Raine; you are of no use to anyone acting like this, especially Jack."

I look up and see Lila looking down at me. Great, out of all the knights of the light I get the bitch as my caregiver.

Chapter 18

God it hurts. The pain is just too much, I want it to stop. Please someone make it stop. I know I am close to death so why won't someone just put me out of my misery. All around me is fog, like I am swimming in a sea of it. I reach the surface for just a split second before I am pulled under again. I can't breathe. I can't move. Help me, please?

I am surfacing again and I see her. Raine is over top of me; she is crying and saying something to me. I can't hear her. I try and tell her that I don't understand but nothing comes out. I am in her arms. She feels warm. I try and smile to let her know I am okay with this. I needed to save her from him and I did. She found her own power and now she can protect herself. My job is done. Let me go. I am at peace with dying I just want the hurt to end. I am back under. I cannot see her or feel her. I think of my life, it was a good life. I did something not many have, I defended the world against the darkness. They will never know but this is a good thing. My life was not wasted. I surface again to see it is no longer Raine's arms I am in, Aaron is holding me.

My friend. He looks upset. I want to tell him he was the best person I have ever known and he should go on and be happy. He deserves it and love. He needs to find love, it is a pity to miss out on such a wonderful thing. I sink back into the abyss. It is getting darker and the fog thicker. I don't know if I can come up again it is heavy and I want to let go. I feel my body one last time and there are many hands on me. What are they doing? It doesn't matter it is too late. I release myself from this form, I am leaving, the pain stops.

Chapter 19

I don't respond to Lila. She has no idea what I am going through or what I have been through. She stands over me as if she is my prison guard, maybe she is. I move to a sitting position and look around. We are in a grassy area and the light is warm on my bare arms. I have not felt warm for a long time.

I am still sobbing and have no intention of stopping. I want to cry until I pass out, which I hope is soon. Jack is not going to get better, I know the knights will try but he was too far gone, he had lost too much blood.

I feel empty inside, like he was a large piece of me and now it is gone. I should not have screamed. I should have let the dark leader do what he wanted, then Jack would still be alive.

Lila comes over to me and crouches down.

"What the hell have you done? Why is Jack bleeding to death and how did you get here?"

I look at her and realize I want to rip her face off, literally. What right does she have to judge me? I guess she is one of the leaders of the knights and Jack is a knight, or is he? He killed Smith and became a dark creature and I think I changed him back. I don't know how but when I touched him with that light he transformed. I will always be grateful that he got to leave this life as his beautiful knight self. He deserved it.

I look up at Lila and decide to answer her best I can.

"I don't know what happened, he was attacked by the dark leader and I knew he was not going to make it. I wished us safe and somewhere he could get help. The next thing I knew we were here in the light."

I am not going to tell her about Jack being a dark creature or that I now have the power to change dark into light. She has not earned the right to that information yet.

"So you brought you both here? You have the power to enter our realm? I do not know if this is a good thing Raine, you are proving to be much more than you lead us to believe."

"I really don't care Lila. I am here and Jack is dead and whatever you want to do with me is fine. I was in the darkness for a long time and do not want to ever go back. I will help you defeat the dark creatures but you must do one thing for me in return."

"And what would that be?" she says with a sarcastic snarl.

"I get the king, the dark leader, he is mine."

I say this with the knowledge that this day will come and I will defeat him.

She looks at me and seems to be contemplating what I have said.

"You think you are so special that you can make the difference in our war? You are but a little girl with some strange power that I don't think you even know how to control."

"I have nothing left to say to you Lila, why don't you go back to your boss or whoever and tell them what I have proposed. If you want my help fine, if not let me go and I will find and kill the dark leader alone. Either way it will happen so let's just get on with it."

I turn my back to her and lay my head on the ground, I am done. I don't want to talk anymore. All I want is to think of Jack.

I hear her leave me a few seconds later. Tears are still falling, I have no control anymore. I must pull myself together, the dark leader will be after me now and I don't have much time. I sit up with a start. My family, he has probably already got to them. And how many others I have cared about in my life, how many other deaths are on my hands. I am a murderer. Just like the dark creatures. How am I any better than them?

I hear someone approaching. I look up and see Aaron. His face is streaked with dried tears. I caused him this pain. He bends down and pulls me to my feet. Quietly he brings me into him and whispers in my ear.

"Raine you have to leave. They have decided you are too dangerous and plan on executing you. They say they have reason to believe you are working with the dark realm and are here to sabotage us."

I look at him as if he is speaking Chinese. Why would I come to them for help if I was a bad guy? Lila, she is twisting everything and making them think such things.

"Aaron, I can't leave. I don't know how and I don't really care enough to run. Let them do as they will."

Death would be peace.

He shakes me as if to wake me up.

"Raine, stop it. You have to fight. You have to live. Smith gave his life for you and Jack needs you to be safe."

This gets my attention. Jack needs me safe, why?

"Jack?"

"Yes Jack, he cannot protect you against all the knights especially in his condition. You must get someplace safe and wait until we can figure out what to do next."

I fold under the weight of my body, Aaron holds me tight.

"He, he is alive?"

I search his face for any signs of a lie.

"Yes Raine, he is alive. He is in bad shape and is not out of the woods yet but he is breathing. We will do everything we can to save him. And he would want you safe so please do as I ask."

I cannot think. Jack is alive!

I want to jump and scream and kiss Aaron. But I must go, I need to get away. I nod at Aaron and stand on my own. I have no idea what to do but I will try. I close my eyes and think of the human world, I see my crappy apartment. I have not thought of this for what seems like years. I see my cranky landlord and my front door. I wish with everything I have to be there. When I open my eyes I am staring at my front door. I look around and see if Aaron has made the journey with me. I am alone, alone in the hallway in front of my place. I grab the key from above the door frame and go inside. Everything looks the same, just as I left it only a few days ago. I am shaking and feel as if all my nerve endings are exposed. I am raw to the bone. I look around the room and have no idea what to do now. I stay frozen for a while and just wait. For what I have no idea.

Jack is alive and that is all that matters. He will heal and come for me. I hope. I decide finally to take a shower. God knows I could use it. I have blood and tears and sweat and dirt and monster grime all over me. I go through the motions of it but feel very disconnected. When I am done I put on some clean pj's I had left in my dresser and go sit on the couch.

I sit and sit and sit. Hours pass and still nothing. I have no motivation to move. I am waiting but still don't really know for what. Am I waiting for Jack? Yes, but I know he will not come yet, he is still in bad shape. Am I waiting for James? Yes, but I know he would not dare come here. The look on his face the last time I saw him makes me believe I now have the upper hand. He is scared of me and that makes me feel ever so slightly happy. I begin to think I may never move again when there is a knock at the door. I get up and go see who it is. I open it cautiously and am totally thrown off by who is behind it.

"Dad, what are you doing here?"

My father is standing in front of me. I have not seen him in years. He looks older and stressed. I look behind him for any signs of my mother. He is alone. He just stares at me and says nothing.

"Would you like to come in?"

He pushes past me and enters my crappy apartment. I motion for him to take a seat on the couch and I sit down across from him on an ottoman. He looks as if he has seen a ghost, he is pale and keeps staring off into space.

"Dad you're starting to freak me out, what's going on?"

He looks at me then and a single tear leaves his eye. It rolls down his cheek and falls to his shirt.

"We thought you were dead. We mourned you and had a wake and everything. They found the remains of a girl a year ago and the evidence said it was you."

I sit back and take in this information. My family thought I was dead. I feel bad for never contacting them and letting them know where I was and that I was still okay. But, how did he find me if he thought I was gone.

"Dad, if you thought I was dead why are you here? How did you find me?"

He jumps to his feet then and looks almost deranged. I am afraid, I have never seen my dad like this. He comes over to me and yells directly at me,

"You are supposed to be dead! And now instead your mother is and it is all your fault!"

I start to gasp for air, mom is dead.

"How?"

Is all I can manage to squeak out.

"They killed her and then they told me to come to you and tell you that you screwed up. If you had just done what they asked she would still be alive!"

The darkness, they got to my parents. I knew there was a possibility but I thought they might want to negotiate now that I know I can kill their leader and he knows it too.

"Dad, I am sorry. I never meant for this to happen. I am so sorry."

I plead with him to believe me. I never wished any harm to them, even when they wanted to lock me up and pump me full of drugs. They were doing what they thought was best, I know they always loved me. And I never stopped loving them.

I must think, what to do now. They have taken my mother, who knows what else they will do. I try and get a grip and clear my head. It is up to me to figure this out.

"Dad, listen to me, did they say anything else? What do they want me to do now?"

He falls to the couch again looking absolutely defeated. He is a broken man.

"I don't know. What kind of mess have you gotten yourself into? They were not normal looking Raine, they looked like monsters, real live monsters."

"I know Dad, they are after me and they went for you and mom to make me come back. You will never know how sorry I am about all this. You were never supposed to know."

"It's all true then? Your nightmares about the darkness and the monsters, you were telling the truth?

I want him to think I am crazy, it would be easier for him that way.

"Yes."

I go to the kitchen and give him a moment to absorb this information. I need a minute myself. They killed my mother. She was a beautiful person who had so much life left to live and she is gone. Another death on my hands. I don't know how much more of this I can take. I don't break down this time though. The tears no longer come; I guess I have run out.

I return to my father sitting again as if in a trance. I have no idea what to say to him. He is angry and has every right to be. I destroyed the love of his life; he is now alone in this world. I will never be his daughter again, not after what I have done.

"Do you want to lie down or something, are you hungry? What can I do for you Dad?"

I need to do something.

"No, I just had to deliver that message to you and now I should go."

He gets up and starts towards the door. He reaches for the handle and stops.

"I am sorry we didn't believe you Raine. Maybe if we would have listened all of this could have been avoided. I failed you."

He then opens the door and is gone. My father is gone, out into the world now knowing the truth and he is all alone to deal with it. I know I should go after him and care for him but the farther he is away from me the better. The fight has barely begun and he needs to be nowhere near it. I will protect those who are left, my dad and Jack. I must figure out my power and how it works. Fast.

There is no need to involve anyone else, the dark leader wants me and I him. We will finish this and everyone else will be safe.

It is up to me.

Chapter 20

The pain has finally stopped. I am hesitant to open my eyes. What if my crime against Smith has kept me from the higher plane? I want so desperately to be there with Smith and all the other knights that have passed before me. It is strange, I feel as if I am still in my body. I guess no one knows what death feels like. I just had always pictured the feeling of weightless and no more ties to my vessel. I must open my eyes.

I slowly do. I am seeing light, bright white light above me. It is not as it should be though. There is a ceiling, why would there be a ceiling? I look around me and see I am in a room, a familiar room. I am getting the sneaking suspicion I am not dead. I see a table with a pitcher and bandages on it. There are beds lining the wall. I am in the infirmary in the light realm.

How is it possible? I felt myself let go, I was leaving this world. Then nothing, all went blank. That must be when they brought me back. Raine must have somehow got us here into the light and my brothers saved me. Where is she? Is she alright? Why is no one around? I try and call out but nothing happens. I reach up and feel the bandage around my neck. I cannot speak. I am starting to panic, I need someone to tell me what is going on!

I try and get to my feet but am too weak. I fall back onto the bed and feel as if I might pass out. I hear a noise at the far end of the room and look up to see Aaron coming towards me. He is smiling from ear to ear.

"What are you trying to do Jack? You must stay in bed and rest, you almost died you know."

He lifts my legs back onto the bed and places the blanket over me. I look at him and shake my head no. I try again to get up but he has much more strength than me. He holds me down.

"No Jack, you can't leave!"

I plead with him with my eyes. He needs to tell me what's going on.

"Jack stop, I will tell you everything, just stay in bed."

Okay, I lie back down and wait for him to start talking.

He takes a seat on the edge of the bed and begins in a hush voice.

"Raine is safe. I sent her away when you got here. The others think she is dangerous and want to do away with her. They think she is working with the darkness."

What the hell? She saved my life and brought me here and they think she is against us. This is crazy. I realize something. Raine brought us here and she changed me back. I look at my body and see I am human again. She shot me with her light and I transformed back. I wonder if they know I was a dark creature. And why I was one. I need to speak; Aaron must answer my many questions.

"Don't look so upset Jack, you are healing and hopefully soon you will be well enough to speak."

I look at my friend and urge him to continue.

"I know Raine is not what the others are saying and we can't seem to locate her. She has some sort of block up that is preventing the knights from finding her. I told her once you were well enough you would go to her."

I smile at Aaron, he has done so much for me. I owe him a lot.

More foot steps are coming down the corridor. Charles and Lila come to my bedside. She is the one that has everyone against

Raine, I know it. Charles looks at me with concern and Lila with contempt.

Charles speaks,

"Jack you are looking much better. We were very worried for awhile there."

I nod in response.

"Well I am sure Aaron has informed you that we are looking for your friend Raine, she escaped us earlier. Do you have any idea of where she might be?"

I shake my head no. I would tell them nothing even if I could speak. Charles is a smart man, why does he believe all this? He knows she is the key in the final battle, does he really think she would fight for the dark. He met her and knows she is only filled with light.

"Do you think she went back in the shadows? Is she with the dark leader planning their attack on the world?"

You are insane.

I again shake my head no.

Aaron then stands and asks the others to leave saying that is enough for today. I need my rest and will answer any other questions tomorrow. I lay my head back and close my eyes. I want them gone I cannot stand to look at my closest allies and know they are hunting her.

Aaron stays and waits until they are gone for sure before speaking again.

"I will try and get a message to Raine letting her know you are okay. She is blocking us from her whereabouts but I think I know where she might end up."

I know what he is saying and smile at him to let him know he is on the right track. Aaron then leaves me to rest.

Days pass, and I am frustrated. Every day they come, the knights, to aid me in my recovery. Aaron has been here the most telling me what he can about the plans for the war and for Raine. They are no closer in finding her which is good but Aaron has not managed to get word to her either. We both thought she would be either at her apartment or at mine. She has not been at either. I am starting to get worried. Where could she have gone?

My health is improving everyday but much too slow. I can manage a few small sounds but this is not enough. I am beginning to gain strength and am now able to get out of bed and take a few steps. I am sick of being a patient. I need to find Raine. She is going to do something rash, I just know it. She is looking for revenge against the dark leader and will not wait long. I know this because I would do the same thing. Charles has visited me a few more times, always with Lila by his side. He asks me the same questions about Raine and I reply the same way every time. They don't trust me, which is fine. I am no longer fighting for the light. I am fighting for Raine. She is what matters to me. Don't get me wrong I don't want the darkness to win and want nothing more than the king dead but my priority is Raine.

I keep seeing her standing there in my arms. I am a monster but she looks at me as if I am the only thing in her world. There is light pulsing through her hand and into my chest. It feels warm and makes me remember the light. She then tells me that she loves me. Her eyes are filled with promise. I play this over and over in my mind. I have never felt such belonging in my life. She is my home and I must find her again. I pray she will wait for me, she cannot fight them alone.

Chapter 21

I let out a scream of absolute disappointment. I have been working at this for days and nothing. A little spark here or there but nothing like the power I felt in the dark realm when I was ready to kill the leader. Then I felt it, I was full of heat and electricity, no one could stop me. I have been held up in this abandoned warehouse for three days. I am running out of food and water but refuse to leave. I must get it. I have managed to knock over a couple bricks but big whoop. I know it's inside of me I just don't know how to release it. I have tried meditating and even went for a walk down in the gang bang district to see if I could scare it out of me. I got scared all right but nothing more than a slight tingle in my palm.

I have heard nothing from Jack or Aaron and am worried maybe Jack is not okay. And Lila, who knows what she has the knights doing. I am sure they are after me.

It is kind of a weird situation to be in. The bad guys want me so they can use me in the battle and defeat the good. The good guys just want to kill me because they think I am a bad guy. When you look at it like that it really makes me want the bad guys to find me first. At least they want me alive. And I will have the chance to kill James.

I walk over to my makeshift bed and grab a bottle of water. I am exhausted but I will not stop. I must figure out the trigger. I replay everything in my mind over and over. Nothing seems to help. I told Jack I wasn't a very good superhero, I don't even know how to make my power work.

I have been thinking of going to the light realm and checking on Jack. I don't want him to come here. He is safest if he stays where he is. If I could do it without anyone knowing I would be there already. I know I have done something to make them not be able to find me. I feel as if I am in an invisible bubble and no one can enter. I put it up right after my Dad left me at my apartment. I just thought about how I want to be alone and there it was. It doesn't really look like anything but I can feel it surrounding me. I don't have to consciously keep my mind on it,

I just wanted some protection and there it was. If I can keep it up and enter the light at the same time they should not be able to track me. Is it worth the risk? I pace back and forth and contemplate this. I know Jack is in good hands, they see him as a knight again so they have an obligation to help him. But they know he was with me and that he got injured by the dark king. I don't know if Jack is as safe as first thought. Maybe he should be with me.

I decide to try it. If they sense me I will get the hell out of there and back to my bubble.

I picture Jack, I see him in a bed. I am guessing they have some sort of hospital for their wounded. I stay perfectly still and wait to be transported to him. I feel my bubble still protecting me and close my eyes. A power surge goes through my body and when I open my eyes I am in a room. I quickly duck behind a bed and stay perfectly still. After a minute of silence I take a peek over the top. I am definitely in an infirmary. There are rows of beds lining the walls and only one looks occupied. It is at the far end of the room. I check in both directions and see no one around. I also see if my protective bubble is still there, yes it is. I think I am safe. I silently get to my feet and sneak down the corridor. I pray it is Jack in that bed, if not I am sure to be found out. I get closer and closer, all I want is to see if he is okay. I am but a few feet from the end of the occupied bed when I see the man start to stir. I freeze hoping I have not woken him. As I am about to duck for cover I see black curly hair fall to the side of the pillow. It is him. I move in closer and bend down beside the head of the bed. Jack has a big bandage around his neck and is pale but other than that he looks great. He is alive and healing. I am filled with such joy. The last memory I have of him is one of horror, I thought I could never erase that memory from my mind but as I see him here in front of me that image is already fading.

What should I do now? Do I wake him? I want to talk to him and tell him how sorry I am. I want him to know I am going to fix everything and light will be victorious. I don't know how yet but I am going to do it. I can't, I can't tell him anything. He needs to stay here and get better. I must leave, I have seen he is alive and that is what I needed. I decide to leave before I am found out and before he wakes. I lower my head and ready myself to leave when a hand touches my shoulder.

I look up to see Jack's deep blue eyes staring into mine.

He touches my face and smiles at me. I smile back and press his hand tighter to my cheek. He pulls my face in close and softly whispers in my ear,

"Are you okay?"

I can barely make out the words and realize he is not right. He can't really talk yet. Of course, his wound was to his neck. I grab his other hand in mine and squeeze it tight.

"Yes Jack, I am fine. I needed to see you. I have been so worried. I need you to know I am going to take care of everything. You just get better okay."

He removes his hand from my face and grabs me by the shoulders. Jack shakes his head back and forth violently and holds me tight. He knows what I am planning on doing and he is pissed about it.

"Jack you have no choice, I must finish this once and for all. No one else has to get hurt."

He quietly says the word no over and over. He then let's go of me and gets out the other side of his bed. I don't understand what he is doing. He grabs a shirt hanging over the chair and begins putting on his shoes.

I run over to him and stop him.

"You are not coming with me! You are not healed yet. You have to stay here and be safe, I can't do this if I know you are not safe."

He glares at me and continues getting dressed. Just then the doors at the far end of the room swing open. I immediately duck down behind the dresser. Jack stops and places himself in front of it to shield me more. I check for my bubble and it is still up.
That doesn't mean they can't see me though, it just means they can't feel me. I should wish myself out of here before they get any closer but I can tell it is Lila approaching by the footsteps and I want to know what she has to say and I really don't like the idea of her being alone with Jack. I guess I am the jealous type.

Jack leans back against the dresser and waits for her to approach. I can see the muscles in his arm tense as though he is ready for a fight. I hope he keeps his composure.

"Jack you are up. I thought you would still be in bed."

Why would she come see him if she thought he was still asleep?

I guess Jack nods or something in response because Lila continues,

"I just wanted to let you know that we have found her. Your little friend, the one that has betrayed us all."

I tense, she knows I am here. I am about ready to jump out and fight for all I have when I see Jacks arm come down by his side, the one Lila can't see and tell me to stop.

"You must be so relieved; you don't have to be afraid any longer.
We will have her soon enough and that will be that. We can all go back to the way things were."

Jack grabs the corner of the dresser and looks as if he might just rip it into pieces. I peek around the dresser, I can't help myself.
She is coming in close to Jack. She leans into him and presses her body against his. I am about to explode with anger when I feel it. The tingling in my palm. It radiates through my entire body. I have the power again. I want to throw it all at Lila but realize she is not worth it. I can't expose myself or Jack because this slut is making moves on my boyfriend. That sounds weird, is he my boyfriend?

She touches his face and he grabs her hand and puts it back at her side. She gives him a wicked little smile and runs her hands down his chest.

"Come on Jack, no one will know. I can be very discreet."

He again places her hands back at her side. She looks ticked. I don't think many men say no to Lila. It's as if someone has flicked a switch, Lila becomes irate.

"She is as good as dead Jack! Then you will see what she really was. She played you for a fool. Raine is a dark creature in disguise and you ate it up. You are a naive and pathetic little boy!"

With that she turns on her heel and heads for the door.
Jack doesn't move until the door is shut closed.

I slowly come out from behind the dresser and Jack is right there. He picks me up and brings me into a tight embrace. All jealousy is gone, he is mine and that's that.

He puts me down and whispers,

"You are not going without me."

I look up at him and smile. He is right, I am not leaving him here. I am stronger with him by my side.

"Are you sure you should leave? Are you well enough?"

Jack nods yes. He grabs my hand and looks at me waiting.

"I guess we are ready then?"

He nods again.

"Are you going to get us out of here or do you want me to do it?"

I am not sure if he is healed enough but want to give him the option. He points to me.

"They will know if I use my light."

His voice sounds sore. I am making him speak too much.

I pull his hand in close to me and see the warehouse. I guess this would be the best place to go, no one knows about it. I picture us amongst all the debris and we are transported. Still holding hands we look around the open and dirty space. This is getting much easier for me. I am now able to move myself almost instantly to where I envision and others too. I feel a little embarrassed to show him where I have been living. But I have stayed safe and that's what matters. Jack takes a few steps away from me and checks out the room. He walks over to the bricks I have piled up and picks up one of the ones I have managed to damage.

"I have been practicing, trying to get my light thingy to work. I haven't had much success."

I go and grab the brick from his hand. I wish he could talk more. I need his advice and guidance on so many things.

Jack takes the brick out of my hand and places it on the ground. He turns my hand over and looks at my palm. He looks back up at me and gives a little smile.

"You can do it. You have to not try so hard."

As he speaks he rubs the centre of my hand with his thumb. He then steps behind me and holds my hand out and away from us. He whispers softly in my ear.

"Just let go, let yourself feel your pain."

I lean into him and close my eyes; I do as he says and let myself feel. I had turned everything off the moment my father walked out that door. All I felt was vengeance but I think Jack is right, my power is not one with hate. When I felt at my most powerful I was feeling love and then heartbreak. And just now in the light realm when I felt it again it was protection I was feeling. So I let myself go and remember. I remember my mom and the love I will always feel for her, she loved me till the moment she died, that I know for sure. I start to feel the tingles move up my arm radiating from my palm. I think of my love for Jack and how I almost lost him and Smith, he gave his life for me because he thought I would bring peace to world. My body begins to vibrate, I can't hold it all in. I open my eyes and see my body is glowing.
Light is shooting from my fingertips and I feel electricity pulsing through my entire body.

"Jack, stand back!"

I need space, I feel as if I am about to explode.

I direct all my pain and love and loss towards the concrete wall at the other end of the building. I release it, everything I have been holding inside and it is gone. I fall to my knees. Jack comes over and picks me up. There is dust and pieces of concrete falling all around us. I look to the wall and see it is gone. There is nothing there. We are looking outside into a parking lot. I took down a concrete wall with a wave of my hand. I guess I am a super hero.

I turn to Jack and smile a triumphant smile. I feel light and happy.

Jack does not.

"What's wrong? Are you hurt?"

He shakes his head no and looks at me with sad eyes.

"Jack your scaring me!"

"You disappeared. When you released the light you were gone."

He says this in a whisper but I can feel the anxiety coming off of him.

"What? I was here the whole time. I saw the wall come down."

He grabs me then and holds me tight as if he thinks I will disappear again.

Chapter 22

I don't ever want to let her go. I want to run away with her and never look back. The world can fight without us and especially without her. I know now what she is and I cannot let her use her power ever again. She will not understand at first but I must make her. I have heard stories about this and about her. She is the greatest power there is and will ever be. But for her to fulfill her destiny she must die and that is not an option.

I cannot believe she is the one. I thought all this talk of the key meant she was special but not this. Seeing what she just did proves it, not the destroying the wall part but the way she transformed when it happened. She disappeared and then became something else. She glowed with the light of all the heavens and I saw a piece of her leave her body. She probably does not feel it gone but it is. If she uses her power again she will keep losing bits of herself until there is nothing left and she disappears all together. She was sent here for the war, to stop the darkness just as all the stories say but she is Raine, my Raine.

She is in my arms now and I must keep it that way. I need my voice back, please god give me my voice so I can explain this all to her. We need to run NOW.

I let go of her and find her hand.

"Do you trust me?" I manage to say.

"Of course I do, why?"

She looks confused. I have no time or the voice to explain it to her now.

"We must go, now!"

I put as much punctuation in my voice as possible trying to get across the seriousness of it.

"Jack, did I do something wrong?"

I shake my head no and head over to her stuff. I grab her back pack and shove her few belongings into it. I turn to her and get her hand in mine. I pull her towards the door.

"Jack, we can go anywhere in the world, just tell me where and I will wish us there. We don't need to walk."

"Raine, yes we do, you cannot use your powers. Do you hear me, no powers!"

My voice seems to have a bit more strength to it.

She looks baffled by my tone and what I am saying to her but she does as I ask. I drag her out the door and into the world. We must move quickly. What she just did in there will alert both the dark and light. It was so much use of pure power, it will never go unnoticed. I am raking my brain trying to figure out where we can go. They can't track her she has somehow shielded herself to them. They can however track me and I am sure they have noticed I am gone by now. They would have figured out I am with her or looking for her, in which case they would send someone to follow me.

I need to go back to my house. They will definitely look there but first they will investigate the warehouse. I think we have enough time; I have something I must show Raine. She needs to understand what is going on.

I pull her up and down various streets and she stays silent, letting me lead the way. We are about a block from my house when I decide we must now proceed with caution. I slow my pace and take a back alley. She follows. I am sure she knows where we are headed and why we are taking the back way. I look back at her and she just nods in response. We silently creep up the alley towards the back entrance to my home. I stand for a few minutes with the back door and windows in view. There is no sign of movement. I motion to her to follow and we proceed up my back steps. I feel no presence of any of my brothers. I open the door and we enter the back porch.

I give a sigh of relief as I close the door behind us. We are alone for the moment, but there is no time to waste I must retrieve it and get out.

I head into the living room and look amongst my many books. It must be here somewhere. Raine stands at my side silently waiting. I am searching when Raine places her hand on my shoulder and reaches out in front of me. She pulls a large book off the shelf and there behind it is what I am looking for. She gives me a soft smile and I grab the small red covered book. I stand and look at her,

"How did you know what I was looking for?"

My voice is still not at full strength.

"I don't know. I was just drawn to it. Why are we here for a book?"

"I will show you once we are safe. We have to go."

We head to the back door and I make sure they are not outside. Nothing. I feel no presence of our kind.

We make our way quickly out the back door and back down the alley. I grabbed whatever cash I had on our way out and it should be enough to get us somewhere out of the city. We must get to the bus station. They won't think to look for us there and I am hoping whatever is shielding Raine may also shield me.

"Raine, you are putting up some sort of block so no one can find you right?"

It really does hurt to speak.

"Yes, again I don't know how but I just didn't want to be found so I have a protective bubble around me. Can the light find you? Should I try and put you in my bubble?"

She looks anxious and scared. I need to tell her what is happening.

I nod at her and slow my pace so she can try. We can't stop moving. I see her concentrate and look around us. I think she can see something I can't. I don't want her to use too much power but she is not glowing and this may just be worth it. If she cannot shield me as well then I will have to leave her. I would give anything not to do this but she needs to be protected.

She gives a smile and smacks me on the arm.

"I did it! You are in my bubble. You have to stay close though and it is not as strong around you as me but you are definitely in it."

I must stay close, that won't be hard. I don't want to leave her side, ever.

I grab her hand again and we head to catch a bus. She looks at me out of the corner of her eye. Just wait Raine. I will show you everything, I just need your patience a while longer. We are almost there.

She pulls me to a sudden stop.

"Jack, stop! You are bleeding."

She reaches for my bandage on my neck. I knew I felt a little worse but we have no time to worry about this now. I try and continue walking, we have to go. She doesn't understand they will be swarming the city soon and they may even freeze everything so they can find us faster. She steps in front of me with her hands on her hips.

"We are not going any further until we look after your neck."

She looks around and sees what she needs.

"There is a drugstore right across the street, we have to go and get you some more bandages and see what damage we have done to you."

"Raine, we can do that later. We have to leave now!"

God, it really hurts. I reach up and feel the blood seeping through the bandage. I feel weak. My vision is going blurry; she is fading in and out of focus. I feel her put her arms around my waist.

"Jack, Jack hold on. I will fix you up."

She drags me over to a bench and sits me down. Raine pulls up the collar of my jacket as we are beginning to get some stares from passer-by's. One pedestrian stops and asks if we need help. Raine waves him away and tells him I am a diabetic and just need my insulin. Good thinking I want to tell her but can't.

"Jack I have to go to that drugstore, I don't think I can keep you shielded if I am over there. Do you think you have enough strength to come with me?"

I look up at her and give her a little nod. She picks me up and basically carries me to the store; I am trying my best to look somewhat normal. We get in the store and there is a chair by the door. She gently helps me sit and takes off down the isle. She is back within minutes and pulls me up. I am losing a lot of blood I can feel it dripping down my neck. I keep my jacket up tight so as no one can see what is happening. We are back out on the street, where to go? Raine is a girl on a mission she drags me down the street and into a building, I don't have the strength to look around and see where we are. She reaches in her pocket and throws money at a slimy looking man behind a desk. I then realize we are in a sleazy hotel. I guess she can't bandage me up on the street can she.

We get to our room and Raine places me on the bed. I feel so pathetic and weak. I lie down and close my eyes. Raine is over me saying something about what she is going to do and it may hurt. I don't care I just need to get my strength back so we can leave. She unzips my jacket and starts to take off the bandage around my neck.

"Jack its bad. I will re-bandage but I don't really know what else to do."

She gets the old bandage off and I can feel blood trickling out of the now open wound. She is working fast but doesn't really know what to do. I look up at her and see she is in deep concentration, she looks worried. I hate being so needy. I am knight of the light realm, sworn to protect and fight for those needing our aid. Now I lie here a patient unable to heal fast enough to help Raine. I feel helpless and like a complete loser.

I feel pressure on my neck, she is done. I watch as she goes into the bathroom and discards the bloody rags. I feel sleepy and think I need to rest. She comes back in.

"How does that feel?"

I nod and give her a smile. You did great. Thank you.

"I am going to take a shower, you should try and sleep. We are safe here, besides I paid for the night."

She is trying to lighten the mood. She is right though, we should be safe, for now.

Chapter 23

I get into the bathroom and close the door. I lean on the vanity and take a deep breath. Jack is in rough shape. I should never have brought him here. He needs more time to heal. I did the best I could but I am not a doctor, the wound looks like it is getting infected and he needs real help. He is in such a hurry to leave town and I am not sure why. I have control of my power now and he is more scared than ever. I don't get what is happening, I blew up the wall and he freaked. He said not to use my power and we need to run. I need answers and the only one that has them can't communicate with me. I guess this is teaching me a lesson in patience. At least Jack is resting now and I will get cleaned up and maybe get some rest myself.

After my much-too-long-and-hot shower I throw on my semi-clean clothes and head back to the bedroom. Jack is passed out but seems to be sleeping peacefully. I move as quietly as possible and crawl in beside him. The bed is lumpy and hard but feels better than anything I have slept on for a long time. I make sure not to disturb Jack as I get comfortable. I lay my head on the pillow and stare at Jack. He again looks quite pale. I am worried. I watch his chest rise and fall and feel my eyelids are starting to get really heavy. I test my bubble one last time before I drift off, it is still in place. I am in the in-between almost instantly. I haven't visited this place in awhile. It looks the same but there is a slight difference. No one is around. I don't feel the presence of the light or dark creatures here. It is like a big empty abyss. Everyone is gone, but where? This is a silly question, I know where. They are all here looking for us. Or the war has begun, either way something big is happening and I am not a part of it. I am hiding and don't understand why. I decide to leave the in-between. I have never had control over it before but now when I make up my mind I can. I open my eyes and see Jack still sleeping beside me. I don't think much time has passed. It is still light outside. I should try and sleep, who knows what lies ahead for us. I may not get to rest again for a very long time. This time I close my eyes and will myself to not go into the shadows and I don't. I sleep and do not dream.

I feel an arm go around me and bring me out of my slumber. I tense instantly and feel my palms start to tingle. I am ready. I open my eyes cautiously and feel silly when I see Jack still asleep with his arm flung over me. He is still sound asleep. I decide to enjoy this moment of peace and cuddle into his side. He is so warm. I close my eyes and imagine we are a normal couple, lying together without a care in the world. What a life that would be. Instead we are in a grimy hotel room, I am wearing clothes I have been wearing for days and Jack is covered in blood with his neck bandaged from where he was stabbed by the dark leader. Not your typical couple no matter how you look at it.

I almost laugh at how crazy this is.

Jacks arm tightens around me and pulls me in even closer. His head is right by my ear and he whispers,

"This is how it should be."

I smile at how he is thinking the same thing as me.

"Yes, I know."

We are having a moment, a moment of peace. It feels so right.

"Jack, how are you feeling?"

I don't turn to face him, not quite ready to let go yet.

"Better."

Is all he says and I feel his breath in my ear. It sends a warm feeling through my body. I try and stay perfectly still, afraid at my own actions if I give in the slightest bit. I have never wanted anyone so much. I have to get a grip, he is severely hurt, this is the last thing on his mind.

He gently begins to nuzzle my neck and his hand is rubbing the side of my hip. This is really not helping. I roll over ready to tell him to stop when his lips find mine. We are kissing. It is tender and slow. I don't want to hurt him so I gently lay my hand on his waist. He is a wonderful kisser. I want to stay here just like this forever. We are completely in the moment enjoying each other when Jack pulls away. His hand goes to his neck and he begins to cough. I sit up immediately and inspect the wound. I pull back the bandage slightly and see that it does not look any worse than earlier. There is no blood leaking out. He is still coughing and I know that is not good for the wound. I jump up and get him a glass of water. I help him drink a bit of it. The coughing subsides for the moment.

"I guess you are allergic to kissing me."

I again try and lighten the mood. Jack smiles at me and pulls me down to his lap.

"I don't think that is it."

He says almost silently. I lean into him and gently place a kiss on his lips. It is not one of passion but one of affection and love.

Again the coughing begins. Maybe it wasn't a joke; maybe he is allergic to me. I sit on his lap and wait for it to subside. It doesn't. He is getting worse. I move to sit by his side. I need to get him to a hospital. I don't know what a regular doctor can do for him but it is more than I am capable of. I get up and collect my things. He watches me as he continues to cough and gasp.

"I am taking you to a doctor. You need help, more than I can give."

He shakes his head no but he is in no shape to argue. I turn my back for a second and when I face him again he is turning blue. His eyes are wide and he looks as if he might explode. I run to his side and am not sure what to do. He can't breathe! I lay him down and start pushing on his chest. I think I remember how to do cpr. I give a few short and hard pushes and am about to do mouth to mouth when he lets out a large sigh. I feel relieved and look up to see his eyes are unmoving. He is not moving at all. He is not breathing or blinking. He can't be gone! He was here but a minute ago. I freeze for a moment thinking this is just a bad dream. Okay Raine wake up!

I am not in a dream; Jack has just died right before my eyes. No! This is not happening. I feel my body start to charge with electricity. My palms are sparking to life without me even thinking about it. He is not allowed to leave me, I need him. I rip open his shirt and place my hands over his heart. I press down and realize I am crying. I haven't cried in days. I thought I was done with tears. I had used up my supply and they would never start again. I guess I was wrong.

Tears are hitting his bare chest as if it is raining on him and my hands are pulsing with my light. He said to not use it but he was wrong. When I do this it feels so right, this is what I was made for.

The light gets stronger and brighter my whole body begins to glow. I will fix this. I wish for life to be brought back to him, to make him whole and healthy. I shoot it into him with everything I have. It is just as powerful a shock as I did to the concrete wall but this is going into a person. I think for a split second it might be too much but I don't care. I can't make him more dead. The explosion enters his chest and radiates thru him. I see light jolt up and down his body. He convulses and writhes under my grip. The light finally settles in his throat. It looks like currents of light racing back and forth under his skin. I tear the bandage off his neck and watch as the injury begins to repair itself. I am amazed at what is happening. His body is becoming healed.

When the light finally fades, I feel all my strength leave my body. He is still not moving. I collapse on the floor.

It takes but seconds before I hear him take in a breath. I jump to my feet and stare. He sits up with a scream. I see the wound on his neck is completely gone. He no longer looks pale. He is glowing with strength. I leap onto him and fling my arms around his neck. I kiss his neck where his wound was and touch his body all over to make sure he is in one piece. He finally manages to grip my arms and stop me from moving.

"Raine, stop!"

I look him in the eyes and begin to cry again.

"You are alive. You were dead and now you're not. Don't do that to me ever again!"

He looks at me with confusion.

"I was dead?"

"Yeah, I saw you take one last breath, then nothing. You weren't breathing and the life was gone from your eyes."

He reaches up to his neck and feels for the bandage. He looks at me and almost screams in my face.

"What did you do?"

Jack jumps to his feet and looks into the cracked mirror over the bed. He is studying his neck and looks down at his chest. There is dried blood everywhere but no more injuries.

"What did you do Raine?"

"I used my power."

I say in a low guilty sounding voice.

"No, you can't Raine. This is bad, very bad."

I am starting to get upset. I can think of many bad things and saving Jack isn't one of them. He should be thanking me not scolding me. I get up from the bed and walk to his side.

"Jack, this is not bad. You were dead and I saved you. Don't you think you should be thanking me instead of freaking out?"

He turns to me and looks as if I have killed his pet. Anger is boiling inside of him. What the hell kind of reaction is this?

"Raine you don't get it. You used your power. Besides the fact they can track us now, you just killed another piece of yourself."

He goes over to my backpack and grabs the small red leather bound book we retrieved from his house. He throws it at me and takes off his shirt. I ripped the shirt beyond recognition. He goes into the bathroom and slams the door. I stand dumb founded by what is occurring. He is mad at me for saving his life. What a jerk.

I hear the shower start and realize he is getting cleaned up. I am sure we will be on the move again as soon as he is done so I get my stuff together and put on my shoes. I carry around the book with me as I go, not wanting to open it. Something inside has to do with me and I am afraid about what it might say. A few minutes pass and I decide I should probably look at it before he comes out. He will be waiting for my reaction I am guessing. I sit on the side of the bed and open it up. It is old looking and written by hand. There are pictures of dark creatures and also of the knights. It describes the war that they are about to face and what the darkness" intentions are. I don't know how long ago this was written but it seems to give the knights the upper hand. If they have known this all along they should be properly prepared. I am skimming the pages not too into what is written, I have been living it so I know most of it. I am about to close it and yell at Jack when something catches my attention.

"The Key", below is a picture of a being made of light. Not the kind Jack and his knights make, it looks different. It is hard to describe, it is made of something different, bolts of electricity.

Like what I do when I use my power. My hands begin to shake. This is me, I really am a key. The being looks powerful, more so than the other images on any page in the book. It is raised above the others looking down on the light and dark. It's face is full of pain and agony. It looks so sad. I run my fingers gently over the face of the key. She is beautiful and tragic all at the same time. Why? I wonder.

I read on and see why Jack is so upset. It states that with such power one must give up pieces of itself each time the power comes to be. It says that in the ultimate last battle the key must sacrifice itself to end the war. That the key is made solely for this purpose and when its duty is fulfilled, it is time for the key to return home.

I am numb. I cannot stop staring at the words on the page. I have so often thought of death in the past few days and almost welcomed it once or twice but to have it spelled out for you is very unnerving. I will die at the last battle, no choice. My life is predetermined by something I can't control. I was not born with free will. Well that sucks.

Chapter 24

Why did she do it? I know why, because I would do the same for her in a heartbeat. That doesn't change the fact that she shouldn't have done it. I don't know how many times she can use her powers before she is gone completely. The book says she will die in the final battle. I am going to do everything I can to make sure that doesn't happen. I am a chicken for making her read it alone, I should be out there with her, supporting her as she finds out her fate. I can't, it rips my heart out even to look at her. I have never loved anything so much and to know that the entire universe is against it and her, is all consuming. So I hide here in this bathroom and wait for her to find out her fate all on her own. I am a coward.

I need to go back in the there and make sure she is okay. I slowly open the door and proceed over to the bed where she is sitting, her back to me. The book is in her hands. I go around the bed and see she is staring at the page, the one that tells of her fate. She is white and shows no emotion. I kneel in front of her and take the book from her hands. She gives me a blank stare, shock. I think she is in shock.

"I am sorry Raine. This doesn't have to happen, we can run and keep running until the war is done. I will keep you safe, I promise."

I need her to hear me, I am not going to let this happen to her.

"What? You can't keep me safe, nobody can. Didn't you see it? I am the one that ends the war, it is up to me."

She shakes off my hands and stands. She is speaking in a calm voice with no emotion. This scares me.

"Raine, it doesn't have to end that way. Please listen to me."

She does not turn to me, she grabs her backpack and slings it over her shoulder.

"I need to go and get you some clothes. You can't go around covered in blood. I will be back in a minute."

What is she doing? I go and stand in front of the door to block her exit. She must snap out of it, we need to move, they will be here soon.

"Raine, stop it! We need to go. Now!"

I give her a little shake to see if I can wake her out of this zombie like state.

"Why?"

She looks at me like I am speaking gibberish.

I grab her then and pull her in close to me; I find her lips with mine and kiss her hard and with purpose. I am hoping this snaps her back to reality. She kisses me back not very enthusiastically at first but then something changes, she pushes me against the door and pins me there. She is in control now and having her way with me. She is strong, much stronger than she should be. I cannot push her away. I am a grown man and a knight and she is man handling me like I am a child. Her body starts to heat up and I see the start of a glow around her. Her emotions are attached to her powers; I can't let her get out of control. I manage to free my mouth from hers and yell at her.

"Raine! Stop! Your powers!"

She releases me then and takes a staggering step back.
She looks at me with sad eyes.

"Jack, I'm sorry. I don't know what happened."

She turns her back to me and collapses to the ground. I go over and sit beside her on the floor.

"Don't apologize. You did nothing wrong. You just need to watch your emotions, the more powerful you feel the more power you have."

"I am such a freak! You need to get away from me, I will hurt you."

"No you won't. And I am not leaving your side. We are in this together. Until the end."

She turns to me then and touches my arm.

"I read it. I know what is going to happen to me. You can't control it anymore than I can. There is no point in me running. I can protect you though, you need to run. They know by now that you are helping me. I mean it Jack, I think I can give you my protective bubble. I have been practicing while you were in the shower. I can send it with you and they won't be able to track you."

What is she talking about? I will never leave her side again.

I shake my head no and am about to protest when she says,

"Don't argue with me. I need to know you are safe. If I know that then I can face anything. I can die knowing you are still a part of this world. Please let me have that Jack."

"No. Do you not know I feel the exact same way about you? If you insist on not running then I will stay with you. I will be there with you at the final battle. You cannot ask me to leave you, I love you."

I tell her this with as much emotion and honesty as I have. She will not do this alone. I want to save her and will figure out a way to do it. But if it comes down to the battle I will be there for her.

"I love you too." She says.

"What do you want to do now?" I ask her.

I have no idea what her plan is.

"I was serious, you need a shirt. And I would like to go out for something to eat."

I laugh.

"So we are going to act like there aren't creatures after us and that the end of the world could be here any second?"

"Exactly, we are going out on a date. If they want me so bad they can find me at a restaurant with my boyfriend enjoying a nice meal. I am not going to cower in the corner, they cannot harm me. Neither the dark nor the light can do anything to me, and since I have no choice in how my life ends I will decide how to spend it until then."

She laughs then and stands up. She has made up her mind and I think she is the bravest person I have ever met. Every bone in my body wants to grab her and hide her, keep her all to myself but Raine wants to go out on a date, so that is what we will do. She really is crazy.

Chapter 25

Okay, I think I have convinced Jack to stay and not run away. I don't want to run anymore. I have spent my whole life doing that. I ran from my family and friends but this I will face. I am willing to sacrifice myself to save all those I care about. It didn't take me long to realize that if I do not participate in the final battle there will be nothing left, the light and dark will destroy each other but the dark has the numbers and the skill to come out on top. Then the human world will come to an end. I cannot have that on me. What kind of "key" would I be if I ignored it all and ran away. I know Jack doesn't understand but this is how it has got to be and I want to enjoy what little time we have left.

It's funny how he has made me feel normal for the first time ever in my life and that is because I really am not normal. I am this strange other thing that isn't of the light or dark and I am not an ordinary. I feel like I belong nowhere. But in reality I think I belong everywhere. Something inside me is telling me that is right. I may not have free will when it comes to my death but I do have free will when it comes to which side I choose. I can back either one and make them victorious. This power is almost overwhelming. I can feel it now surging through my body, I feel electric and alive. I will help the light to win this war, it is the right thing to do! The ordinaries deserve to live in peace and never know of the other realms. Look at my Dad, he was faced with the truth and now he is probably in a nut house somewhere.

My Dad….I don't remember what he looks like. I know I just saw him a few days ago. I can't picture him at all or my Mom. I don't remember anything from my childhood either. Nothing, it is a blank slate. This must be what the book meant by losing pieces of myself. It is gone. I look over and see Jack putting on the shirt I went down the street and bought him. It looks nice on him. Plain and black but fits him just right. We got most of the blood off his jeans and his jacket so now he looks respectable. I can't tell him I don't remember these things. He must think everything is all right. I don't want to cause him any more pain than I have to. I will keep it to myself but I am freaked out at what else I may be missing. I think of everything about my life I possibly can. From the age of 18 till now I remember every detail but before that is gone. I have lost it forever. I am not that sad though I still remember Jack and that is what I want to take with me when I leave this place and go home to the unknown.

He turns to me then and tries to put on a brave face. I know he hates that we are staying and that I am acting like nothing is going on but that is how I want to play this out.

"Ready to go?" he asks me.

I give him a big genuine smile and grab his hand.

"Let's go out on our first date."

With that we leave the sleazy hotel and go to a nearby restaurant. It is nothing fancy but I love how ordinary it feels. We are surrounded by many couples enjoying a night out. Some are laughing and others look to be in deep conversation. Everyone seems happy and content with the here and now. I am studying all the faces around us when Jack interrupts my train of thought.

"Raine, what are you thinking?"

"I am just so in awe of all these people. They know nothing of what is happening to their world; that there is a huge war going on over who gets to control it and if the dark wins they are all as good as dead. Here they sit planning their futures."

I make eye contact with Jack then and realize I have upset him. It was not my intention to hurt him I was just telling the truth.

"Raine, the dark can't win and these people do have futures and it will be because of you. They should be bowing at your feet for what you are about to do for them."

He sounds pissed. I reach across the table and stroke the back of his hand.

"Jack, it is going to be okay. You are right, they should be planning their futures and you know you have one as well. Are you going to remain a knight after it's... it's over?"

He needs to go on after I am gone. He is too good to let himself waste away as an ordinary. He does not answer for a bit so I sit patiently and wait.

"I see no future for myself. If you are gone I want to be as well. I have cheated death twice now and I think that is enough."

He is not looking at me but I can see wetness touch his eyes. He loves me too much. He must realize he can go on without me.

"Jack listen closely to me, you will not die at the battle. If I have to zap you someplace safe that is what I will do. This world needs you and you will fulfill your destiny just as I will fulfill mine."

I want him to look up at me so he can see how serious I am about this. If it is the last thing I do, he will be alive when I die.

"You can't do that to me Raine. You are willing to kill yourself but

I am not allowed to go with you? What if the tables were turned, would you want to go on without me?"

No.

"I wouldn't want to but I would. I would honor your wishes and live out my life the best I could. You must do the same."

The waitress comes over then and brings us our food. It looks good, some sort of pasta with bread and salad. She excuses herself and I dig in. Enough talk about life and death, I want to enjoy the here and now. Jack pushes his food around his plate and looks absolutely defeated.

"Don't you like your food? Mine is excellent."

He just looks at me and frowns.

"Jack, please. I am sorry I brought all that up let's try and enjoy our time together. You know I have never been out on a real date. I mean I had a date to prom and graduation but never out like this. You are my first."

I smile at him and wait. He shakes his head and sits up straighter. He is going to play along with me. That's all I ask, I need a moment of normalcy.

"Well I have been on many dates and this one is by far the best."

He starts to eat then and I let myself relax a bit.

"Really, you are a ladies" man then? I should have guessed."

He laughs and it seems genuine. He is beautiful when he laughs; his whole face lights up and his blue eyes look so alive and happy.

"Yeah, that's me. If you haven't noticed I am surrounded by men. Besides Lila, you are the first girl I have even spoken to in almost two years."

Lila, I wish he wouldn't have brought her up.

"Speaking of Lila, I don't like or trust her. And what's up with her rubbing all over you like that? Does she do that often?"

His eyes are still twinkling.

"I knew you were the jealous type. You were about to do something to her in the infirmary weren't you? And no, she doesn't do that to me often, just when she thinks it will get her what she wants."

I blush a little. I didn't know I was jealous but yep I most definitely am.

"I am confused. She is a knight of the light realm and yet she is not made of the same light as the rest of you. You all beam white and pure and she has a haze around her. Why is that?"

I have been wondering this from the first time I saw her.

"What are you talking about? I have never seen anything different about her light. Maybe because she is a woman. They told me there have been other women knights but she is the only one I have ever met."

Something is occurring to me. It is tickling at the back of my mind but I can't quite get to it.

"She is different Jack and I know she is not pure of heart. Something is up with her, I am not sure what but she is not right."

We sit quietly and contemplate this, what is up with her?

After the waitress comes and clears our plates it is time to go. Where? I have no idea. I suggest taking a walk. I think I will let down my protective bubble once we are outside. I didn't want to do it yet; I wanted to enjoy my first and only date. There is so much I am going to miss out on. I will never get married or become a mother. Not that I had ever really considered those things a possibility for me. I went crazy before I was even able to think of stuff like that. But now, walking hand in hand with a wonderful man, I must admit I am sad about it. My life has taken such a weird and fantastic turn. I must look at the positive. I am not crazy and I am the one that is going to give all these other people the chance to do what I never will. That is a good thing, a very good thing.

It is getting dark and the street lights have come on. There are people mulling about going in and out of pubs and restaurants. The air is crisp but is not really cold yet. The seasons are changing. I will miss the change of seasons. Stop it Raine! I must keep my mind on what is about to happen. I hope it is the dark that finds us first, I want a chance at James before everyone else arrives and the battle begins. I need him out of the way so I can fulfill my duties without being distracted. He need not be part of the fight.

We turn the corner and are by the park where I have often sat and watch children play. I feel a chill run up my spine. I look at Jack and he suddenly drops my hand and looks as if he is ready to pounce. He turns to me then.

"Raine they will be on us any second, please run."

He does not have much hope in his voice. I smile at him and copy his stance. He watches me and shrugs his shoulders. He knows I will not leave, this is it.

I start to feel a cold sweat begin on my forehead. This is how it started last time. It is the light that has found us. Great. I feel weak in the knees and need to sit. I don't. I will myself to stand beside Jack and look as brave as I can. I see the world start to slow down and then all is still. Out of the trees come knights, lots of them. I see Charles and Lila in the lead. Aaron is off to the side. They all look very serious and lethal. I give Jack a sideways glance and see he has not moved from his protective stance. He is by my side, until the end. I decide to take things down a notch and stand up straight and put my hands up in a surrendering position. I know the knights are here to kill me but I don't want anyone to get hurt. After all they are the good guys right?

"Charles, it is nice to see you again."

I figure a pleasant greeting might help to set the mood. Jack glances at me and smiles. I think he thinks I am nuts.

Charles slows his pace and the others follow suit. They are now about 30 feet from us.

"Raine, Jack. You two have been very hard to track down. Jack you are looking remarkably well for someone that was on death's door such a short time ago."

I will answer. Jack needs to take a back seat on this one. I want him to have a job to go back to after all this.

"I healed him. And you can find us now because I am letting you."

I don't sound angry but all the pleasantries are gone from my voice.

Lila lets out a chuckle. I don't understand why the others can't see her the way I do.

"You! You are just an insignificant little girl who happens to have some sort of powers. You don't decide what we can or can't do."

She is getting a little worked up. This is good. I will egg her on a bit, just for fun.

"Lila, it's so good to see you again. The last time I saw you was when you were trying to seduce Jack in the infirmary."

She turns beet red then and looks as if she may explode. I laugh at the sight, I can't help myself.

"I was not! How dare you say such things to me."

Oh, I can say whatever I want to you.

"Lila, it's okay I am sure you have tried it with most of these other men too. Right, Charles?"

Jack comes over to me then and whispers for me to stop. I smile at him and give him a knowing look that says I got this. I turn back to see Charles giving Lila an ominous glare. She takes a step back then and lets Charles take the lead.

"Enough Raine, you know why we are here. I am sorry but this is how it must happen. You are too dangerous to let live."

He seems saddened by this, he really is a noble knight. Jack then decides to speak up. I wish he wouldn't.

"Charles, no. Raines is of no threat to us. You need to understand. She is…"

"No Jack, you need to understand! You have betrayed your brothers. We don't look kindly on what you have done. You are helping her and she is evil. And you killed Smith. You are not one of us. You will never be again!"

Charles throws the words at Jack with such hate that it takes me a second to get my head back straight. Jack does not respond but looks to the ground and takes a step back. They have hurt him in the worst possible way, he is a knight down to his core and they have stripped that from him. I am getting worked up. I need to keep myself under control but when I see them treat Jack like that I feel rage, it's beginning to boil. I need to take a second and calm down. I guess Jack can see it to. He comes to me and places his hand on my back. He whispers so only I can hear,

"Raine, don't. They are not the enemy. You need to calm down."

I close my eyes and try my hardest to get the rage under control. Jack is sticking up for the people that have just renounced him. He is good. Better than any of them. I take a couple breaths and feel my body calm. When I open them again Aaron is coming over to us, he looks tense.

"Aaron, what are you doing? Go back over there."

Jack says to his friend. Aaron looks from me to Jack and gives a little grin.

"Raine, I believe you are not what they say. Jack, I was there. You are not a murderer, you are a savior. I am where I need to be. My heart guides me and it is telling me they are wrong."

I can't help it, I throw my arms around Aarons neck and give him a big hug.

"Thank you Aaron."

I whisper in his ear. I knew he was a good guy. I am happy he has made a stand but now I have one more person to protect. My attention now has to be split three ways instead of two.

"Aaron, what are you doing?" Charles calls out.

"I am choosing. As a knight we are taught to follow our hearts as well as our heads. Mine is leading me here."

Aaron steps over beside Jack and looks calm and ready.

"So you are a traitor as well. I can't believe you two stand beside her. She is evil and will end us all."

I am really getting used to being called evil. I know they are wrong so it doesn't even faze me.

"Enough with the dramatics. You are here to kill me and I am telling you that you can't. As Jack was trying to tell you before you so rudely interrupted, I am the key. The one you have been searching for. I want to fight with you not against you. I told all this to Lila when I brought Jack to you. I guess the message somehow got lost in the translation."

Charles darts a glance at Lila, she simply stands with her nose in the air as if I haven't said a word.

"You cannot be the key. You are trying to trick us."

"I am not. Why would I bother? The darkness has forces like you have never seen. They have hundreds of soldiers waiting to tear you to pieces. I want to help."

Why can they not get this, they are the most paranoid bunch of superheroes I have ever met.

Just then Lila takes a step towards us and throws her light at me. I see it leave her fingers and want to turn to Jack and say, "see her light is different." There is no time, it is coming fast and aimed right for my head. The next thing I know I am down on the ground, my face against the dirt. I was about to kill the witch and now I am on the ground. I roll over and see Jack on top of me.

"Haven't we done this before?" I say to him.

He looks like he is ready to rip Lila's head off.

"Stop joking around! They are not going to listen to you and I am not going to let you use your powers so may I suggest we run now!"

Aaron then yells over to us.

"Guys, get up! They are coming and I can't hold them all off!"

Jack jumps to his feet and I see his light begin to glow. Aaron is ready as well. I look to the knights, there are too many of them. These two don't stand a chance. So I do what I can to help. I picture Aaron and Jack gone and poof they are. They are going to be pissed, but it is my job to keep them safe.

The rest of the knights stop dead in their tracks. They look at each other and then at me. I get to my feet and wipe off my jeans. I then look at them and feel the electricity begin. They cannot hurt me, but I sure as hell can hurt them. I raise my arms over my head and hear them gasp at the sight. My arms are tingling and I am starting to glow. I look at my body and see I am not pure white light like the knights; I am a rainbow of every color imaginable. I feel the power wanting to be released but I hesitate. I cannot kill all these beings of the light. They need to be there in the final battle. I cannot defeat the darkness all on my own. It is written that both sides be present. I look into Lila's eyes and see her smirk. Everything clicks into place. I know what she is trying to do. I know whose side she is on.

Chapter 26

I am about to release my light with all my power when I see an empty field before me. What is going on? I blink and look around; Aaron is beside me with the same look on his face. Raine did this, she said she wouldn't but she did it anyway. Aaron and I were about to fight, to protect her and she made us disappear. I let the light in my hands fade and walk over to Aaron.

"Raine did this didn't she?" He asks me.

"Yes she did. We need to get back there, now!"

Aaron just nods his head in agreement and we simultaneously are gone back to the playground. She may be able to wish us away but we can wish ourselves back.

I let out a huge sigh of relief when I see her standing there. She has countless knights but a few feet from her and she looks pissed. She starts to glow. No. She can't use it. We are across the park and not close enough for her to notice we are back. I start to run and pray I will make it to her before she does something stupid. I yell at her to stop. She needs to get control and killing all these knights will not help anything. I am almost to her when I see her start to lower her arms. She is staring at Lila, I look and see Lila is smiling. Why does she not look scared like the rest of them. I get to Raine's side and grab on to her.

"Don't do it."

"I'm not going to. You sure got back fast."

She looks up at me and seems fine. Her emotions are in check. I turn to the knights and address them all.

"Do you see now? She is like nothing we have seen before. I swear to you all that this is the truth. Raine is the key. I have fought by your sides many times and I want to again. I have not betrayed you; Raine is what is going to make us win this war.
Look at me my brothers and tell me that I am lying."

My friends look back at me and one by one lower their light. They are beginning to see the truth. All except Lila, she stands ready to strike again. Aaron is on the other side of Raine and I see he is keeping a close eye on her as well.

"What did you prove? She glows pretty colors when she is mad. I would hardly call that our savior."

I see now what Raine has been saying, the light in her hands is tainted. It is not pure and bright, but dull and muddy looking. Why did I not notice this before? I guess because I was not looking for it.

I look to our leader, he looks confused. He is wrestling with what he thought was the truth and what is reality. I have always admired Charles but now see he is under the influence of Lila. He looks to her now as if waiting for instruction.

"Charles, you are our leader. Why do you look to Lila? You must make up your mind for yourself."

Charles turns his attention to Raine. I ready myself, if I must take him down, I will. As everyone stands in silence, Raine makes a move. She has locked eyes with Charles and is walking towards him. I am about to follow when she turns to me,

"Jack, it's okay. I need to talk to Charles alone."

I let her go, Charles takes a step forward and they are very close. I see her reach up and touch his cheek. He seems a little embarrassed by this move and starts to blush. I have never seen him blush before. She strokes his cheek and I see his eyes widen. What is she doing to him?

Charles then grabs her hand and places it back by her side. Something has happened between the two but I have no idea what.

He whispers something to her and she nods. When she turns back to Aaron and I she looks calm. Charles turns to the knights and addresses them.

"I was wrong, Raine is not our enemy. We will let her be as well as Jack and Aaron. They will come to the final battle and stand with us."

Raine takes her place between Aaron and I and does not say a word. I want to know how she did that. I want to make sure she didn't use any of her power.

"Raine, what did you do?"

"I just showed him the truth."

She gives a little wink as she says this. She is a strange and different creature. The knights are all talking amongst themselves and seem to be relaxing a bit. I have that all familiar feeling, the world is about to become alive again. Charles is readying the knights to depart. I am not sure what we are supposed to do. Raine whispers to me,

"We are going into the light with your brothers. The war is upon us at any minute and we need to be together when it begins."

She grabs mine and Aaron's hands and gives me a nod. She is letting me take us there. Take us to my home. The last thing I see before we depart is Lila, still standing in the same spot almost frozen. The look on her face is one of shock and hate, lots of hate.

We spend the next few hours together with the knights. Some are apologizing for not believing us and others I can see still have slight hesitation towards Raine. She sits amongst them all and speaks to whoever wants a word. She is being very gracious considering they were all about to kill her just a short while ago. I on the other hand am not. I am mad that this group of warriors of the light were so blind. If they would have stopped for a moment and really looked at her, they would have known the truth long ago. How could they be so blind? I sit to the side and watch. I am ready to jump in at the slightest inclination that they are going to harm her. Aaron is doing the same. He has become as protective of Raine as I am. Finally Charles asks the knights to leave and get some rest. No one is to go back to the human world. Most of us have homes there but we will all stay in the light until the battle is over. Charles finally comes over to the three of us and says his goodbyes. He asks Raine if she will go and speak with him after some rest. He would like her input on the dark creatures and how she thinks it would be best to go forward. I think of this and it makes me laugh. Raine is now the strategist in the ultimate war? I hope she has some idea of what she is doing. I stand as Charles exits the room. Aaron says his farewell to us and we are alone. Raine comes over to me and rests her head on my chest. She is exhausted.

"Jack, where do you think Lila ended up? I have not seen her since the playground. Did she not come back?"

"I don't know. I saw her as we left but she didn't look too good.
You were right by the way, her light is different and I think she wants to kill you no matter what Charles has decided. We will need to watch out for her."

"Jack, she doesn't want to kill me. She wants me to use my power. She knows that the more I use it the further away I go.
That's what she has been trying to do all along. She is bad Jack. I mean really bad. I don't know how she is doing it but I think she is part of the shadow world."

I look at Raine with both shock and understanding. Raine is right. Lila has been provoking Raine from the start. She knows about the prophecy; she knows Raine will disappear when she has used up too much power. My body goes rigid, I want to find her and rip her head off. She is evil and she has been one of us for so long. She is a spy for the darkness. It all makes sense. That is how the dark leader knew of Raine and how they always know when and where we are going to attack. Lila is behind it.

"We must tell Charles. He needs to be on the lookout..."

"Jack I did. I showed him. When we were in the park and I touched him, he saw it all. I let him into my head just like I did with you. He saw the dark leader and the shadow world; he saw what you have done for me. He saw Lila. He knows everything."

"You are pretty smart aren't you?"

I am so proud of her. She figured out a way to convince them of the truth without using her power and no one got hurt.

"Yep."

"You look worn out, do you want to go and rest?"

"Yes, I am tired. Those knight buddies of yours can sure yap. Where do you guys sleep when you are here?"

I lead her out the door and into the courtyard. There are rows of small cottages on each side of us. I point to one at the end of the row.

"This is where I stay. Usually Aaron bunks with me but I think he went to another one for the night."

Raine looks at me and gives a huge smile. She grabs my arm and poof (as she would say) we are in the small one room house. I laugh at her and wrap her up in my arms. She is so different from anything I have ever known. She doesn't follow rules or care what others think. She does what she wants when she wants and seems so free. She is teaching me to let go and live. I owe her so much for that. I push the dark thoughts to the back of my mind. She is here now and I must enjoy this time with her. I need to be happy for her sake.

"I am glad you didn't let me blow everyone up tonight. This is so much better."

She is right, this is better. Now we can be alone for a moment without being in danger and without me dying on her.

"What did Charles whisper to you after you showed him what's in your head?"

"He said he will take care of Lila and he thanked me. He thanked me for being the key."

"Well I am glad for that."

I lean down to her and gently kiss her perfect little lips. She responds and we embrace. She pulls back and begins to laugh.

"I guess I can't get too riled up. I become some sort of hulk and may hurt you."

She says this in a mocking tone and I grab her under the arms and fling her onto the bed. I jump on top of her and wrestle her arms until they are by her sides.

"Okay you win! You are a big strong man and I am not."

Again mocking.

"I am glad you are not a big strong man, this would be rather awkward then wouldn't it?"

I lean down a kiss her again. I move my lips to her neck and gently place kisses along her collar bone. I am happy, I am enjoying this time with this amazing girl and am doing as she asked, living in the moment. I let the rest fade away, for now. She lets out a small moan and I continue back up to her lips. She gets her arms free from my embrace and grabs at my shirt. She pulls it over my head, her eyes are sparkling with excitement as I am sure mine are. She runs her hands up and down my back, I want her totally. I grab her thigh and press down onto her. I feel electricity pass between us. She is hot, I mean really hot. I pull up and see she is starting to glow. Shit!

I roll to my side and leave her gasping. She immediately sits up and takes a couple deep breaths as do I.

"God, that sucks! Every time I want to get lost in my emotions I begin to heat up, literally."

She places her hands over her face and collapses back on the bed.

"Raine, it's okay. You did nothing wrong."

She is still covering her face. I try and pull them away but can't.

"Raine, look at me!"

Cautiously she moves her hands away and I see why she is hiding. She is completely pink with embarrassment. I lower myself to her side and rest my hand on her stomach.

"You have nothing to be embarrassed about. You can't control how unbelievably sexy I am."

Laughter explodes from her and she reaches up and touches my face.

"Thank you."

"You're welcome."

I lean in and give her a tender peck on the lips.

"Let's get some sleep; I think we are in for some heavy training tomorrow. Charles likes to have all his bases covered when going into a fight."

Raine looks at me and I melt. I love this girl and am going to do everything I can to keep her happy. She deserves it.

Chapter 27

He is staring at me with so much love and promise. My heart is breaking. I want to stay with him more than anything. He makes me feel so powerful yet so vulnerable at the same time. I want to tell him that I will always remember him, no matter where I go after this, he will be with me. I want to hold him close and never let him go. He has made me happier than I ever thought possible.

I get up from the bed and ask him if there is anything I can wear to sleep in. Jack rummages through one of the three small drawers in the room and finds my some of Aarons jogging pants. He is smaller than Jack but still a lot bigger than me. He also gets me one of his t-shirts. I discreetly bring it to my face when he is not looking and smell it. It has his scent and I am excited to have it on. I excuse myself and go into the small bathroom attached.

As I change I can't help but wonder if there is actual plumbing here. I will have to ask Jack.

I go back into the other room and see Jack has changed as well. He has on pyjama pants much like the ones he was wearing the first time he saved me. I look like I am wearing my big brother's hand me downs. Not so sexy.

He turns to me and gives me a funny little grin. I must look silly.

"You look like you are drowning in those. Do you want me try and find you something else?"

"No, I'm fine. Besides the only other girl here is Lila and I don't think she is the sharing type."

"Yeah, I guess you're right. Are you ready for bed?"

"Yes. I am really beat."

I go over to the bed and jump in. It is a very comfy and cozy feeling in this small cottage. It feels like camp. Although I don't know if I ever went to camp. I try and remember, but still nothing. Jack climbs in beside me and cuddles in. I get into the crook of his arm and lay my head on his chest. I keep telling myself that I will remember him forever. But what if I don't? I will use up all my power at the final battle right? So does that mean I will have erased my whole life? This scares me more than dying. I want to remember Jack. If there is only one thing I can take with me it is his memory. I hope and pray this will happen.

I feel his chest rise and fall under my cheek; his slow breathing is lulling me into slumber. I feel warm and safe. I am fading and going into the in-between. I stop myself. I do not want to spend what might be my last night here in the in-between or the shadows. I want real sleep, the kind where you can dream and in it things are better and you feel free and happy. I want that kind of sleep and I think I deserve it. I let my thoughts drift into the air and tell the universe to give me this and it replies with a resounding yes. I get to sleep as a normal person and it is magical.

I wake to Jack getting out of bed.

"Where are you going?"

I want him back here with me snuggling.

"I have to go, the others all left hours ago. You were sleeping so peacefully I didn't want to wake you. You can go back to sleep if you want."

"How long was I out?"

"I am not sure but at least nine or ten hours. You were talking in your sleep to. I heard my name many times."

He is smiling at me. I feel myself blush. I was dreaming of him and all the things I cannot do with him in reality.

"Yes, you were there. They were great dreams."

I jump up and go get my clothes off the chair. If he is not staying with me then I am going with him. He puts on a t-shirt and I find myself frowning. I wish he would go shirtless all the time. He really is doing the world a disservice by covering up. He catches me staring.

"What? I have to put clothes on Raine."

"I know. Wait for me okay. I will be ready in a sec."

I run into the bathroom and throw on my jeans. I decide to leave on Jack's shirt. Mine is dirty and ripped and this way I can smell him all day. I tie it in the back to make it not look so much like a nighty. I splash some water on my face and comb through my short hair. That's as good as it's going to get.

I see Jack as I enter the room, he is on the front small porch talking to someone. I do not recognize this knight but he is again large and pretty like all the rest. I go out the door and stand by Jack. I don't care if I am interrupting, if it is something important I should know too. The man glances over to me and gives a slight nod. I return in kind and he excuses himself. Once he is gone I turn my attention to Jack and see he looks concerned.

"What's up?" I ask.

"That was Devon. He is Charles" right hand man. He was sent to give us an update on Lila. She is still missing. They can't find her anywhere. If she really was one of us we should be able to track her easily."

"I know she isn't one of you. She has your powers but hers are tainted. I think the reason you can't find her is that she is in the shadows with James."

He does not seem any less tense at my suggestion of where Lila may be.

"I don't think she is done with you Raine, she wants you gone and I think she will be back."

He is probably right but I don't really care. She can't hurt me and if she is working with James then I want her gone too.

"Don't worry so much Jack. I can handle myself."

I start to walk down the stairs and realize I have no idea where we are going. Jack must see this on my face.

"Raine, you are supposed to go and talk with Charles. He has been waiting for you."

"Okay, let's go."

Jack shakes his head in response but doesn't make eye contact.

"I have to go to training. Charles wants to discuss things with you in private."

"Why, you know as much as I do about what's going on. I don't want to go without you."

"You have to. Charles is our leader and if you want me to stay a knight, I must listen to him. And that means you must listen to him as well."

He gives me a quick peck on the cheek and starts walking away.

"Jack, where do I go?"

Thanks for helping me find my way around. He calls over his shoulder at me to follow the path towards the other cottages and his is the first one. Why is Jack in such a hurry to leave me? I think something is up. I go and find Charles place and quietly knock on the door.

"Come in Raine." He calls from inside.

I enter the small cottage that looks almost exactly like Jack's except there is a tiny desk in the corner. Charles is behind it looking at something familiar. It is the red leather book that tells of my future.

"Charles, why did you ask to see me alone? Jack knows everything that is going on. I have no secrets from him."

Charles looks up from the book and a moment of panic crosses his face before he gets control, but I saw it.

"I never said he couldn't be present here."

Okay then, Jack is definitely up to something and I am a little worried. I shake it off and try and get down to business. The sooner I answer Charles questions the sooner I can go and find Jack.

"So, what can I help you with?"

I take a seat in the small chair on the opposite side of the desk. I guess I am done with manners and such. When you only have a limited time left there really isn't time for niceties.

"Why do you refer to the dark leader as James? Jack told me that is what you call him."

"He is right, that is his name. Before he became the leader of the dark realm he was James a business man. You see, when I went to the shadows I found out I could see the dark creatures as they were, before they became monsters."

Charles leans forward on his desk and contemplates what I have just told him.

"Really, that's interesting. I wonder why you would need such a gift."

I shrug my shoulders and tell him I have no idea why. But it made me be able to see the real Jack, for that I will always be grateful.

"What else do you know of their plans?"

"I know they want me, they think that with me on their side they can obliterate the knights and take over the human world. They have the numbers, I think probably close to five hundred. And I know they are scared of James. I have watched them for many years and I have never seen them cower like they do to him."

Charles sits very still as I tell him all the details I know of their camps and their weapons. I have told him most of this before and am becoming inpatient with retelling it.

"Charles I really must go and check on Jack. Can we finish this up later?"

I get up and am walking to the door when Charles calls after me,

"Raine, you are not going anywhere. You must stay with me until we are done with Jack."

I was right something is going on. I turn to Charles and feel my palms tingle. I do not like to be threatened and that sounded like a threat.

"What are you doing to Jack? You have better not hurt him! He has been through so much and you saw in my head, you know he has only been looking out for me. If it wasn't for him I wouldn't be here and your stupid prophecy wouldn't be coming true!"

I am getting worked up and need to calm down; he had better give me some answers, now!

"Raine, calm down. We are not hurting him. He is just not allowed to see you right now. We need you focused on the battle and he is a distraction to you. He has been sent somewhere where not even you can get to him. I am sorry for keeping this from you but you are the key, not some silly school girl with a crush on a boy. Jack has played his part."

His part. What the hell does that mean? Is he trying to tell me that Jack was acting? I won't believe it. Jack loves me and this meeting is starting to tick me off.

"Charles I would watch what you are saying to me. You are not my boss and I am pretty sure I can kick your ass if I want to. I will say this one last time and please give me a straight answer.
Where is Jack?"

I have come back over to the desk and am leaning as close as I can to Charles, this man is not intimidating to me and he needs to know it.

"He is no longer apart of this story. Get over him and get your head into what is about to happen."

Charles stands and I notice he is at least a foot taller than me. My palms are starting to tingle, I need answers and he is not going to give me any. I will find someone that will. Aaron. I turn around and head out the door without another word. For a guy who should really want me on his team, he is not producing the best environment for me to trust him. I march down the path back to Jack's cottage. I head inside, not sure what I am looking for but decide it is a place to start and I can call Aaron to me without a bunch of prying eyes. I sit on the edge of the bed and call for Jack first. I try and try but he does not come. I feel betrayed, by Charles and by Jack. He knew something was happening and he didn't warn me.

I take a deep breath and call for Aaron instead. I think I can trust him. Within seconds he is standing in front of me. He looks surprised and then focuses and sees me sitting in front of him.

"I had nothing to do with it Raine. I just found out myself. They had me at training hours ago, I guess so they could take him without any problems from us."

He looks upset and I know he is telling me the truth.

"Do you know why or where they took him?"

"I don't know where but I think I know why. I don't think you are going to like it though."

I urge him to go on. I must know, even if it is going to hurt.

"That first time we met you at Jack's house Charles told Jack something as we were leaving. I wasn't supposed to hear, but I did. He told Jack to befriend you and make sure you trusted him."

I feel my chest getting tight and hold back the tears with some effort. I will not cry, I will not cry.

"So I was just a job for Jack? He was acting?" No.

"I don't think he is acting now. He really does care for you Raine. He wouldn't have followed you into the dark realm if he didn't. I think at first he was doing what he was told but then it turned into more. You have to believe that Raine."

"Why didn't he tell me this? I would have understood."

Now I am just pissed but then I would have understood.

"I think he didn't want to upset you, especially now when the battle is so close and you are going to…"

"Die."

I complete his sentence for him as he didn't look like he wanted to say the words. Aaron nods his head. We both are silent for a moment. I don't know what to do now, do I look for Jack, do I just get on with it or do I say screw it and take off.

"Aaron, where were you? I can send you back there if you want."

I want to be alone and figure things out and no point in Aaron getting in trouble.

"It's okay, I will walk back. I am sorry Raine. I know he means a lot to you. If I find out anything I will let you know."

"Fine."

I feel deflated. I thought I would spend this day, possibly my last with Jack and now that is not going to happen. I must decide what my next move is. So many options and so little time.

Chapter 28

She is going to hate me now for sure. By now they have told her I betrayed her. That my job was to be with her. I don't think I could ever convince her otherwise. Charles is very persuasive and he needs her to do as told so I am sure he has told her everything to crush her spirit and keep her docile until the fight. I knew this was a possibility but I thought maybe, just maybe they would let me stay with her until the end. I was wrong.

I guess it's better that she hates me and not all the knights. They still need her help. I can feel her every once in a while. She is calling me to her but I can't go. They have me on lock down. This place is so far out of the light realm that my powers are nonexistent and Raine's barely reach here as more than a tickle. I was told this is where I will remain until it is all over. I can't believe I will never see her again. When they called me away I thought it was to a meeting about my actions against my brothers. I thought I would be reprimanded for Smith. They tricked me just as they did Raine. Before I knew it they had me zapped here and I am now alone and powerless. Strategically it makes sense but on a human level this is cruel to both Raine and me, but the knights no longer think as humans.

So here I sit waiting, waiting for the war to end and waiting for Raine to die. I don't think I can be a knight after this. I can't go back to being a emotionless soldier. We are beings that fight for good in the world but are not necessarily good. Otherwise we would be allowed to experience love and connection with others. How can I become that person again? Raine has made me human down to the core and I will be forever grateful for that.

Hours pass, I sit here thinking and praying. I need out, I need to be by her side in the battle. Even if she hates me, she needs to know she is loved at the end.

I stand again and try my powers, I don't know what difference this makes but at least I am trying something. I can't give up. I try until sweat in dripping down my back and my head feels as if it may explode. I collapse on the ground and scream out in frustration. "This is not fair! Let me out, I need to be with her!"

I sit and wait for a response but nothing. No one is listening and no one is coming.

I am absolutely defeated. I roll to my back and stare up into space. I try and sleep; if I can sleep maybe I will see her. She won't be gone and we can be happy. I will myself to dream but no luck. I am awake. I think of the first time I saw her and thought her to be a strung out homeless person. I was so wrong.

I had just found the key and didn't even know it. I wonder how different things would have been if I knew. We probably would have never even gotten a chance to speak. Charles would have taken her away immediately and put her somewhere so she could prepare for the fight. I am glad that part worked out the way it did at least. I am also glad Charles put me in charge of gaining her trust. He could have easily given this job to Smith. He after all was the most trained and highly trusted of all the knights. And he would have never got emotionally involved. At least that is what Charles thinks. Smith is the reason Raine is alive and on our side right now. I wish he was here now, he would help me.

I feel it again. Raine is trying to call me to her. I am happy she is still trying but she needs to worry about so many other things right now.

More time passes and I am sure I have now been gone for at least 24 hours. I cannot rest in this place and my senses are dulled. I feel weak and so very powerless. Not just because I have no powers here but I have no say in what is happening. I wonder how long they will keep me secluded. I wonder if they realize what kind of mood I am going to be in when finally released. I can't ever trust them again. I don't think I will hurt them but I will not fight alongside them, ever. Maybe Aaron will come with me. He sees them as I do. We can go and fight against evil on our own. Once the darkness is gone there won't be much left to fight but I am sure there will be some. Not all bad is going to leave after the shadows are gone. I am sure new and more horrible creatures will emerge and we can be there to stop them before they get organized and turn into what we have now. The world is still going to have bad and so the world is still going to need us.

I think on this for quite some time. I hope Aaron will join me, I don't want to be alone and I most definitely don't want to be with them.

I lay in my daydreaming state and hear a voice. It takes me a minute to realize it is not in my head. I look around my cell and see no one. The voice is muffled and low. I can't make out what it is saying. I stand and listen carefully. The voice is getting louder and louder but I still can't make out what it is trying to tell me. Maybe it is in my head. I sit again and close my eyes. I try and think of something else but the voice is too loud. Maybe I am going insane. I have been alone for some time, I think I have snapped.

The voice is getting too loud. I cover my ears and try and muffle the sound. I finally tell it to go away, leave me alone!

The voice stops. I slowly uncover my ears and stand. I still see no one. What was that?

Something catches my eye in one of the corners of the room. It is a shadow and moving slowly. I go towards it, not scared just curious.

The object is floating and has no real shape or form. The voice begins again. The closer I get the clearer it is. I am but two or three feet from it and see its eyes. They are glowing and familiar. The open gap of black in the place of the mouth speaks.

"Come closer Jack. We need your help. Please come closer."

I am drawn to it until inches are between us. I am searching my mind trying to figure out why the eyes are so familiar. They are not Raine's. The voice is pleading. I respond,

"I cannot help you, I am powerless."

"But you can, we need you."

"Who are you?"

The shadow moves then swiftly to engulf me. I am covered in it. I try and fight it but it is like fighting the air. I struggle as I feel it grip me. The voice begins to laugh,

"Oh Jack, you will please him so. We must go now, it is about to begin!"

I guess I am getting my wish. I know what is about to begin and I will be there at the end but not with Raine, instead I will be with her, the one that has betrayed us all, Lila.

Chapter 29

I need out of here. I need to clear my head away from Charles and the rest of the knights. I don't belong here without Jack. I decide to go to the one place I can think in peace. So I wish myself to Jack's house. I don't care if they come looking for me. I will put my bubble in place and that should buy me some time. As soon as I arrive I try Jack again. Still nothing. I have no idea where he is. He cannot be in the dark realm and he is not in the light. He also is not in the human world or the in-between. There must be more places than I had thought. I search his book shelf and find nothing, just a bunch of stories of how wonderful the knights are and how they have kept the darkness at bay for hundreds of years. I do find one interesting book on creatures I had never heard of before. The Zilotons. I sit on the couch and begin reading. These things have been extinct for a hundred years it reads. They were enemies of both the dark and light and their only mandate was to create chaos. They could enter any realm and appear as any creature. They tried everything they could to keep both sides from achieving their goals. The knights finally banded together with the dark realm in just one instance to set up the Zilotons and destroy them forever. They were obliterated and their kind has never been seen again. I sit and wonder how bad these creatures must have been for the dark and light to fight alongside each other. I am glad they did, at least now there are only two sides, good vs. evil.

I get up and go to Jack's fridge. I haven't eaten in more than a day. There isn't much but I manage to find an apple and some juice. I stare at Jack's walls as I eat and imagine him here. This is his home and I am sure he will return here when all this is over. I am heartbroken that I will not be returning. This is it my last look at the human world and all I want to do is stay in this house near Jack's things. I head back to the living room and find a pad of paper and pen in a drawer. I open the curtains and let the sun spill in. I sit on the floor in the sunlight and begin to write. I tell him that I loved him more than I ever thought possible and I want him to go on and have a wonderful life. I want him to know I am not mad at him about leaving me, I know he had no choice and I know he truly did love me back no matter what they say. I tell him he made my last few weeks here like nothing I ever imagined. I thank him for believing in me and making me feel capable of doing anything.

After I complete my first and only love letter I seal it in an envelope and place it in the pocket of his brown leather jacket hanging on the back of his bedroom door. He will find it there.

I feel at peace with this and ready to go. I just needed to say goodbye to him and now I did. I take one last look around his home and take it all in. I say a silent thank you to the air and wish myself back to the light. I am ready to face the darkness and the knights. Bring it on.

I pop back into the cottage and let my bubble of protection fade away. As soon as I do this there is a knock at the door. I go and answer it. Charles is standing there with that Devon guy and Aaron by his side.

"Raine, where have you been?"

"I needed a moment Charles, you really upset me before and I needed to cool off."

I see Aaron give a little smirk and I do as well. Charles may be the big boss man here but I will not allow him to bully me.

"Fine, whatever. We must ready ourselves, it is time. The place of the final battle has been established and the dark realm is already there."

I feel as if someone just kicked me in the gut. I know it was coming and thought I was ready but I am suddenly terrified. I am not ready. I manage to nod my head but can do little else. I am not ready. Aaron reads my face and comes over to me. He steps in front of the two other men so they cannot see me. He places his hands on my shoulders and looks into my eyes.

"Raine, you can do this. You are more powerful than all the rest of us put together. I believe in you and so does Jack."

I stare at him and feel myself calming just a bit. I hope I don't fail them. The light deserves to win no matter how crappy they have treated me. I whisper thank you to my friend and take a couple deep breaths. When I nod he takes a step back and lets the others see me again.

"Charles, what do you need me to do?"

Charles looks relieved that I am calming down.

"You must come with me. We will not be going with the first wave of knights. They will go and flush out the enemy and kill as many as they can. I know the dark leader and how he performs in battle. They will have traps set for us, we must wait and make sure all their schemes have unfolded before we show you."

"So the first knights to go you are sending to their deaths?"

I am appalled at what I am hearing. They are going to sacrifice their own like it is no big deal. I should go in first and just get it over with, no one else has to die.

"They all know the sacrifices they are making, that is part of being a knight and they will gladly die to protect the human world."

He sounds as if I have insulted him.

"Charles it doesn't need to be that way. I can go in first and do my thing. None of the knights have to die."

"That is not what the prophecy says, we will all stand together in order to achieve success. You know that. Now get ready we leave shortly."

With that he turns and leaves. What a pompous ass. He is right though that is what is written but why do we have to do exactly what it says in the silly little book? I am my own person, for now at least, and I think we should try other ways so as not so much blood is spilt. They won't listen to me. I am just their weapon and nothing more. Aaron does not leave with the other two; he instead sits down on the step and leans on the post. He looks worried. I sit down next to him.

"Aaron what's wrong?"

He glances over to me and gives a little nervous smile.

"I have never been in a battle without Jack by my side. We always watch each other's backs."

I see, Aaron is scared as am I but as a knight he is not allowed to possess this emotion.

"Aaron, I promise you I will have your back. You will come out of this alive. Jack needs you."

He looks at me with grateful eyes. I need to ask him this just for my piece of mind,

"You will look out for him for me right?"

"Raine, he is my best friend. I will always be there for him and I will do my best today to be there for you too."

"Thank you Aaron."

I give him a tight hug and he does the same. We are both scared and this gives me more comfort than I would have thought. He is a knight but he feels like me, I will not be alone today.

We sit for a while longer in silence. There are knights going this way and that, they have on battle gear and look quite focused. I watch as they help each other with this and that and as they practice with their light. Everyone looks very intense. I finally tell Aaron to go and get ready. I on the other hand have really nothing to do. I don't need amour, I can't practice with my weapon so I sit and watch. It's ironic how I am again a spectator for the moment. Things have really come full circle. I have now witnessed the light and the dark prepare for battle. I know both sides equally and understand them equally as well. The thing is if the dark wasn't trying to take over the human world, I would probably just walk away. They are evil yes, but each and every one of them had the choice to become what they are as did the knights. No one on either side is forced to do anything. The darkness is full of hate but that is where they want to be. Just as the light is full of good. I have seen that both sides can be corrupted and that means neither is fully good or fully bad. They need each other and I am not sure of the effects once one side is gone. That is a somewhat scary thought. I push it to the back of my mind and try to remember that the light needs to win or else everyone in the human world will be lost to the shadows. The light will at least keep life the way it is, I hope.

They seem to be forming a loose circle in the middle of the court yard. Some are talking quietly; others have their game faces on and are off by themselves. Charles enters the open grassy area and looks ready to lead. He has a regal presence about him and the others all respond to it. Aaron comes back as well and looks just as tough as the rest. I get to my feet and proceed over. I am still in my jeans and Jack's shirt. I look like the tag-along little sister that everyone is annoyed about. Who would guess that I am going to save most of these big macho men's lives? I am hoping most anyway. Charles addresses the troops and gives them what I imagine to be the normal "let's go get 'em boys" speech. The knights seem to eat it up and are looking pumped. Men will be men, it doesn't matter what realm you are in, they love to feel powerful and like they can beat the crap out of everyone. Pump up their egos and they will fight to the death. I can't imagine this to have the same effect on a bunch of women.

The first wave of brave knights is readying themselves to leave. The air is palpable with intensity. I watch in complete horror as Aaron joins the group. No, this is not happening. The first group faces death almost for sure and Aaron is with them. I will not let this happen. I push through the crowd of guys and find Charles. He is busy speaking to Devon. I interrupt,

"Charles, Aaron is not going now! He goes when I go."

Charles looks at me with disdain, like I am a child interrupting his important business meeting.

"Yes he is Raine. I meant it when I said no distractions. Aaron has become one now, so he must leave."

This man really is letting power go to his head. I have had enough.

I glance over at Aaron and he is shaking his head no, silently begging me to stop. I am not going to listen. Aaron needs to be there for Jack. Jack would never forgive me if I let him die.

"Charles, I don't think you understand me. Aaron is going to fight when I go. He is my friend and I don't care what you think. You are not in charge here, I am. I can leave whenever I wish and you will lose. Do you get that Charles? What I say goes!"

The other knights all hush themselves to listen in on our exchange, good. They need to hear this as well. Charles raises his hand as if to strike me, I don't budge. I lock eyes with him and he sees the power within me. I am daring him to strike. There will be nothing left of this man if does. I am ready. He slowly lowers his arm and squares his shoulders. Let's see how he gets out of this. I can't imagine the others would like it very much if he pisses off their savior.

"You are a foolish little girl."

He whispers to me. Then he turns to address the masses.

"Do you all see now why women do not make good knights? Their emotions lead them instead of their heads."

He laughs then and turns to Aaron.

"Do you wish to go with the knights and fight the good fight, or do you wish to be commanded by some silly girl?"

Very well played Charles. Make Aaron feel like less of a man in front of the rest of them so he will bow to your peer pressure. I am not sure how Aaron will take this.

"Yes, Charles. I would rather be commanded by some silly girl when she is the one that is going to save us all and the human world. I would watch my tongue if I were you. You never know who is listening."

Aaron strides over to my side and gives me a wink. He is like the big brother I never had and I am so grateful to have him with me.

The others react as if he just smacked Charles across the face, which I guess he did. They are so ridiculous. Without another word to me or Aaron, Charles orders the first wave to go. I have a pang of guilt as I watch them leave; they are not going to survive.

We all stand in silence and wait. I look up at Aaron and he grabs my hand and gives it a squeeze. I know this is where I should be and what I should to be doing. This is right!

Chapter 30

I am engulfed in the shadow and being carried away. We are not moving like the knights or Raine, this is slower and darker. I feel her all around me but she is not solid. Her breath is in my ear as she giggles with delight. I ask why she is taking me to the battle and why she is helping the dark realm. She never answers she just keeps laughing. Wow, she really is crazy.

Finally after a couple minutes I am released from the smoke and dropped hard on the ground. I get to my feet and take in my surroundings. I am in a field. It is empty and wide. There is nothing for miles. It looks to be a farmer's field but nothing is planted here. Just dirt. The air smells fresh and clean but I know soon that will not be the case. I see the shadow of Lila settle down a little ways from me and decide to see if I have my powers back. I let my light come to life in my hand behind my back; it does but takes great effort. My powers are not as they should be. I am worried that they will not be back to full force before this all begins. I try and leave, get myself to Raine but I cannot. I am stuck here waiting for the battle with Lila. Once she is solid she heads straight over to me. She looks so proud of herself. She stands right in front of me and smiles,

"Jack, I am so glad I could rescue you from that place. It was so dark and lonely wasn't it? Aren't you thankful?"

She reaches up and strokes my hair. I do not move. She is totally insane and I have no idea what she is capable of. I answer as calmly as I can,

"How did you do it Lila?"

She claps her hands and starts walking around me, touching me and never letting her hands leave me. I am repulsed but can't let it show.

"Well Jack, you see I am not a knight. I guess you already know that don't you. I am also not from the dark realm. I am something entirely different. My kind has not been around for a long time so it was easy to fool you."

"What do you want?"

"Oh, I want this! I want the war and I want the darkness to win!"

"Why?"

"Don't you get it Jack? With the darkness in charge the world becomes one of complete and udder chaos. People will go insane when they see the dark creatures enter their reality. Thousands of battles will be fought and millions will die. Doesn't that sound like fun?"

I bite my tongue and try and keep control. What kind of creature would want that? She has lived as one of us for so long and she has learned nothing of peace. She is evil, more so than any dark creature I have ever encountered, including James. I have nothing to say. It seems she has lots to get off her chest. She is stroking my back as she continues,

"It wasn't that hard actually. I went to James in his sleep and showed him great power. He was a man of morals and had good in him. That made him the perfect one. You see Jack, it is much easier to manipulate a creature of good than one of darkness. They are so trusting and fall in love at the drop of a hat. I made him do horrible things and become what he is today. I then told him of the power he could have if he took it a step farther. I told him of Raine and that he should make her his queen. That she is the key and he deserves to have her for himself."

My body tenses at the mention of her name. I can't help it. Lila feels it and lets out a big victorious laugh.

"I needed her out of the picture Jack. Nothing personal. I was a little upset my plan didn't work. I never thought you would be willing to kill for her."

She is now right in front of me with her hands on my chest. I want to reach down and wrap my hands around her neck and squeeze the life out of her. She did all this. She tried again and again to kill Raine and she is the reason we are here in this field. I have never felt such loathing in all my life, to look at her is to see the devil himself.

The sky then turns dark and the field is full of shadows and darkness. They are coming and there are many. Lila turns her back to me and places herself directly in front of me like she is shielding me with her body. I want to laugh. She is now going to protect me after she ruined my life. I try and bring my light out but it is still only a spark. I am contemplating whether I should just start beating her with my bare hands when the smoke parts and James walks through. The last time I saw him was right after he stuck a knife in my throat. Then he looked scared, scared of Raine but now he walks as if there is nothing standing in his way. He sees Lila and smiles and then sees me. He looks confused. She begins to explain. She again is acting the part. She speaks as if he is her superior and she is but a humble servant. I don't think he has any idea of what she is or what she has done.

"James, I brought you a present. But, you are not allowed to kill this one okay?"

"What do I want with some knight? How could he possibly be any use to me?"

"James, dear. He is the one Raine loves. With him at our mercy she will not go through with the prophecy."

I am trembling with anger. That is why I am here. She is using me against Raine. Why did I not see that coming?

"But, how can that be? The last I saw of him he was a dark creature. How did he become this?"

She takes a step towards the dark leader and soothes his concerns.

"There are many things that you do not understand my king. This is one of them. That is why I am here, to help aid you in your quest. We will be victorious as long as we keep him alive."

She gets closer to him and strokes his mangled face. He looks at her and gives a nod. She has him under her control just as she said. She also had Charles. She definitely knows what she is doing.

I am now surrounded by dark creatures, hundreds of them. As they see me they start heading in my direction. If I can get one of them to kill me before Raine arrives she will do as she is meant to. I take a swing at one close to me since I have no powers yet. I connect with his face and knock him to the ground. I am then jumped on by at least five or six more. This is going to be painful but I have no other choice. Just then the weight is lifted off me. James is standing over me and yelling at his followers.

"This knight is to remain unharmed! No one is allowed to touch him! If you do you will be dead."

I lay looking up at the beast and wanting nothing more than for him to throw another knife at me.

"You will not win. Raine knows what she must do and I will not make any difference in her decision!"

I don't know if this is true, but I hope so.

The dark leader looks down at me and says nothing. He goes back to the middle of the field and prepares them all for the battle. Lila stands by his side, looking ever the proud parent. I get to my feet and stand off to the edge. I know this field is enchanted and I will not be able to leave until the fight is done. That is how we always do it. I am helpless. There is nothing I can do until it all begins.

I stand and wait, wait for my brothers to come and be slaughtered. I know Charles and he will send in a first wave to flush out any secret attacks and of course James is planning many. These brothers will be killed. I am so very saddened by this and all that is about to happen. Lila comes through the crowd of creatures and takes her place by my side. She is giddy with anticipation.

"Jack, don't think of trying to get involved in any of this. I know Charles better than anyone and Raine will not be here in the first attack. Of course James doesn't know this, that makes it all the more fun!"

"Fun. This is not fun, this is mass slaughter. Our brothers will be killed. Why do you not care?"

"They are not my brothers. And I don't care because I have no idea what emotion that is, I feel many things but caring and concern are not among them."

I go to leave her and find somewhere else to stand but can't. I cannot move. I look at Lila waiting for an explanation.

"Oh yeah, sorry, you can't move. I have put a spell on you so you will stay put. I don't want you going and throwing yourself on someone's sword and trying to be a hero. Your roll is simple, you will be our bait for Raine and when it is over then you can die."

She leans over to me and kisses me on the lips. I can do nothing to stop her, my arms are pinned at my side and I can't even turn my head. She then whispers softly in my ear,

"If you don't wish to die I can take you with me. I have always wanted to play with you."

"Lila, go back to hell where you came from. I would rather die a thousand times then ever kiss you again."

A moment of anger crosses her face before she puts back on her act.

"It's about to begin Jack. Hope you enjoy the show."

I look to the centre of the field and see it glowing white. James readies his creatures. They are surrounding the glowing mass ready to attack instantly. As the glow becomes solid, knights explode from the centre of it. They attack with accuracy and strength. Every creature in their way is killed in an instant. I look eagerly among their faces searching for Aaron. If he is here and I can get his attention he can go back and warn Raine. He is not here. I watch as the second wave of dark creatures comes in from the shadows, they have been hiding in wait. The knights are overwhelmed just by the sheer numbers. Slowly one by one they are brought down, their lights extinguished. They cannot hold off the hundreds of monsters the dark leader has created. James is nowhere to be found. Saving his presence until Charles and Raine arrive I am sure. Lila is standing by my side watching as if this were the best comedy movie she had ever seen. Laughing and jumping around. She disgusts me. As my brothers and friends die one by one the dark creatures cheer with delight. There is but a handful left when the light begins to shimmer again.

I would do anything to stop this from happening. Raine needs to save the knights and the light realm. I pray she acts first and does not take any time to look around and see me. If she hesitates my brothers are all dead. The light is forming into solid and again more of my brothers pour out onto the field. I can't look away; Lila has made sure of that. I see a familiar face emerge. Aaron. He is ready for the fight and immediately attacks the creatures. He is a good knight and has great skill when it comes to war. I should be by his side, we have always fought alongside each other protecting each other's backs. I see a big toothless deformed creature come up behind him. It has a huge mallet-like weapon that it is about to swing at Aarons head.

Aaron is preoccupied with two other beasts and doesn't see him coming. I scream out for him to watch his back just as the monster swings it at him with full force. Just then I see her, she is standing in the centre of all the commotion with her eyes focused on Aaron. With one look Aaron is gone; he is standing beside Raine, ready for whatever is approaching. He does not look even the slightest bit surprised by what she has done. They are working together. She looks so small and frail compared to the knights and the dark creatures. She doesn't look like she belongs in such a world and I am right. She belongs someplace better. She is focused though, she is watching everything and trying to protect the knights, she moves others out of harm's way, they look nothing like Aaron at this, and they are shocked. It takes them each a moment to get their bearings and continue fighting. I struggle to free myself from my invisible confinements. Lila watches me and lays her arm on my shoulder.

"We must get her attention, don't you think? It would be a pity if she didn't get to see you one last time."

"Lila, please don't. I will do whatever you ask of me, don't do this!"

"Oh, Jack. This is so not about you and your love for one girl, sorry."

And with that I am thrust into the air above the fighting, being held there by Lila for all to see. Raine looks up and pauses.

Chapter 31

I must be seeing things. It's Jack. He is in the air above us as if he is flying. This is not one of the knight's powers, is it? I stare at him and see he does not look happy, more tortured is like it. He is staring at me with sad regretful eyes. I must do something; he looks to be in pain. As I stare up at him and try and will him down to me I feel the earth turn cold. I look away from Jack and see James approaching. Aaron steps in front of me and Charles is at my side. The sea of knights and monsters part and all the fighting ceases for the moment. I guess we are going to have a talk before I end this. I glance up at Jack again and see he is trying to tell me something. I cannot hear him. I desperately want to speak to him, to tell him I love him one last time. James interrupts my train of thought.

"Raine, my dear, so nice to see you again. I was hoping you would show up here. This would be a very uneven fight otherwise."

He glances over at Charles and looks down his misshapen face at the knight's leader. I didn't think anyone was as big an egomaniac as Charles, but James just might have it.

"James, why is Jack hanging above us? Did you do this to him?"

I don't want to talk to this monster but need to know what the hell is going on. I made a promise to myself when James tried to kill Jack that he would die first and by my hand alone. I want to keep that promise very badly.

"Oh, yes Raine. Do you like it? My beauty brought him here for me. He is here to help you make up your mind."

"What are you talking about? I have sided with the light if you haven't noticed. And you can tell Lila to go to hell."

I am trying to sound very brave but am afraid I may not be pulling it off. I look to Aaron but he is staring up at Jack, I think trying to figure out what he is saying. I see her then; she steps beside the dark leader and takes his hand. I knew it. She is with them and always has been.

"Lila, I don't get why you have Jack up there. I can destroy you all right now and he will be just fine. Why don't you just bring him down here so we can get on with it?"

"You think you have this all figured out do you? Well you are right, you can destroy the dark creatures but I am sorry to inform you I on the other hand was not made like the rest of these creatures. You cannot harm me just as I cannot harm you. And Jack stays where he is."

I see James look sideways at his "girlfriend". He did not know this.

I had a suspicion she was one of those things from that book I read at Jack's but now it is for sure.

"What do you want from me Lila?"

"I want you to decide. You can save Jacks life by letting the darkness obliterate the light. I promise you that Jack will be safe and you can go on living with him. You don't need to destroy yourself; you and Jack can live long and happy lives together.
Doesn't that sound better than killing yourself and in turn killing the only man you have ever loved?"

So she wants to bargain with me. I must give up and let the dark realm win or watch as she kills Jack. I know now what he is saying to me. He is telling me to not give in. To fight these creatures of evil. I can't help it; the thought of him being dead is not an option for me. So what do I do now? The only thing I can think of.

"James, why do you let this creature control you? She turned you into this you know. She is the reason you killed all those innocent women and children, she is the real evil, not you."

I need James to believe me, he is my only hope in turning this thing around. Lila turns to James,

"She is lying; you are evil through and through my king. I did not make you this, you did."

I am losing my temper. She is in control here and I need her not to be. I beat myself up, I knew she was evil and I did nothing about it. Maybe if I would have pursued my suspicions she would not be here now. Her kind thrives on chaos and that is exactly what she has. She is winning.

Charles steps forward then and addresses the dark leader.

"Are you prepared to die? Raine will not cower to your demands. She knows her part in this and she will not give in just to save one man. This is bigger than one soul; we are here to save them all."

I want both these leaders to be quiet. They are not in charge, do they not see that Lila and I have all the control. Lila looks at me and we exchange an almost kindred look of disgust at the men at our sides.

With that James the dark leader motions to his creatures to continue the fight. Everything turns loud and chaotic. Men are screaming as they are killed and I am the only one that can stop it. How? I try something. I don't think Lila knows all my abilities so it is worth a shot. I throw up my protective bubble and send it around Jack. It forms around him but not fully. Her powers are very strong and so different from the others. Hers are made of both light and dark, that I guess is why no one is immune to her skills. But aren't mine different also? I am neither light nor dark. It is written in the book that I defeat the dark and tells nothing of her kind being present. She is rewriting the prophecy so that means maybe I can too. I have a feeling of hope rise in me. I have not felt hope for so long. I have come to accept I will die today but maybe Lila has given me a way out. I again look up at Jack, no one can see the shield I have placed in front of him but it is there. I try again to pull him down to me but fail. I turn to the crowd around me and see Lila has disappeared again. She is a bit of a chicken I think. James and Charles are eyeing each other. Charles glances at me and yells,

"Raine, what are you waiting for? Do it!"

I feel the tingling sensation begin in my arms and it shoots throughout my body. I am beginning to glow. One of the dark creatures attacks me from the side but I barely notice. They are consumed by my power instantly. No one can touch me. James backs away and looks as if he may run. That is not an option. I put up my hand and with one single motion bring him to me. He is powerless, this king of the darkness. I stroke his face as he had always done to me. I think about licking him but that is a little too gross so I just smile instead. It is a strange thing to hold someone's life in your hands. I feel no pleasure in it but I also feel no remorse. This is the creature that killed my mother and almost killed Jack. He wants to destroy the world and I can stop him. Suddenly I feel it, someone is trying to get to Jack. My protective bubble is being destroyed. I drop my hand away from James and see Jack is gone. He is no longer above us. When I look back at James, Lila is again by his side and Jack is in her arms. She is hugging him like they are a couple except she has her light aimed at his heart. Her hand looks to be on fire, the light is red, blood red. Jack is convulsing in pain. I feel someone by my side, it is Aaron.

"Raine, you have to destroy them all, now! Charles has gone and we have few soldiers left. Please!"

I speak to him never taking my eyes off Jack,

"She is killing him. I have to save Jack."

Jack looks up at me then and speaks through the pain,

"Raine, do as Aaron says. This is bigger than us."

I want to collapse and cry. I want to be a girl again and feel. I cannot, I must do what is right. I close my eyes and concentrate. I let my body take over. As the strength courses through me I feel nothing but pure power. I open my eyes and see I am again a rainbow of colors; light is shooting through me and out into the ground. I think of what I want to do and immediately all the dark creatures collapse to the ground, all but two. I look around at the few knights that are left and wish them away. Home to the light realm. All but two. I feel excruciating pain surge through my head. I can feel it this time; a piece of me has gone. I wonder for a fraction of a second what is missing when I am brought back to what is happening. Jack screams out in pain, he is dying in front of me and I cannot stop her. James lunges towards Aaron at my side. If the dark leader gets his hands on him he will be but ash. I do not move but bring Aaron behind me. James is pure rage. I have ruined his plans and he has no army to follow him. He lunges towards me and that is it. The most powerful force of evil is gone. He is consumed by my light. Now there is only one thing left, Lila. The field is silent except for the heavy breathing of Jack. Aaron is still with me but I need him to go. What happens next needs to be between me and this creature. I look over to Aaron and smile. I am still a kaleidoscope of colors and know I have little time left. I remember these people in this field but that is really it. I have no idea how I got here or how this started all I know is I must save Jack and there is only one way to do it.

"Aaron, thank you. You must go now."

He looks at me and shakes his head no. I send him away.

Lila has been silent for some time. I think the calmness in which I am approaching her freaks her out. She likes chaos and I am giving her the opposite. Everything is silent and still.

"Lila, I think we will end this now. You do not deserve to be a part of this world any longer."

"What the hell are you talking about? You ruined everything! You cannot kill me, but I can kill Jack."

Her hand returns to its glowing red and she pushes it into his chest Jack does not scream, he looks at me and smiles. I feel my body swell with love and a single tear escape my eye and fall down my cheek. I reach my hand out to him and with that he is brought over to me. Lila cannot stop him. He comes to me and I bring him into my light. We are but one engulfed in the light of every good and honourable being that ever existed. I was given this power by more than just the light, I was given it by every good thought and deed done by every creature that has ever existed. My power is immeasurable because good continues to happen and with each act I grow stronger. I cannot be killed because goodness cannot be stopped. I embrace Jack and look into his eyes. He has taught me so much and given me everything. Tears roll down his cheeks because he understands as well as me that this is it. I was made to destroy evil and there is but one thing left to do. I hug him tightly,

"Jack, if I take anything with me, it will be you. I will remember."

I kiss him softly and release him out of my light. He tries to fight me but cannot.

Lila is staring; she looks shocked and a little scared but cannot move. I made sure of that.

"Lila, you are a being of darkness and hate and your kind should have never been created. You are chaos and the world needs no part of you."

"You can't kill me!" She is almost shrieking.

"You are right, but I can take you with me."

I almost float over to her and let my light seep into her. She is fighting and screaming but I will not release her. My power is fighting back and with every wave of release I feel pieces of me fall away, almost like I am shedding my skin. She continues to thrash about but it will do her no good. I am taking her wherever I am going and she will be of this place no longer. I do not know what is going to happen to us but I do not fear it. I am thankful for my life and for what I have experienced. We are fading into the light, Lila and me. She begins to quiet when she notices what is happening. I look out one last time and see Jack on his knees looking up at us. He is full of pain and I feel so very sorry for him. He is suffering so much more than me. If I could take it away I would, I would make him forget me and all that has happened. But I think that is not how it is supposed to be. He needs to remember so he can continue on and fight for the light. He needs to tell others that good can always win if there is love. I look upon his face one last time and try to remember it. He will be the last thing I see in this realm. Goodbye Jack.

Chapter 32

The world is quiet. I sit here on my front porch and watch and wait. For what I have no idea. I have been doing this for days. I sit out here and watch the people go by. They have no idea what has taken place and what almost came to be. I wish they knew... they knew all that she did for them. I can't bring myself to even think her name. I am so deeply hurt over losing her. She didn't need to do it. All the dark creatures were destroyed, she could have walked away and left Lila for now. We could have figured out some way to destroy her together. I am angry with her. She never let me tell her how sorry I was or that I loved her. She just left, destroyed herself. Now I am alone and have no reason to go on. I did not return to the light realm after she was gone. I came here. They have called for me but I do not go. They took her from me as much as the darkness did. I hate them all. Aaron has been by a couple times but I have nothing to say. He cannot help me. He tells me how sorry he is and that he is here if I need him. He asks me to come home and be with my brothers. I am as polite as possible for I know he was always on my side, he is not to blame for this. I should have known about Lila. This is really all my fault, if I were a better knight I could have stopped her. I guess this is why we are not supposed to have emotional connections with anyone. Our job is nearly impossible when you care so deeply. I have been trying to turn it off. To forget her and the way I feel. I have not been successful yet but am still trying. Smith managed after his wife died. He must have turned off his feelings in order to go on. I wish I could ask him how he did it.

Another week passes. I have stopped waiting on the front steps and now am pretty much confined to my room. I lay I bed all day and think. I think of what might have been and what I could have done differently. I wait to feel better, even a little bit but it does not happen. It is as if it happened moments ago, so fresh in my mind. Raine telling me goodbye and lifting herself and Lila up into the heavens. It was the most beautiful and horrific sight I have ever seen. I can think her name now a least. Aaron stopped by again and said he is dragging me out of this house tonight. He is taking me to dinner so I can see there is still life and people still need us. I think he is full of crap but do not have the strength to argue. As if on cue I feel him enter. He enters in the living room and is alone. That is good; he threatened to bring some of the other knights if I don't snap out of it soon.

"Jack are you still in bed? Get up!"

I have nothing to say so just stay where I am. He comes in and looks disgusted with me. He throws a towel at me and tells me to get in the shower. I do as I'm told. I don't want to fight; I don't even want to speak. I stand in the shower and let the water fall down my face and body. I feel nothing. I am a robot going through the motions of living. I go back to my bedroom and put on the first thing I find. When I go back into the living room I see Aaron looking at a book. I think little of it until he turns to me.

"Jack did you see this? I was cleaning up and found this on the floor near the couch, did you put in there?"

I shake my head no and sit down. I feel dizzy and weak. I can't remember the last time I ate.

"It was turned to the page where it speaks of Zilotons. I think Raine must have found it."

"What are you talking about?"

"This book, it tells of Lila and what she is. I think Raine figured it out long before we did. I know she left the light after you were confined to that cell. She was gone for quite some time. Do you think she came here?"

"I have no idea. What does it matter anyway?"

He shrugs his shoulders and returns the book to the shelf.

"I guess it doesn't. I just think maybe Raine knew all along at the battle that she could take down Lila. I think that was her plan."

Great so she knew what was going to happen and didn't warn the knights or me. I know she couldn't but I still feel betrayed.

"Jack, let's get you out of here and get something to eat. You look like crap."

"Thanks Aaron, I feel like crap too."

We head out the door and Aaron stops.

"Jack get a jacket, you are just in a t-shirt you'll freeze."

I don't feel cold but again do as I'm told. I go back to my room and grab my leather jacket hanging on the back of my door. I throw it on and head out. We walk a few blocks down and eat at a little restaurant on the corner. I guess the food is good, Aaron says so. I eat what I can and am at least feeling a little less weak. Aaron jabbers on about the knights and how Charles is looking to recruit more. How we lost so many in the battle and once the darkness starts again we will need more bodies. I half listen and nod when I think it is appropriate. I am out in the world and still feel nothing. We finish up and head home. I tell Aaron I am tired and thanks for getting me out. He leaves me on my front steps and I reach into my pocket for my house key. I feel something there. I pull it out and see it is an envelope addressed to me. I sink to the ground. It is in Raine's handwriting. I hesitate not knowing what to do. Do I want to see something she has written? Can I handle it?

I decide I must. She left me a message and I owe it to her to read it. I open it and begin to read. I almost laugh at the irony of it. I was grieving so hard about the fact I couldn't tell her how sorry I was and that she wasn't just a job to me and here she is forgiving me all of that. She tells me how much she loves me and that she will always be thankful for our time together. She tells me I must go on living and I need to find happiness again. She is giving me the pep talk I need. I laugh and cry as I read on. She knows me so well; it's hard to believe we were only together for a short time. I feel weight leave my shoulders and most importantly I feel. I read it again and again. She will always be a part of me and I her. I don't feel so alone anymore and realize if

I want to honor her and what she sacrificed; I must become part of the world again. I will always miss her and long to have her by my side. I know I will never love again but I guess that doesn't mean I can't care. I should care about Aaron and my brothers. I should care about the human world and how to go on protecting it. I should care about myself and remember I am not dead. I am here and owe it to Raine to go on and fight for us both. I decide to go home, not in this realm but in the light. If I want to heal I need to help and I will start with helping my family. I go into my house and am about to transport myself into the light when I feel it, she is calling me……………

BOOK TWO - UNVEILED

Chapter 1

Where am I? What's going on? I don't understand. I feel sick and dizzy. I can't stay awake. My eyes are so very heavy. I need to get it together. Come on get a grip. I open my eyes again and try and focus on something, anything. I see a wall in front of me. It is grey and dirty. I feel pavement below me, it is cold and wet. Okay I am getting my bearings. I listen to see if I can hear anything familiar. There are voices in the distance and what sounds like a congested road; cars are honking and people yelling. I am still woozy but get myself in a sitting position. As I do something comes out from behind a dumpster that I am beside. I scream as the furry rodent darts right in front of me. I jump back and stand against the wall. The rat pays me no mind and goes on his way not ever noticing me. I look down at myself for the first time and notice I have nothing on. I am completely naked. Why am I naked? I cover myself with my hands and look for some sort of clothing in the dark alley. There is a piece of cloth sticking out of the dumpster, I grab it and see it is an old soiled linen table cloth. I wrap it around myself like a toga. I look like something out of a cave man movie. I can feel my hair is matted to my face and I am covered in dirt. What to do now?

I have no idea where I am and even scarier I have no idea who I am. I remember nothing. My last conscious thought is waking in this alley. I have no idea how I got here or why. I try and try to remember something. It is so strange; I know what things are and the names of them. I knew the rat was a rat but no idea what I am. I guess I am a human being. That is what I look like anyway. I study my body and see it is female. I feel my head and realize I have short hair. I have no scars that I can see. Maybe if I could find a mirror I will remember me. I walk cautiously up the alley towards the sound of voices. I know I am not dressed like a human and I will stand out. I must find some clothes and figure this out. I am getting to the entrance to the street when two men approach me. They are big and have tattoos covering their arms. They look at me and smirks appear on their faces. I feel heat hit my cheeks and realize I do not like the way they are looking at me. One comes very close and grabs my arm.

"Look at this Gabe. This chick looks as if she hasn't seen a shower in years. Isn't she about the homeliest thing you have ever seen?"

I struggle against his grip and push him away. I do not want them near me. The other one just laughs and comes in closer. They are forcing me back down the alley where we will be alone and no one can hear me. I think for a second and decide all I can do is fight. I grab a hold of the first one and kick as hard as I can between his legs. He hits the ground instantly, I feel strong. I look over to Gabe and approach. He is swearing at me and telling me I am in for it now. I lunge at him and throw him to the ground. I pounce on top of him like a cat and start striking at his face. I punch again and again. He is a bloody mess when I stop. He looks at me with great confusion and agony. I release him and get to my feet. I turn and look for his partner. He is gone. What a coward.

I look down at my make-shift robe and see it is covered in blood. I look to the hulk of a man I have just beaten the crap out of. He is wearing a t-shirt, big but it will do.

"Give me your shirt."

He looks at me and does not move.

"Give me your shirt!"

I go towards him and he quickly pulls it off over his head.

"Who the hell are you? You are definitely not a hooker!"

I take off the dirty table cloth, I obviously don't care for modesty that much as I am standing completely naked in front of this stranger. He hands me the shirt and I pull it down over my head. It is so large on me it looks like a dress. I turn to leave, I hear him struggle to his feet behind me. I don't turn, he would be an idiot to attack me again. This time I make it out onto the sidewalk. There are people hurrying this way and that. Nothing looks familiar. I feel no sense of ever being here before. I make my way down the street to a playground. I see parents and children running and laughing. Beside the playground is a bathroom. I go inside and look in the first mirror I can find. As I stare at the face looking back at me, I am in disbelief. This girl is small and weak looking. How did she just beat up two huge men? Her hair is very short and her eyes are green. She is nothing special to look at and seems very ordinary. I study every feature and see nothing I recognize. Nothing. After some time staring I realize this is getting me nowhere. I do not know her. I do not know me. I wash my face in the sink and drink some water from the fountain. I need to do something but no idea what. I feel a pull, like I need to be somewhere, it makes me feel nauseous. I need to go. I leave the washroom and again start to walk. I walk in the direction my heart is telling me to go. I walk and walk. I am barefoot and the pavement hurts my feet. I am wearing pretty much nothing and it is getting dark. I am cold and hungry. I am alone and feel abandoned by life. Maybe I am a druggy. That is why I can't remember. I fried my brain beyond repair. Or a lab experiment. Scientists wanted to see if they could erase someone mind completely and they are watching me. Or I guess the most logical explanation is that I was in an accident and hit my head so hard that I have a whopping case of amnesia, but why would I be naked in an alley then? Nothing makes sense. I can walk no further. I find a bench and sit. People keep giving me sideways glances, who knows what they are thinking. I don't really care.

I sit for some time watching the people pass. Maybe a hospital. If I check myself in to a hospital they may be able to find out what is wrong with me but for some reason I feel I shouldn't. I still do not even feel human, that I am in this shell but not really one of them. I shake my head and try to look at this logically. I am human and have just had something very traumatic happen to me and that is why I feel so disconnected. The streets are clearing, it must be getting late. The town is quieting. I have nowhere to go. I lay my head down on the bench and curl into a ball. I feel drained. I close my eyes and fall into a deep sleep.

There is nothing except peace here. I feel a complete sense of belonging in this place. Light is radiating through me and I know here I am in my true form. Colors bounce all around me as if they are speaking to me. I reach out and try and touch them, the colors are warm and inviting, calling me home. I want to stay here and never go back to the human world. I beg the heavens to let me stay but I know their answer. I must go back, I am still needed. I have no idea why. I know nothing of that world. I feel tears run down my cheeks as I am being sent away, I plead with the colors to let me be with them. They fade into the distance. I am alone. I look and see not all the light has left, there is a spark of light. I run for it and when I reach it I see it is not my colors but pure white. I hesitate to go to it, it is not familiar to me. It comes closer and starts to change. It forms into a human man. I am scared. He steps out of the light and reaches for me. I pull away and run. I will not go with him. He yells for me to stay but I don't turn, I run with all my strength into the darkness until there is no light left.

I awake to being shaken with great force. I open my eyes and see a police man standing over me.

"You can't sleep here miss. There is a shelter just down the street, they should have some empty beds."

I slowly get to my feet and apologize to the policeman. I walk the way he has pointed. I have no intention of going to a shelter so I just keep moving. I am so very upset that my home does not want me. I know now from my dream I was right. I am not human and do not belong here. I was sent to perform some task

and will not be allowed back until it is done. They could
have given me some sort of clue as to what that may be.

I picture the man from my dreams. Maybe he is the clue I need.
I do not recognize him at all. He was trying to tell me something
but I did not stop to listen. I don't trust him.

I look up and see I am no longer downtown. I am in a residential
area. Duplexes line both sides of the street. Out of nowhere I feel
a strange sensation take over my body. The hairs on my arm
stand up and I am tingly all over. I am alert and ready for
whatever is about to happen. I see no one on the streets with me
and very few lights are on in the houses. There is something
here and I don't think it is good. I feel a presence behind me, as
I turn to face whatever is on me I waste no time. I lunge at him
and knock him to the ground just like the man in the alley. My
only thought is to protect myself and destroy whatever gets in
my way. I raise my arm above my head and am about to strike
when he looks into my eyes. He looks scared, really scared as if
he has seen a ghost. He is completely white and a whisper
escapes his lips.

"Raine?"

I have no idea what that means. But I do recognize him. He is
the man from my dream, he has found me. I punch with all my
strength at him and jump to my feet. He does nothing but stare.
I run. I need away from him, he is after me in both of my
realities. I feel something sharp puncture my right foot. I can
feel blood seeping out of the wound as I sprint across the road
and down a back alley. I need to get away. Why did I not finish
him off when I had the chance? Now he will catch me and I am
injured. Panic is beginning to rise in my stomach; I cannot let
him get to me. I turn a corner and glance behind me, I see no
one. Then smack! I run right into something hard and
immoveable. I fall back and land on the ground. I look up and
see another man. This one has lighter hair and is somewhat

shorter than the first. He smiles at me and reaches his hand down to help me up.

"Sorry Raine, I didn't mean to knock you down. Are you alright?"

Raine, that must be my name. That is what the other one said as well. My mind is racing. So I have been here before and people know me. I have not decided if this is a good or bad thing yet. I look up at the man and do not feel scared; I let him help me up. As soon as I am on my feet he scoops me up and hugs me tight to his chest.

"We thought you were dead. How did you get here? Why haven't you let us know you were alive?"

He looks at me waiting for a response. He seems genuinely concerned for me. I have no idea what to say. I push away from him and he releases me back to the ground. My foot is throbbing so I balance on the other one. I am about to speak when I hear the other man approach. I turn and scream. The dark haired man stops in his tracks and puts his hands up in a surrendering gesture.

"Raine it's me. Don't be scared."

I see the man is crying. Why would he be crying? I didn't hit him that hard. I look back and forth between the two and have no idea what to do.

"Listen, I don't know who you are. I don't know who I am. Please just leave me alone."

I am crying now also but not sure why. This is too overwhelming. I feel light headed, I see the men coming closer to me but there is nothing I can do, the world is spinning out of control, my head is pounding and then all goes dark.

Chapter 2

She is alive! She is right in front of me and she is alive. I feel peace, I haven't felt this way since the last time I saw her. I watch as she lies on my couch not taking my eyes off of her. She has not woken yet; I think her mind needs time to process what has happened to her. Aaron and I brought her here right after she passed out in the alley. She does not know us. This is going to make things more difficult but she is here and that is all that matters.

I wish I knew why she is so scared of me. Aaron said she didn't have the same reaction to him; she let him touch her and even give her a hug. I wonder if Charles knows what is happening to her and why she is back. I would like to think she came back for me but if she doesn't remember anything I don't think that is the case. I stroke her hair softly and ache for her to awake and remember. She needs to know that she is safe and loved. Aaron wanted to take her to the light but she is not ready for that. She looks like she has not eaten or bathed in weeks, she needs to recuperate and get her strength back before we can tell her everything. Although her strength isn't that bad. She managed to throw me to the ground quite easily and when she punched me in the face it almost knocked me out. Why is she so strong when she is not glowing or using her powers? I have so much to ask but it must wait until she is healed.

She begins to stir and I back away so as not to frighten her again. She opens her eyes just as Aaron comes back into the room. It takes her a second but then she is on her feet. She wants to flee.

"Raine please just stop. We are not going to hurt you. I promise you are safe here."

She looks to me and I see nothing in her eyes, she doesn't remember me at all. This hurts so very deeply but we will get through this.

"Is that my name? Raine?"

She stays in her protective stance. She really does not know who she is either. Why would she be sent back to me like this? I find this to be a very cruel punishment for both of us.

"Yes, your name is Raine and I am Jack and this is Aaron. We are your...friends."

Aaron comes in closer as she studies us from head to toe. I guess she is looking for something familiar.

"Aaron, you are my friend?"

She is addressing him and not me. I feel jealousy rise within me, I fight to get it under control, she is not herself.

"Yes we are friends. You saved my life."

She smirks at this and I see a tiny piece of the girl I use to know emerge. I remain quiet.

"I saved your life? Aren't you a little big to need saving by some girl?"

Aaron laughs then and so does she. She glances over to me then. Her voice changes and becomes harder.

"Did I save you too then?"

I have to look away. I cannot begin to tell her how much she has saved me.

I don't get into it and simply reply yes. She again looks to Aaron,

"I would like to get cleaned up if that's okay, can I use your shower?"

Aaron looks awkward and turns to me, I simply nod and have to leave the room. She does not know me but even more hurtful is she does not seem to like me at all.

I hear my friend telling her where the shower is and towels. She says thank you and goes into the bathroom. I am standing in the kitchen feeling both overwhelming happiness but also complete sadness. This is so cruel, to give her back to me but not all of her. She promised she would always remember me and I am so disappointed she did not keep that promise.

"Hey man, you all right?"

I look to my friend and shake my head. Words can't describe how I am feeling.

"Jack, she is just confused. She doesn't remember anything and for some reason she thinks you are a threat. I don't know why but it will pass. I know it."

My friend is trying to make it better. He has been trying for weeks but now his job should be done, Raine is here and that is all I have been praying for.

"I know Aaron. I am just a little overwhelmed by all of it I guess. Thanks for not taking her back into the light. I think she needs some time to process."

"Yeah I think your right."

We stand silently for a couple minutes trying to decide what our next move should be. I hear the shower shut off and am about to go and get her some clothes to put on when she waltzes into the kitchen, naked. Aaron turns around immediately and I grab the dish towel hanging on the oven. I cover her up and she just looks up at me surprised.

"Did I do something wrong?"

I look into her beautiful green eyes and am lost for a second. This is as close as she has let me near her.

"No, nothing wrong. Just we don't usually go around with no clothes on. Why would you think it is okay?"

"I don't know. I guess I just didn't think about it. Sorry."

I laugh then and tell Aaron I will take her in the other room and get her some clothes. She looks a little apprehensive at being alone with me but she sees that Aaron is not going to look at her like this. She shrugs her shoulders and follows me to the bedroom. I am sifting through my drawers trying to find something that may fit her somewhat when she moves to the back of my door and touches my jacket. The one she wore that first night when she was attacked by James, the one she left her love letter to me in. I watch her stroke the sleeve of it and close her eyes. Is she remembering? She shakes her head and looks upset.

"Do you remember something Raine?"

She turns her attention to me and looks sad.

"I thought for a minute I was feeling something familiar but then it was gone."

"It's okay you know. We have lots of time to figure this out. I am just glad you are here."

"Why? Why are you glad I am here."

I don't know what to say. I cannot tell her the truth it will be too much for her.

"Because I care for you. We are very good friends and I was very sad when you left."

"How long was I gone for?"

"You were gone for too long. About three weeks."

"Why did you look so scared when you first saw me?"

She comes closer to me studying my every expression. She is looking to see if I am lying. I will tell her what I can without totally freaking her out.

"Raine, we thought you were dead. I never expected to see you again and when I did I was in shock. Sorry, if I freaked you out."

She is still standing there with a small dish towel covering herself up. I reach into the drawer and pass her my pyjama pants. She lets go of the towel and puts on the pants. I turn my back to give her some privacy, not that she cares. She seems to have lost all sense of inhibition.

"Do you have a shirt for me? I guess this is your place and not Aarons, sorry I didn't know. And you didn't freak me out, I was freaked long before I ran into you."

I give her a t-shirt and then turn to face her.

"What happened to you Raine? What do you remember?"

"Not much. I woke up in an alley, naked. Two men attacked me but I beat the hell out of them. I wandered around looking for some clue as to who I am and where I am. Nothing jogged my memory and then I fell asleep on a bench. I dreamed and then...."

She looks at me and shuts up. She doesn't want to tell me what happened next. It can't be the in-between or the darkness. They no longer exist. She made sure of that.

"Raine, you can tell me anything. No matter how crazy you think it sounds I will believe you."

I am so completely in the moment with her I don't hear Aaron coming down the hall until he is standing at the doorway.

"Jack, I have to go. They are calling me and I don't want to get them suspicious."

Raine looks to Aaron.

"Do you have to leave? I would feel better if you were here too."

Another stab in the heart. Why is she so trusting of him and not me?

"Raine, I am sorry but Jack is going to keep you completely safe and I will be back tomorrow to check in."

I can't even look at my friend, he is being polite and a complete gentleman but I just want him to leave.

"Fine."

She says and looks back to me and gives an apologetic smile. She knows she is hurting me but does she know why. Aaron says his goodbyes and leaves through the front door. Probably a good idea not to blast out of here in front of her.

"Are you tired, do you want to go back to sleep?"

I will not press her any further; she needs to trust me again.

"No, I would really like something to eat if that's okay. I am starving."

"Of course, let's go into the kitchen and see what I have."

I have barely eaten in three weeks so really have no idea what is in my fridge that is edible. I search the cupboards and refrigerator. I have cereal and some milk that has not yet gone bad. She takes it happily and starts chowing down. I watch and see to my delight she still eats the same way. I try not to stare but still can't believe she is here. Just hours ago I was in my bed mourning her death. When she is done she heads into the living room and starts looking through my shelves of books. I don't know if this is the best idea as they are all of the knights and other creatures not of this world. Does she know about such things anymore? I sit down and watch as she slowly reads binding after binding. She glances at me a few times but quickly looks away when she sees me watching her. She comes to the book that she removed weeks ago to show the red leather bound one hiding behind. The book that told of her fate. It is still in the light realm with Charles. She grabs the book and removes it, she looks behind it. She remembers the book.

"What is it Raine?"

"There is something missing here. I am not sure what but I know there is suppose to be something here."

"You are right. There was a small book hidden there."

I am excited to see she is recalling something from her past, something that ties in with me. She smiles brightly at me then. It is her genuine brilliant smile.

"I remember something!"

Chapter 3

I know it is not much but I have some sort of recall of my past. I don't feel so alien here now. I was here before and in this home. I do know these men. I still feel a little uneasy around Jack.

There is something about him that makes me not feel right. He tells me we are friends but that is not right either. When he says these words to me he looks very sad. I am right here but he is seeing someone else. I don't know how to act around him, he has expectations for me and I can't live up to them. I see none of this in Aaron. He is calm and just plain happy to have me here. I think I like Aaron, he is my friend, I believe that.

I am standing by the book shelf and realize that the room is in rough shape. There are books lying on the floor and it looks as if no one has cleaned up in some time. This is surprising because Jack seems the type to have everything in its place. He is sitting still staring at me. I want to tell him to stop but don't want to hurt his feelings. I try and remember my dream, the one with him reaching out to me. What was he trying to tell me? I see his lips moving but cannot hear him. I was so busy being scared that I never stopped to think maybe he wasn't after me, maybe he was delivering a message. I glance back over to the shelf and think to myself how none of these books are ordinary. They all have titles that seem very foreign to me. They speak of knights and realms. Jack must know. He knows I am not ordinary and maybe not even human. He has answers and I need to know the truth.

"What am I Jack?"

He seems a little taken aback by my question.

"You are Raine."

"I know that is my name but I am not human am I?"

It sounds crazy but he said he would believe anything I said. Let's see if he was telling the truth.

"Why would you say that? Do you not feel human?"

"No I don't. I know something is different about me. I do not feel the way a person should. I am disconnected, like I don't belong here."

I am being honest; I hope he shows me the same courtesy. He gets up and comes over to me. He looks hurt by my words and I have no idea why. He looks at me with no hint of anything but love in his eyes. Love? I see it there and realize why he has been acting the way he has. He loves me. Things are starting to click into place. Jack is in love with this person standing before him. I feel my body tense; he sees my reaction and takes a step back. His eyes leave mine and turn away. He speaks in a low hushed voice.

"You are something I have never seen before. When we first met I thought you were just a girl but you are much more. You saved me and my kind and the whole human race in a massive battle. I don't know the name for what you are but you are right you are not of this world."

His voice is shaking and I can hear he is holding back his emotions the best he can. I should go to him and comfort him but I feel nothing for this man. He is just a person that is helping me remember and as much as I try he is nothing more. He does not turn back and walks to his room. He tells me he is tired and says goodnight never turning to look at me. I stand frozen until his door is shut. What am I supposed to do? I found my way back to him for some reason but it seems cruel to stay and torture him like this.

I sit down and think about everything that has happened today. I was reborn in a sense with no preconceived ideas of anything. I am a blank slate and whomever I encounter is writing on it telling me who I used to be. If I was once capable of love that means I must be somewhat human. But was I in love with Jack or was it a one way street. Was I pretending to have feelings for him? I could see that. I think I am quite capable of faking any human emotion. Maybe he was just a tool in my last life to help me save the world as he said. What a funny thought. I saved the world. I wonder how you would go about doing such a thing. I obviously wasn't that great at it because I did die. And then was brought back. I sit and stare at my surroundings wondering if anything else will spark some distant memory. I fold my legs up and remember my injured foot. I look at the bottom and the wound is gone. Did I imagine it? No, I cut it bad, there is no way it could heal so fast. Before thinking I get to my feet and go and knock on Jack's bedroom door. He comes immediately looking very concerned.

"What is it? Are you all right?"

"Yes I am fine. Why is my foot healed? I cut it badly running from you in the street and now it is fine, what happened?"

He looks both relieved and sad again.

"I healed you Raine. I am a knight of the light realm and we have the power to heal others."

"You've done it to me before haven't you? Healed me I mean."

I know this is true. I don't remember specifically but I feel he has helped me before many times.

"Yes, I have."

"Thank you. You are a good man, I know that now and am sorry I treated you so badly before. I was scared of you but now know I don't have to be."

Jack is good. I see it all around him, he is full of light.

"Why? Why were you scared of me and not Aaron, you never answered me before."

He is leaning against the door frame and listening intently. I see now why I would be attracted to such a man. He is very good looking and has a beautiful body. He looks as if he could save you from anything, if I needed saving that is.

"When I slept, you were in my dream. I was trying to get home to where I belong and then you were there and I thought you were trying to stop me. I ran from you and then when I saw you in the street I thought you were again trying to stop me from something."

He does not seem the slightest bit phased by the fact I am telling him this crazy stuff.

"It's okay Raine. I would never try and stop you from anything you were trying to do. I really am on your side."

"I know that now. You are in love with me aren't you?"

Might as well get this out of the way. I need his help and he needs to know that if he can't handle it I must move on. I want to go home and to do that I have to get whatever I was sent back to do over with. He says nothing and grips the door for support. I should have used a little more subtlety I guess. I don't remember how.

"How do you know that?"

"The way you look at me, Aaron looks at me as a long lost friend and you look at me as if you want to hold me and never let me go."

Blunt and to the point, I wonder if I have always been this way or if this is a new attribute. Jack falls to his knees and looks up at me. He looks so tortured. I feel something then as I look down at him, I try and place the emotion. When I realize what it is I again feel bad. I am feeling nothing more than pity.

"I am sorry I hurt your feelings Jack. I know I am meant to be here and that I need your help but if this is too hard for you I will leave."

I turn to go and he grabs my hand. Something happens then, a spark passes between us. I pull away and study my palm.

"Did you feel that?" I ask.

"Of course, I feel it every time we touch. You cannot leave Raine. I just got you back and I will help you any way I can just promise me you will stay."

I kneel down beside him and grab his face between my hands. The spark is back and it is getting somewhat painful, I try to ignore it. I don't understand my actions but it is as if someone else is making them. I look deep into his blue eyes and see myself there. I am in his mind.

"Jack, don't move!"

He does what I say. I am actually in his head. I see me as I use to be. I see Jack and myself in a field. I am consumed by my colors, the ones from my dream. Jack is sitting just out of reach and staring at me. I am leaving and have someone in my grasp. The person is struggling but no match for me. I am powerful. Jack watches as I rise above him, I continue up into the sky far above everything. He sits and watches until I am completely gone from sight. He then collapses to the ground. Aaron appears and picks him up. Jack is done, every emotion is gone from him. He is dead inside.

I release his head and fall back against the wall. I am panting and sweating.

"Were you just in my head? What did you see?"

"Yes, I saw my death."

Then I pass out. My last thought is that I seem to do this a lot. I have done it now twice in the past few hours, for a super human save the world type I can't seem to handle too much.

When I come to I am in Jacks bed and he is by my side. I feel stupid. I am feeling all sorts of things now. I was a robot before but now seem to be getting more and more human. Maybe the longer I am here the closer I am getting to being the person I once was. He sees I am awake.

"Raine, are you okay? You scared the crap out of me. Would you please stop fainting?"

I laugh at this. Laughter, why would I pick now to do such a thing? I have just witnessed my own death and somehow I think it is funny. Wow.

"I am fine. That was weird. Being in your head I mean. Could I do that before?"

"No. I can do it but you never could. You let me in your head once but if you wanted to, you could block me."

"So I am different than before. That's interesting don't you think? Why would I have different powers?"

Jack looks at me and smiles. He seems very pleased with me for some reason.

"I don't know but you are starting to sound more and more like yourself. I meant what I said before, you can't leave. I will help you figure all this out. I know you don't feel for me what you used to but I am okay with it. I just want to be with you, if you don't mind."

I don't mind. I want to stay. Why the change of heart? Why do I suddenly feel the need to be with this man? Am I changing back into my former self?

Chapter 4

She is in there. I see her. Glimmers here and there. She was a stranger just hours ago and already she is beginning to act somewhat like herself again. This gives me hope. I want her to hurry up and come back to me but I must be patient. She will come back but in her own time. I have no idea why she was sent back to me and what she is here to do. She seems to think she has some sort of mission to accomplish. I hope not. I just want her here so we can get on with our lives. I want to be with her and feel normal. I don't know if that is possible but I will keep wishing for it. Her powers are different which probably means she is right, she is meant to do something. Hasn't she done enough? Can't the universe let her be?

I tell her she should get some rest and I leave her to it. She is again in my bed and this is playing déjà vu with my mind. The first night she stayed here and our adventure began; I did not know I would fall so totally in love with her. She was a job then, an order given to me to get close to her and see what information I could extract. It's almost laughable that I thought that was all it was going to be. She has changed me forever and now she needs my help. I decide we should probably do some investigating tomorrow and we should start with me trying to get into her head this time. If she lets me, maybe I can figure out what she is doing here. And maybe, just maybe I can break down the barrier in her mind so she can remember who she really is. I just pray it is still in there. I close my eyes and try to rest. I woke up this morning alone and in mourning and now I am renewed. I sleep peacefully for the first time in weeks. No bad dreams and no painful memories.

When I wake the next morning I smell something cooking in my kitchen. I jump up thinking Aaron must be in there making me breakfast. He has done that a few times in the last while trying to get me to eat. I enter and see it is not him. Raine is over the stove making what looks like omelettes. When she sees me she flashes me her heart-melting smile. I want to go to her and take her in my arms and kiss her. I do not.

"Good morning. Did you sleep okay?"

She asks me in the sweetest voice.

"Yes thank you. The best I have slept in weeks. And you?"

"Yeah, me too. I hope you don't mind I went and got a few groceries while you were sleeping. I found some money in the drawer by the front door. It was the strangest thing; I knew it was there before I even looked for it."

She is remembering more and more. She knows my home as if it was her own and she is putting the pieces together.

"That's fine. My home is open to you, whatever you need you can have. And that isn't that strange, you know everything about my house, it is one of your more unique abilities. We never could figure out why you would need such knowledge but maybe this is why."

"You think me knowing where you keep things is important?"

"Maybe."

She shrugs her shoulders and plates the food. It looks great. I had no idea she could cook. She has never made anything for me before. We are about to sit down when light fills the living room. I see she can sense it too as she looks to the other room. I know it is Aaron. He comes into the kitchen and Raine greets him with a huge open smile. She still feels very drawn to him. I can tell. I know they bonded when I was taken and they fought together in the war but I wish she would look at me like she does him. She offers him a plate and he graciously accepts. We all sit together and consume our food. We fill Aaron in on what we learned last night and what she is remembering. He is pleased and she is excited to tell him. We do not get into the fact that she knows I am in love with her and she does not feel the same for me. I am glad not to share this with him, it is still too painful for me. I am doing my best to suppress my feelings for her but it is taking a lot of effort.

After breakfast I go and change into some clothes and realize she has nothing to wear. She can't live in my pyjamas. I hear her and Aaron jabbering on in the living room. They get along so well. He is telling her of the light realm and what we are, she is asking all the same questions the first time she found out about us but this time it is not me answering them. I go back to the others and let them know what I think we should do next.

"Raine, I think we should take you to your place so you can get some clothes and maybe it will help jog your memory."

She looks to Aaron to see if this is what he thinks is best. I take a deep breath and try to calm myself. I have never played second best to my friend and this is very hard for me. Get over yourself Jack! Aaron gives me an apologetic look, this is not his fault.

"Yes you should do as Jack said. Do you two need me to tag along?"

My friend is feeling uncomfortable with the situation, good. Raine interrupts my thoughts.

"Of course you should come. I feel very comfortable around you Aaron I know I can count on you to have my back. Don't know why but I just want you around. That's okay with you isn't it Jack?"

She turns to me and waits for my response. I don't know what to say. I will do anything for her and if she wants Aaron near her how can I say no.

"Of course he can come. Whatever you want Raine."

I will make her happy, even if it makes me miserable.

"Great, let's go."

She heads towards the door. She looks like some sort of gangster in her oversized clothing. She also has no shoes.

"When you went out this morning what did you wear on your feet?"

She giggles a little and points to my runners. She has tiny little lady feet how on earth did she manage in my size twelve shoes. She must have looked like a clown. I shake my head and smile. She makes me smile.

"Maybe we should go in the light instead."

"What is that?"

She looks from me to Aaron waiting for a response. I answer.

"It is how we move between realms and another way we get from place to place fast."

She smiles brightly and looks excitedly at us.

"Yeah, let's do that!"

Raine comes over to me and grabs my hand, mine and not Aarons. I feel somewhat triumphant at this. Childish I know but I I don't care. Then it happens again. She looks up at me and the current flows between us. She releases my hand instantly and silently goes to Aaron's side. He does not understand what just happened between Raine and me. I suck it up and smile at her. She needs to know I am okay with it. I'm not but she needs to think I am.

"Let's go."

I say in my most manly and confident voice. What a fake. Aaron gives me a "what the hell" look and I decide to fill him in when I have a chance. He deserves to know.

We simultaneously let our light fill the room. I watch as Raines eyes widen with delight. She loves this stuff. Both this time and the last she seems so comfortable here in the world of the different. We arrive at her apartment her hand still in his. I go over immediately and tell her where she can find her things. She looks around and says she sees nothing familiar to her. She seems disappointed. As she excuses herself to change I finally have a chance to speak to Aaron alone. He has the same idea and wastes no time.

"Jack what is going on? Why did you two seem so comfortable when I first got to your place and then when you touched she acted like you were poison or something? And why is she always so happy to see me?"

He looks completely confused.

"She trusts you Aaron. I don't know why but she doesn't have the same level of trust in me. She figured it all out last night. She knows of our past and I think she feels awkward around me because she doesn't feel like that for me anymore. I am trying to deal with it but I have to admit it's rough."

"I am so sorry man. I know how much you care about her. What about that thing that happened when she grabbed your hand?"

"It happened last night too. I thought it was just me and my feelings for her but it is something else entirely. When we touch it is as if her body is repulsed by me or something. It shocks her and makes her instantly release me. I have no idea what that means."

I didn't realize it before but that is exactly what is happening. Her body is telling her to get away from me. That really helps the whole situation.

"Jack what do you want me to do? I know she wants me here but I feel really weird about it."

"There is nothing to say Aaron. Whatever she wants she gets. I am just happy she is here and if that means me never touching her again that is the way it has to be. I wished with everything in me for weeks to see her again and my wish came true."

"I think you should have been more specific Jack."

"Me too."

I hear a small voice say behind me. I turn and see Raine looking up at me with sad eyes. She has heard our conversation and she knows what I am going through. I didn't want her to know. She deserves to feel no guilt in her actions, none of this is her fault.

"Raine, you weren't supposed to hear that. I am sorry."

She looks to Aaron.

"Could you give us a minute, Aaron?"

He nods and leaves the room without a word. I turn to her and wait for whatever she has to say to me.

"Jack, you have nothing to feel sorry about. You feel the way you feel. I should be the one apologizing. I am trying very hard to trust you. I know I don't want to be away from you. I feel a pull towards you but I do not yet feel comfortable around you. You intimidate me and your strong feelings make it hard for me to talk to you. You want me to be something I am not."

"Raine nothing could be further from the truth. I only want you to do and say what you feel. The rest will happen when it happens. I can suck it up."

I smile at her.

"Do you think we could try something? Will you let me try and get in your head and see if I can jump start any memories stored there?"

She contemplates this for a moment and goes and sits on the couch. She looks over to me and pats the seat beside her.

"How could you like someone that lives in such a dump?"

Raine laughs then. She wants me to feel comfortable and I appreciate the effort. I play along, just like I used to.

"I guess your winning personality out shone your crappy apartment."

"You do have a sense of humour, I was wondering where it was hiding!"

Chapter 5

Okay, Jack is totally head over heels for me that is pretty obvious. I am starting to feel something for him but nowhere near his level of emotions. I am a little freaked at his intensity but feel bad for not reciprocating his feelings. He wants me to hurry up but I don't know how. He needs me to be his Raine again but what if that never happens.

Jack wants me to let him into my head. I have nothing to lose so let's go for it. He is sitting by my side on this couch that is supposedly mine. I recall none of this. I push that away so I don't get discouraged. I remembered Jack's house and his things so maybe this place is just of no importance to me. As I watch Jack sitting beside me this is feeling oddly familiar to me. I think this has happened before. I give my head a shake and realize how stupid that sounds. Yes, he has probably sat on a couch beside me before and I would think this exact one. I am such an idiot.

"So what do you need me to do?"

As I ask this Aaron comes back in the room. He sits down quietly opposite us and watches. He must know what is going on. Jack comes closer to me and I feel suddenly apprehensive. He must see, I don't hide my feelings very well. I figured that out pretty fast. And it is funny that I don't remember how to act all the time. Like coming out of the bathroom naked, the boys looked mortified and I had no idea this was a bad thing. Why do I not remember manners and common sense? I should be embarrassed but am not, I don't feel that emotion at all. I wonder if I did before. Jack breaks my internal dialogue.

"Just sit still and let me hold your hands. I know your body doesn't like my touch but we did touch last night without the electric thing hurting you too bad right? I think you just need to relax."

I nod my head and close my eyes. I try and clear my mind and tell myself over and over Jack is not going to hurt me. I feel him grab my hands and the electric pulse happens again but I do not let go. I open my eyes and see he is feeling it to.

"Jack, I am not letting go. Let's see if it stops."

He nods and holds on. The pain is intensifying for me and going up my arms, everything in my body is telling me to release him.

"Does it hurt you like it does me?"

I ask him.

"No, I don't think so. I feel something but it is not painful. Are you okay."

I grit my teeth and try to smooth out my face. I will hold out for as long as I can.

"Just do it. Try and get what you need from my mind, quickly."

I look into his eyes and wait. I feel him then he is in. I try and leave myself wide open to him so he can find out anything and everything that might help us. It is strange because when I went in his head he didn't know what I saw but I am seeing everything he is seeing as if it is a movie playing out before me. It is dark and there are so many doors, each one locked up tight. He tries one after another, never able to get in. I try and release the locks but cannot. It seems to be hopeless and the pain is now searing through my entire body. My body starts to shake but I grip his hands tighter trying to tell him to keep going. I need to find out anything I can. The doors are endless. It feels as if he has been in my head for so very long. I feel him start to pull back when I see it. Way in the corner, in the darkness is a window.

There is light flickering behind it. I don't let him leave and guide him in the right direction. He is there beside it, look through it Jack. I push him into the light of the window and we see together what is there.

It is me at that field again. This time it is my point of view not Jacks. I am ascending into the light and I am at peace. Lila is in my arms, that is her name. Pieces of my former self are falling from me. With each passing second I am not me anymore. We rise higher and higher until we are above it all. We are in my colors, my home. Lila falls from my arms and is weeping. She looks to me and screams out in rage.

"Why did you bring me here! I don't belong here! Let me go!"

"You are going nowhere. You will stay with me in this place and become part of this world. There is good in you we just have to find it."

I am speaking as a teacher and guide. I am not Raine in this place I am a different creature all together. Lila sobs at me feet. I leave her there and head off into the colors. They envelope and caress me. I am laughing with delight when another presence comes over to my side. It is not a solid but I seem to know it and bow in its presence. It is communicating with me but I do not understand. The me in the colors understands, but the me sitting in the crappy apartment doesn't. We only hear my side of the conversation. I look confused and surprised by what is being said to me.

"Why? Why do I have to go back?"

"But I ended it all. There is no more threat to the humans."

"I don't understand. You do not want me here?"

And with that the shadow casts me off and I am in the alley. I push Jack out of my head and let go of his hands. I have had enough. The pain is scorching me from the inside. I fall to the ground and try and catch my breath. I see Jack on the far side of the couch doing the same. Aaron comes to me and lifts me back onto the sofa. He can touch me just fine. We are all silent for a few moments and then Jack speaks.

"That was you. What are you? And what was that shadow thing saying to you, I could only hear what you were saying in response."

I look to him and begin to cry. That was my home and they don't want me there anymore. I was cast out and have no idea why. I did something bad and I am not allowed back. I had it all wrong. I thought I was sent here to save the world again or something and then they would take me back but I know now that is not what is going to happen. I could tell by my emotions that I will never be back there, in the peace and colors. I am sobbing uncontrollably. I finally choke out a couple words.

"I can never go home."

Why did they do this to me.

"Raine, you are home."

I say nothing to Jack in response. I don't want to hurt him. I am alone in this world and this will never be where I belong.

Chapter 6

Raine is broken. I see that now. She has been cast out from the place she thinks she belongs and is in great pain over it. She doesn't see that this is her home, with me. Inside her head is nothing like it was last time. Before she guided me to what she wanted me to see but the rest was still open and bright. Now it is a place that holds many secrets and she can't even enter to see what they are. I do not understand why she was sent back with no recall of any of her former life. If they truly did banish her from her home realm then why not restore who she use to be so she could have an easier time of it. And why let her still have powers? I would think if she was being punished for something they would want to strip her of all her powers so she would be harmless to herself and others. There is so much I am not getting. I know when she was holding my hands she was in excruciating pain. She is tough though and held on long enough for me to see what she keeps calling her home. It was beautiful I guess and I could see she felt great peace there. But the Raine I know could never want to stay in such a cotton candy and pixie dust kind of place. She loves life and challenge. There was neither present in that place.

I look over and see Aaron sitting with her trying to calm her. She is hysterical with sadness. I cannot comfort her; I have caused her enough pain for one day. I stand by the window and wait for Aaron to do my job. I play back the memory again and again in my mind. It is not making any sense. No matter how you look at it I do not think Raine is being punished. She does of course but she is wrong. She is whispering something quietly to Aaron and he rises and comes over to me.

"Raine wants to be alone. She wants us to leave."

I look at him like he is insane.

"No. I am not leaving her. I will give her privacy but I am not leaving her alone here."

She glances up at me and looks pissed.

"Jack there is nothing you can say or do to make this better. I need space from you guys. I need to figure out my life, alone. I am sorry if this hurts you but I can't care about you right now, I need to look after myself."

She has ripped out my heart and just stomped all over it. I go to protest and she does it again to me. She looks from myself to Aaron and commands us to leave and guess what, we do. We are now standing in my living room and she is in her apartment. I can't help but laugh. Aaron looks at me sideways and I am on the ground laughing my ass off.

"Jack, how can you find this funny? She just ordered us away and told you she wants nothing to do with you!"

"I know. I think I have snapped."

I continue to laugh for a while longer until Aaron has had enough. He bids me farewell and says he will be back tomorrow to check on me. I nod and try and calm myself down. My life has turned into a insane circus where all the characters are never what they seem. It is all an illusion and I will never really understand what is actually happening. I again feel lost and alone. Betrayed and let down. I have no idea what step to take next. Do I ignore the fact that she is out there? Do I get on with my life and hope one day she realizes she loves me? If she was still dead I think I could probably begin to heal but this, this is worse.

I spend the next couple days going through the motions. It takes everything I have not to go to her. I have walked past her place a couple times but do not go in. She does not want me around and I will give her the space she desires.

Aaron stops by and is still begging me to go back to the light with him. I have no intention of leaving the human world with her here. He has heard nothing from her either and this makes me a little happier. It is not just me she wants space from. I find myself walking one day, just wandering and thinking about my childhood. I have not thought about my past in a very long time. I was a spoiled and indignant child. Raised by nannies and never getting close to my parents. How can anyone find more importance in life than being with those you love? I have never understood why they had me if they did not love me. I recall

Aaron's stories of his youth and how much his mother loved him, and the other knights. When they speak of their pasts it is with great love and affection. We are taught when we become a knight that we are who we are because the people that loved us helped to guide us here, into the light. I was not raised in such a way so why am I one of them? Raine asked me once why women did not become knights and that is the reason, they raise knights and to become one is to give that up. It is a mystery to me how I was chosen for this path. I think back to all my different babysitters and none of them ever stuck around long enough for me to get attached. How was I guided to the light with no help?

I find myself wandering towards the training field and decide to enter. This place gives me a sense of peace and also belonging without having to go to the other realm. I walk into the middle of the field and sit. This is the spot where I killed Smith. I look back at that now with no regrets. He came to me in a dream and let me know I did the right thing. He is happy now with his wife in some other place and because of his death the human world was saved. I would have liked to gotten to know him better. He was a great man that did not conform to the ways of the knights but made our way work for him. It is quiet here. The war is over and the darkness is ended. There is only the light now. I have never thought about it before but the balance is gone. Good has won so the scales are now completely off tilt. Can the world work with only one side in play?

Chapter 7

I sent them away. How I have no idea. They were here and then gone. I am sure it is one of my powers but really I don't care. I don't care about anything. I haven't moved in hours, maybe days. Time has stopped for me. There is nothing but unrelenting life ahead for me. I was a being more powerful than any other and now I am here to live out my sentence as a human. How depressing is that? Why would I be left with some of my powers? I think on this for some time and I believe it is because no one can take them from me. I was made with them as part of me and since I cannot be destroyed they can't be destroyed either. I wonder what I can do. Jack said they were different this time. Maybe I have evolved. Finally my very human self can take it no longer I must eat. There is nothing in this place and I have no money. I look through all my stuff and do find a twenty hidden in my sock drawer. I quickly throw on some clothes and head out. I still feel nothing for this place or city. The streets are crowded and people look happy and cheerful. I can't even fake a smile. What is there to be happy about? I find a sidewalk hotdog vender and get two. I sit down and chow down. As people pass they all say hello and exchange pleasantries. The sun is beaming down and the warmth reminds me of my home. I push the thought away and try to stay focused on the here and now. This is my home now and I better learn to accept it or I will be depressed forever.

As i finish up I decide to go for a walk. I pass a park and watch for a minute as the children are jumping around and climbing. They are all laughing and having such fun. The moms sit close by and look as if they are having as much fun and their children. This place is full of happy people today. It must be the weather I decide and continue on. I find myself heading down a street with abandoned warehouses on either side. Something is making me walk right to the end of the road. All that is there is another abandoned looking building. I am a little confused as to why I would want to go here. I look for some sign of life inside the windows but nothing. I am about to turn and go when I see the wall move ever so slightly. My mind must be playing tricks on me. I reach out and touch it. My hand goes right through the brick. I pull it back and study my hand. It seems fine. I test it out again and stick my whole arm in this time. Again when I pull it back it is all still there. I look around one last time to check and see if anyone is watching, I am alone. I close my eyes and take a step into the wall. I hold my breath. When I open my eyes again I am not inside a building at all. I am in a field and I see someone sitting in the middle of it. I know him instantly. It is Jack. He is sitting with his back to me and his face turned up to the sky. The same sun is beating its light here and it is so warm and inviting. I hesitate for a moment not knowing if I want to talk to him or not. I decide that my heart has led me here for some reason and Jack obviously has something to do with it. I silently walk up to him and sit beside him. He turns his head to me and looks a little stunned. I smile at him.

"Hi Jack."

I don't know what else to say. Last time I saw him I pretty much told him to get lost and never speak to me again. Nice.

"Raine, what are you doing here? Are you alright?"

He sounds worried and confused.

"I am fine. I was out for a walk and for some reason I felt the need to come here. This place seems familiar to me. But there is great sadness here, I can feel it. Something bad has happened here hasn't it?"

I feel like I need to cry and have no idea why.

"Yes, Smith died here. That must be what you are feeling, but you weren't here when it happened."

"Smith, I do not know this name."

I look around searching for something to help me jog my memory.

"He was a very good man and knight. He is the reason you were there at the final battle. He is the reason you were able to save us all. He gave his life willingly to help you."

I don't know what to say, to have someone sacrifice themselves for you and you don't remember any of it hurts.

"I am sorry I don't remember him. He sounds wonderful."

We sit in silence for some time just basking in the heat. I remove my light jean jacket and bunch it up to place under my head. The sun warms my skin as I lay down and close my eyes. Jack is still beside me but I do not feel the need to speak, we are comfortable without saying a word. I begin to drift off the sleep. I have not slept in days. I hope I do not dream of my home. It is too painful to go back there every time I rest and have to wake to this place. I fade into the light. I see a door in my dream, not like the ones in my mind this one is white and welcoming. I go over to it without hesitation and open it. I peak in and see nothing but am hit with an emotion so deep and strong it knocks me down. I am laying on the ground and it is sweeping over me and hitting me again and again. It is trying to enter my body but I protest and do my best to keep it out. For some reason I do not want to feel it, I don't know what it is and it scares me. I am jarred awake, I sit up quickly and see Jack has not moved from beside me. He looks at me and gives a soft and sad smile.

"How long was I asleep?"

"Not long. Maybe fifteen minutes."

"I have to go."

I get to my feet and grab my jacket. He also gets to his feet and looks as if he has something to say. I pause and wait but he seems to change his mind.

"Goodbye Jack."

For some reason this infuriates him. He comes over to me and grabs my shoulders. The electric shock pulses through my body but I do not pull away. He yells in my face.

"Don't ever say that to me! Just leave; never say those two words to me again!"

I have no idea what I have done to upset him. I stare into his eyes and see how very tortured he is. I have done this to him. I reach up and touch his cheek; he pulls away from me and turns his back.

"Jack, I just said goodbye."

And then it hits me. I see it, me floating away and him on the ground pleading with me to stay. That is the last thing I said before I left him and he thought I was dead. How cruel of me.

"Oh, I am so sorry Jack. I remember now. I didn't mean it. I didn't mean to hurt you again."

I grab his shoulder and again I feel pain but I no longer care. He is worth a little pain. He shakes me off and walks away. He is done with me and who can blame him. I decide it is time for me to go. That dream really took it out of me and I don't think Jack wants me hanging around. I slowly make my way back to the entrance. I assume I can just walk back through. As I am about to leave I turn one last time and see Jack is again in the middle of the field standing, staring at me. He looks miserable.

Something starts to move behind him. The air is shifting and a bright light starts to glow. I know this is the light of the knights.

But for some reason I hesitate to leave. Jack turns around and sees it to. He looks over his shoulder at me and waves for me to leave. I cannot. He looks worried and I know it is not Aaron that is about to arrive. I stay. My body will not move in the direction I should be going. Instead I am walking towards Jack and the light.

"Raine, they don't know you are alive. You have to get out of here, now!"

I look to him and smile.

"I can't. Everything in my body is telling me to stay. I don't know why but I need to be here."

He shakes his head and comes to stand in front of me as a barrier. He is protecting me even though he hates me. He whispers over his shoulder to me as a man comes out of the light.

"You are really difficult you know that. I don't know what Charles will want to do with you when he finds out you are alive. Raine, please listen to me for once!"

"For once, you mean I didn't listen to you before either?"

I am not scared of this Charles. He stops dead in his tracks when he notices me behind Jack. Jack speaks, trying to ease Charles tense look.

"Charles, it is Raine. She has come back."

"I see that. Why wasn't this reported to me right away?"

"She wanted to be alone; she has some issues she is trying to deal with. She was not returned here the same as she left."

Makes me sound kind of pathetic doesn't it. I step in front of my body guard and look at this leader. He seems pompous and arrogant and quite the tool.

"I don't think you have any right to know where I am or what I am doing Charles. I am not a knight and from what I here I saved your butt big time so just leave me alone, okay?"

Jack lets out a little chuckle before he recovers. Charles looks to me as if I am crap on the bottom of his shoe.

"Raine, you still have that mouth on you. That didn't seem to get lost in your trip back. And Jack, you haven't reported back in weeks. You need to come with me and be with your family."

"No."

I am surprised by my tone. Jack looks at me and is as startled as me at this.

"Raine you have no say in matters of our kind. If you do not wish for our help then leave. Jack is one of us and must do as ordered. We left him for so long because he was mourning you but you seem to be very alive and now he must get back to work."

"No. You are not taking him anywhere. I do not trust you and neither should Jack."

Charles begins to laugh then; a cackle is more like it. He thinks I am just a ridiculous little girl that wants her boyfriend all to herself. That is not what is happening. I feel it surge through my body. He is pissing me off and if he doesn't leave now I will lose it. Jack comes to me then.

"Raine, what are you doing? Charles is not the bad guy. You got rid of all them. He is arrogant and doesn't have the best manners but he is not bad. Why are you acting like this?"

"I don't know. Jack please trust me, you can't go with him, please."

"I will always trust you."

With that he wraps his arms around me and we are gone. We are back in my apartment and Charles is nowhere to be found. I again have no idea why I did that. Jack is staring at me waiting for answers.

"Thank you for believing me. I am sorry you are now in trouble with your leader but you can't go there. They are up to something and it is wrong."

"How can you say that? All you did was look at him. He is still a being of good because if he wasn't he couldn't travel in the light."

I don't know what to say, his argument is sound but I just know in my gut I did the right thing.

"Jack you are right but you said you would trust me so just do. I don't have all the answers right now but I am working on it."

My mind is racing. I am no longer worried about being a human or missing my home. There is something very wrong with this world and it needs my help. Jack's too. I not only wanted to protect him from Charles, I need him on my side for some reason. I wish it wasn't so hard to figure out. Why must the universe give me so little to go on. If they spelled it out for me things would be so much easier but that is not how it works. I must discover the answers on my own.

"Okay Raine. You seem very focused all of a sudden, what has changed?"

"In the field when I was sleeping I had a dream. I was being attacked by something. I couldn't see or touch it but it was trying to get me. It was an emotion. I know that sounds crazy but that's what it was. I did not let it in but it wants me."

I look up at him then waiting for him to tell me I am insane. Jack takes a couple steps towards me and simply shrugs his shoulders.

"Okay so what do you think that has to do with Charles and the knights?"

"The emotion that attacked is the same one surrounding Charles. I felt it all around him. I guess that is why I was so freaked."

"Charles is a being of light. That makes him made of love. Not human love but pure good."

"You are a knight and feel nothing like him. Your glow is not the same as his."

He begins to pace back and forth in front of me. He is in deep thought. He stops.

"Do you know what I feel like? Is it an emotion you know?"

I study him and try and place what he feels like to me. He is not going to like what I have to say.

"Your light is full of sadness, pure and deep. This emotion I understand."

Jack turns his face from mine and looks out the window. I leave him for a moment and go the kitchen. I find a couple glasses and fill them with water. I enter the living room and offer him one. He takes it never looking at me.

"You are right. I feel nothing other than that. I feel as if all is lost to me, you are lost to me."

"I don't understand Jack. How can you love someone so much? We were together for such a short time."

He turns to me then and gently caresses my cheek without actually touching me.

"You have no idea what it was like to feel so totally and absolutely at peace with another person. Love is not about touchy feely crap it is about being safe, safe to share yourself completely. You were a part of me and I was a part of you."

That sounds nice. To be connected to someone and know you are not alone. He lowers his hand and moves away. I want that feeling but no, I cannot have it.

There is work to be done.

Chapter 8

It is very strange to be explaining my feelings about love to the girl I love and she has no idea what I mean. I see she does not comprehend what I am saying. I feel sorry for her. I wish she could remember this emotion; it is the greatest there is. She says I do not have the same light around me as Charles, I wonder what that means. I know I have been out of it for weeks and haven't even tried to use my light. Maybe I can't.

Raine is sure something is wrong with Charles and who am I to say she is wrong. She knows so much that the rest of us do not. She felt Smiths death in the field and she feels Charles is up to something. The thing is what could he possibly be doing? I would think it a very happy and peaceful place in the light right now. I guess I should have ventured back at some point then maybe I would see what she is feeling. Aaron is there lots maybe he knows what is going on. I ask Raine if she can call to him. I explain it is another one of her gifts and she says she will give it a try. She stands away from me and closes her eyes, she is concentrating very hard then in an instant my friend appears in the middle of the room. Raine beams brightly at the fact she did it. I am proud of her. Aaron looks confused.

"Hey Aaron, I asked Raine to bring you here. Hope that's alright."

He clears his throat and looks as if we interrupted him doing something important. He does not have a good poker face.

"Aaron what's up? Where were you just now?"

Something is definitely wrong.

"Jack, you shouldn't have brought me here. I was with Charles. He is furious. He wants to know what is going on with you and Raine. We have been ordered to seek you out and bring you in."

Raine comes to my side and pushes me behind her.

"He is not going with you Aaron. Tell Charles I did this on my own and Jack is gone. He left and is not coming back. Tell him I sent him away. Please Aaron I see your light and you have been infected like Charles but it is not totally surrounding you yet. You need to do this so we can figure out what is happening and save you."

Aaron laughs then, an arrogant sounding laugh that resembles Charles.

"I don't need saving. You are wrong we are happy as is the rest of the world. I will do this one last thing for you but that is it. I am done with you after this. You two have little time left so I would use it wisely if I were you."

With that my friend is gone. Raine is definitely right. Things are getting weirder by the second.

"Raine, what did you see? How did he look infected?"

"That same light that surrounded Charles is eating its way through Aarons light as well he is almost completely encompassed by it. We need to do something before they come for you. How can we protect you from it?"

"Your bubble."

She looks at me as if I have said something in a language she has never heard before.

"That is what you called it. You can put up a shield that my kind cannot track. We will be out of sight from them. I am not sure how you did it, you told me you simply did not want to be found and it appeared."

"So I just can at will make us invisible to the knights. That's cool."

She comes over and stands very close to me. She looks up into my eyes and places her hands on my chest. No skin is touching so I don't think this hurts her, she shows no sign of being uncomfortable. My heart beat speeds up and I am hoping she doesn't notice. This is not the time for touchy feely crap right?

"I need to concentrate could you please calm down. Your heart feels as if it is going to come out of your chest."

She says this mockingly and smiles at me.

"Sorry" Is all I can manage to say.

She lowers her head and presses firmly into me with her hands. A moment later she surprises me by jumping up and wrapping herself around me. I catch her just before she falls to the ground.

"I did it! You are in my bubble. They won't be able to find us. Thank you Jack, for teaching me all these things."

I stand holding her and basking in the moment. She likes me right now, things are looking up.

Her look turns serious, moment over.

"We need to go somewhere else. Aaron will bring them back here once he is fully infected. Where should we go?"

I put her down and contemplate what we should do next. I think of the most outrageous place that the knights would never expect me to go. Not even Aaron my best friend. A place I have never spoke of or rarely thought of since becoming a knight.

"We should go to my home."

"Isn't that the first place they will look?"

"No, not my house. My home where I grew up. They will never even think to look for us there."

"Why not? Isn't it where your parents are? They will surely look for us wherever your family is."

"That's just it. I am not attached to anyone there. They are strangers to me and always have been. I feel nothing for those people and they feel nothing for me in return. It is a perfect place to hide and figure out what is going on."

Raine looks sad to hear me say this but it is the truth. I gave up long before leaving them on ever trying to get them to love me. It was simply a place to grow and move on from, nothing more.

"Okay Jack. You trust me and in turn I trust you. We will go to your home. I don't think you should use your powers to get us there. They can track that can't they?"

"Yes they can, that is why we are going to take the bus."

She throws her head back and lets out a big belly laugh. I don't know why this is that funny; many people take the bus every day.

"Okay then. Let's go and take some public transportation to a place you hate so the good guys can't get us and turn us into one of them!"

Well when you put it like that it does sound a bit absurd.

We decide to not waste any time and go straight to the bus station with only the clothes on our backs. I get out all the money I have on the way and we are set. Raine is unusually quiet. She seems frustrated and on edge. When I ask her what is wrong she tells me she knows she has the answers we need but they are just beyond her reach in her mind. She tries to put on a brave face but I know she is suffering. Once on the bus we settle in for the six hour trip. I stare out the window as we leave the city and enter farm land. I have never left this city without being on a mission and then I did not travel by bus. This feels so normal. This is what ordinaries do.

We sit in complete silence for the first hour of our journey, Raine by my side. She is concentrating so hard that perspiration is forming on her face. She needs to realize this is not all her problem, I can help her.

"Raine, stop. You are trying too hard. Maybe if you relaxed a little whatever answers you are looking for would come to you."

I break her out of her meditation. She looks to me and sighs.

"It is just so dam frustrating. I need to remember my life, not just for myself but I fear for everyone else as well. There are so many questions."

"You are right there is but you can't force it."

"Why not? If I am so powerful why can I not access my own mind?"

"You had to release it all. When you used your abilities to defeat the darkness you had to let go of every bit of yourself to get that powerful. I saw it. You were nothing but a shell by the time you actually left me."

"I was? Did I know that was going to happen? Did you?"

"Yes. I tried everything to keep you away from it. I was selfish I know but I wanted you to stay with me, I didn't care that the world was about to end. But you insisted it was your destiny and you were willing to sacrifice yourself to protect my brothers and the ordinaries."

"And you. I think you were the one I was trying to keep safe the most."

I say nothing and turn back to the window. She makes this all very difficult. I think this is how it is going to be now, me as a stranger to her and then she says things like that. She may never be herself again and I must come to terms with that. We continue on our journey to where I grew up. I feel no anxiety which is weird. I mean I haven't seen these people in years. They must think I am dead by now. I am hoping no one over reacts; my mother always had a flare for the dramatic. I would watch her perform for all her society friends while father drank away all his inhibitions. If they weren't so filthy rich I can't think of a single person that would even speak to them.

I close my eyes and try to rest, Raine is doing the same. I hope she finds some peace in her sleep. And maybe if it's not asking too much, a piece of herself.

Chapter 9

I think I am getting bus sick. Jack is sound asleep at my side but I have found little rest. The rocking motion and smell in this confined space is getting to me. I feel claustrophobic. We must be almost there. We have been travelling for so very long. The sky is dark and there is only the sound of the bus driver's radio.

I have not been able to access any memories and at this point feel kind of hopeless. What was that emotion that was trying to get me? Why was I so afraid of it? And why are all the knights infected by it? If I could name it maybe I would have a chance to conquer it. I go through my list of feelings in my head. If I could figure out what I haven't felt maybe that will point me in the direction of what is after me. Since I have been back I have felt scared, nervous, cautious, anger, loneliness, protectiveness, pity and maybe even a little bit happy here and there. What am i missing?

The bus comes to a stop. I hope this is it. I shake Jack gently and let him know what stop we are at. He lets me know this is the right one and we finally get to leave the big stinky machine. I breathe deeply once we are out in the night air. Jack stretches and looks at the big map posted in front of the small store we were dropped off at. It is now two in the morning and there is no one around. We are completely alone. I check my protection I have up around us and see it is still in tack. They do not know where we are.

"This way."

I follow Jack up a narrow road with trees falling in on us from both sides. This seems to be a beautiful quant little town. It is all quiet now but there is evidence in the driveways of lots of young children. Bikes and skateboards and basketball hoops are everywhere. The houses are large and regal looking. We get to the end of a block and Jack hesitates. We can go no further because of a big gate blocking our way. Jack turns back like he has changed his mind.

"Jack, where are you going?"

"I don't think I can do it Raine. Behind that gate is my family and I don't know if I can face them."

I walk over to him and place my hand on his shoulder. He is frightened of this place. I can see it in his eyes.

"Why are you afraid to face these people Jack? What did they do to you?"

He looks at me; his eyes show just how very sad he is.

"Nothing Raine, absolutely nothing. They never lifted a finger for me so I don't know why I was so stupid as to think they would help me now."

"You said this is where we should go and we would be safe here. We are running out of time and options, you may just have to suck it up. If I am right and the light is up to no good than this is a lot bigger than your mommy issues."

I guess that was a little harsh but we don't have time for this. Jack seems taken aback by my comment and takes a minute before speaking.

"Well when you put it like that...."

He proceeds over to the gate, punches in a code at the side and it swings open. The driveway in front of us is long and decorated with elaborate flower beds and fountains on each side. It looks more like the entrance to a castle than house. Jack is staying a step in front of me not letting me see his face. This place really is a painful memory for him. We come into a clearing and before us is a grand mansion. There are several cars pulled up in front and it looks as if a dozen people must live here.

"Jack, who lives here with your parents?"

"No one, just the two of them, although they could fit several families if they wanted to."

He turns back to me and pauses.

"I am sorry for what you are about to witness. They have not seen me in two years and I am not sure what kind of welcome we are facing."

I nod my head and smile. I don't really care what they are like. If they are that cruel of people they do not deserve to have someone like Jack be a part of their lives. I feel a sense of protection wash over me as he rings the bell. Just as I did in that field when Charles wanted to take Jack away. I am ready for anything, even crazy parents. He buzzes a couple more times and then a light finally comes on inside. We hear someone approaching. The door opens slowly and a elderly man appears in the doorway.

"Do you have any idea what time it is? The mister and misses do not want to be disturbed at such an ungodly hour. How did you even get in here?"

"Sir, I am Jack and this is my home. I would like to speak to my parents please."

The butler or whatever he is takes a step back and stares at my companion.

"You are Jack? I don't believe it. Their son died two years ago. I am going to call the police if you do not leave immediately!"

Jack doesn't waste another moment and pushes past the old man. He heads up the giant staircase at a run. I stand in the doorway for a moment and just stare. The old guy goes for the phone on the side table; I grab it before he has a chance.

"We are not here to hurt anyone and he really is their son."

He takes a swing at me and I duck. I grab a hold of him and sit him in a nearby chair. I am much stronger and quicker than him. He looks up at me stunned.

"Like I said we are not going to hurt anyone. Just give Jack a minute okay?"

He nods his head and says nothing. I am not sure what to do now. I should probably give Jack some time with his parents but I feel this overwhelming need to protect him. If they are as awful as he has said he may need me. I tell the butler guy to stay put and take the phone with me. He seems to be calming down and I don't really care if he does call the cops. Jack belongs here. This is his home.

I proceed up the stairs and down one of the hallways. I see Jack leaning against a wall just outside two beautifully adorned doors that can only lead to the master suite. He is shaking and is as pale as a ghost.

"Jack. What's going on? Are you okay?"

"I don't know what to say to them. Even if they are awful they think I am dead. I am going to scare the crap out of them."

"Yeah, you probably are."

I don't know what else to say. This is going to be a shock for them no matter how you look at it. I decide to get things moving. I go over to the big doors and knock. Jack looks at me and nods his head as if to say thank you. He straightens himself out and comes to stand beside me.

"What is it? Johnson, do you have any idea what time it is?"

The voice is male and sounds pretty upset at getting woken up.

"Dad. Dad it's me....Jack."

No sound from the other side of the door. Sucdenly the knob turns and there standing in front of us is a very distinguished looking older man with white hair. He is shorter than Jack and his eyes are brown not blue. He looks nothing like his son, I don't know what I expected but I thought I would see some similar characteristic between these two men.

"What the hell are you doing here?"

Okay, I am no family dynamic expert but I dcn't think that is the proper reaction to seeing a son you thought was dead. Tears, fainting, screaming but this I didn't see coming. Jack looks totally taken aback by this as well. He looks to me for something. I don't know what. I want to help him but how? I take a shot at it.

"Excuse me sir. This is Jack your son. The one you thought was dead. Aren't you happy to see him."

Jack is unable to speak; he just looks from me to his father.

"And who the hell are you? I knew he wasn't dead and what god dam business is it of yours anyway? Are you one of them to?"

What does that mean? One of what? And if he knew he wasn't dead why would he tell everyone he was? Jack slides down the wall and sits. He is unable to look at his father any longer. He is destroyed. It is as if his father struck him with his hate. I must keep handling this for Jack.

"I am Raine your son's friend. And if I may ask why are you being such an ass?"

With this his father turns his back to me and slams the door. He calls through it.

"There is a room down the hall where you can stay the night. I will speak to you in the morning."

I feel like punching him in the face. What a complete and utter jerk. I bend down and try to get Jack to his feet. He is heavy and not really cooperating. I grab his face in my hands. The pain begins in my palms but I am getting use to it, pushing it to the back of my mind. I can manage it if I do not touch him very long.

"Jack look at me. We need to get you to the room down the hall. Do you hear me?"

He looks at me with dull eyes. This has emotionally destroyed him.

"Jack! Please snap out of it!"

He comes to a little then and put his fingers through mine. We are very close and I feel odd about it. Something is tingling in the back of my mind. I pull away from him and get to my feet. He stands and leads me down the hall without a word. We enter a room with a big embossed wooden bed in the middle of it. Jack peels off his coat and kicks off his shoes. He goes to the bed and lays down. I take off my shoes and place them by the door. I sit down beside him on the bed. His arms are covering his face and he doesn't seem like he is going to start talking to me anytime soon.

"Can I go take a shower?" I ask.

"Yeah, go ahead."

He replies with no enthusiasm what so ever. I leave him to his sulking and go take advantage of getting cleaned up. The water is hot and makes me feel so good. I love showers. I think I did before to. They make me feel calm and grounded. I must have been in there for at least thirty minutes. I find a robe hanging on the back of the door and decide I don't want to get back into my jeans right now. It is warm and fluffy. I quietly re enter the bedroom in case Jack is asleep. I look around and see no one. His shoes and jacket are still here but he is not. I go out the door and start looking for him. I hope he hasn't done anything stupid and if he went too far he will be out of my protective bubble and the knights will be on us in an instant. I race down the hall and check the rooms. He is not here. I head down the stairs and almost run smack into Johnson.

"Sorry. Have you seen Jack?"

"No miss. Sorry about earlier. I was told you wil be staying here the night."

"Yes we are."

"Goodnight then."

"Yeah, goodnight."

That was weird. He must have spoken to Jacks father. I continue looking around the house, when I finally see him. He is in a room with walls lined with books. The official library I guess. Jack is sitting on the floor in front of a roaring fireplace. He has books, no albums strewn all about him on the floor. He is staring down at one not moving.

"Jack, what are you doing in here?"

He glances up at me and immediately back down to the album in his lap.

"I am gone. I am not in a single picture in this house. They have erased me from their lives completely."

"What? Why would they do that?"

I move to his side and sit on the rug beside him. I look at the albums and see smiling faces looking back at me. People at parties and Christmas pictures. Holiday photos and baby pictures. Not one face looks like Jack. No black curly hair or beautiful blue eyes anywhere.

"I don't know. Could you possibly hate your own child so much that you pretend they were never born?"

I take the book from his hands and close it. I close the rest as well and move them all away. This place is creepy and strange. Something is up here, more than just crazy parents. I don't know if Jack can see it but I sure can.

"Jack it's going to be okay. We will figure this all out tomorrow. I promise."

"Raine, thanks for taking over for me with my father. I couldn't even speak. I guess I was kind of shocked at his reaction."

"No problem, whatever you need."

There it is again. The look. The one he gives me when I have said or done something nice. He is a very handsome man and I wish I was feeling something other than friendship for him. I would be lucky to have such a person close to me. I know that, even though I remember very little and don't really understand feelings, I do know that.

Chapter 10

I wish I understood what was happening. I am in my home, the one I grew up in and it feels so totally foreign to me. It is like I don't exist at all. They have gotten rid of any trace of me. I don't think I have ever felt so totally alone. I knew they didn't love me but I thought that just maybe they would feel some sort of loyalty towards me. I was their only child. My brain is fried. I have no idea what to say to these strangers that were once my parents.

Raine is at my side trying to comfort me. I am so glad she is here with me. I think I would have completely lost it by now if it wasn't for her. She has a way of bringing everything back to the basics. She tells it like it is and this really does make things easier. She does not play games or make you guess where she is coming from, it is all there on the table for you to see.

We are sitting by the fireplace where I spent so many nights reading and doing my homework. I loved it in here. My parents rarely used this room so it always felt like it was mine. I know all the books on the shelves and have read everyone. I loved to read when I was young and day dream of a different life full of adventure. I wanted so badly to be an explorer or super hero. To be important to the world and make a difference. I guess I did get my wish. It just came in a different form all together. I never imagined this life. The life of a knight that lives in the light and protects the world from bad guys, as Raine would say. I need to get my head back in the game. We are here for a purpose and that has nothing to do with these people in this house. If they want me dead that is what I will be to them just as soon as Raine and I decide out next move.

"We should get some rest."

She looks at me and smiles.

"Yes we should. And can you please try and remember that my protection shield thing doesn't include you if you get too far away from me. So stay close okay."

I will. I will stay as close to her as she will let me be. We get up and head on up to the guest room. I wonder, just purely out of curiosity what they turned my room into and how long they waited after I went missing to delete me from their lives. I give my head a shake and stop such thoughts. We are in the bedroom and Raine goes over and jumps in the bed.

"It's a huge bed, we can share."

She says this with such innocence that it makes me think of the last time we slept in the same bed. We were getting ready for the war and knew it would probably be the last time we would be that close. Then we couldn't be together the way we wanted because of her powers. Now we can't be together the way I want because she doesn't remember me and also she is actually repulsed by touching me. If I didn't know better I would think the universe is definitely trying to tell us something.

I climb in beside her being very careful not to touch her. She has on a oversized robe so I don't think any skin will touch. She lays her head on the pillow and looks into my eyes.

"Jack, it's going to be all right. We are going to figure this all out and how to save your brothers. I am going to make you happy again. I promise."

She speaks with such confidence. She knows this to be true. Raine is going to make me happy again. The only problem is that all I need to feel good again is her. The rest doesn't matter to me. I smile back at her and thank her once again. We say good night and I turn off the bedside light. I think tomorrow is going to be a very long day.

I awake to the sound of someone out in the hall clearing his throat. I jump to my feet and go to the door. I look back quickly and see Raine is still fast asleep in the bed. I open the door and see Johnson standing with a tray in his hands. It has coffee and tea and toast on it. I take it from him and thank him. He informs me that my parents are still asleep but he will let me know when they have woken. I go back over to the bed thinking I should let Raine know there is food here. She is probably starving. She looks so peaceful though. I am sure she hasn't been getting much rest so I decide to let her sleep. I quietly pour myself some coffee and make up a piece of toast. I am feeling very anxious today. Last night was so strange I have to keep reminding myself it really did happen. I have so many questions.

"Were you going to tell me there is food or just keep it all to yourself?"

I was so deep into my head she startles me.

"I thought I would let you sleep for as long as possible. Do you want something?"

Her expression turns serious.

"Jack, have you done that before? Tried to sneak out on me I mean?"

"No. What are you talking about?"

She is acting weird and her eyes look so very far away.

"Yes you have. I was in bed and when I woke up you were leaving me. I didn't see you again for a very long time. You left me alone."

Raine begins to cry. Is it possible is she is remembering our last night together and how I betrayed her and left her to fight alone.

I go to her side and carefully put my arms around her as to not touch her skin. She leans her head on my chest and sobs.

"You are right. I did leave you and I am so sorry for that."

"Why? Why did you not want to be with me? I was told you were with me because you were ordered to be, is that true?"

She is choking out the words. It is coming back, her memory but not what I want her to remember. She is remembering my betrayal not my love. I try and make her look at me. Into my eyes so she can see the truth.

"Raine, I never meant to hurt you and you were much more than a job to me. They tricked me into leaving you but I should have known."

"Jack, I don't like this feeling. I feel.....hurt. I don't want to feel this. Make it go away. I don't want to remember anything if this is how it is going to make me feel."

She is panicked and yelling the words at me. She is getting angry and who can blame her.

"I can't make it go away. You need to feel everything so you can remember and come back to me."

She pushes me away then and jumps up from the bed.

"You don't understand I don't want to feel everything. It hurts me and I don't want to be hurt! I need to be strong so I can protect you, if I feel too much I can't do what I am suppose to do. What I am here to do!"

Raine stops suddenly and stands up very straight. She is shocked at what she has just said as am I. Is it true? Was she sent here to protect me?

"Jack what is happening to me? I feel...confused."

"I don't know any more than you do. Do you have any idea what you are supposed to protect me from?"

"No."

Just then there is a knock on the door. This is really not a good time. I stare at her across the room wondering what to do. She needs me right now but I need some answers for myself.

"Answer it Jack. This can wait."

She goes over to the window and starts nibbling at her finger tips. I haven't seen her do this in so very long. She is stressed and scared but she is not going to talk to me right now. I can see she is trying to figure things out and she needs time to process. I walk over to the door and again open it.

"Your parents are in the living room waiting to speak to you."

"Thank you Johnson, I will be right down."

I turn to tell Raine I am leaving and see she is already getting on her jeans. She looks over at me.

"You are not going anywhere without me. I am sorry if you were expecting some privacy because you are not going to get it."

There is little emotion in her voice. She is back in suppress-your-feelings-and-protect-Jack mode. I shrug my shoulders and open the door for her. She passes by me and marches down the hall. She is strong and I don't think she likes the fact that I saw past it, to the real her. She stops then and waits for me to catch up. I lead her down into the room where my parents are waiting. With so much going on with Raine I forgot for a moment I am about to see my mother for the first time. We enter the room and there they stand, my mother and father. They look exactly the same as

I remember. Perfectly put together not a hair out of place. I am not sure what to do.

"Hello mother, father."

They look to me as if I am nothing more than a servant and say nothing. Then they both settle their gazes on Raine. My father addresses her.

"Raine isn't it? Why did you bring him here? Did we do something wrong?"

I am totally confused. What the hell are they talking about. I glance over at Raine she is showing no sign of confusion. She looks in control and confident.

"No, you did nothing wrong. We just need a place to stay for a couple days while we figure a couple things out. Is that going to be a problem because the way I see it you have no choice. A deal is a deal."

She glances over at me and gives a quick wink. She does know what is going on. I can't stand it anymore.

"Mom don't you have anything to say to me? It's me Jack!"

My mother turns her attention to me and comes over to stand in front of me. She is much shorter than me. She reaches up and strokes my cheek. She does not seem even slightly surprised to see me.

"Jack. We did what we had to do. I will not feel guilty for it. We have the life we do because of it."

My father speaks then. I can't take my eyes off the women in front of me. I knew she was cold hearted but this is ridiculous.

"Enough. You may stay but for only two days. We are hosting a dinner party on Saturday and you must be gone by then. That is all, we will offer no further support our job for you people is done."

I am enraged by my father. What a heartless and hateful man. I push my mother to the side and am about to attack my so called father when Raine steps in. She grabs my arm and lowers it down to my side. She is stronger than me. I look to her for answers. She whispers,

"I will explain. Just stop."

She turns to the psychos.

"Thank you for the help. We will be out of here in two days."

Raine, still holding my arm leads me out of the room and outside into the back yard. I feel sick. I fall to my knees and heave. My head is spinning and I feel like a lost child unable to make sense of anything. Raine waits patiently while I get sick. She sits at a small table on the patio and stares out into the manicured garden. When I feel I am done I rise and go to her side. She offers me the seat beside her and I except. We sit in silence for some time then I can't take it any longer.

"Raine, what is going on? What were you and my parents talking about?"

"I am not exactly sure but I do know this. They are not your real parents. I think they were hired by someone to raise you. They are cold and callus and care nothing for you. Sorry."

Okay then. She just ripped apart my whole life and told me it was all a lie. I thought I loved her honesty but she could have used a little more tacked.

Chapter 11

I could have said it gentler I guess but he needs to understand what I am telling him. I know I am right. Jack is not one of these people, it is another clue to what is going on.

He has not spoken to me in some time. He is sitting there staring into space looking lost. What am I suppose to do now?

"Are you sure Raine?"

He suddenly says still not looking at me.

"Yes, I think I am. It makes sense don't you think? Why else would they tell the world you were dead and erase you completely from their lives. Your father is mad we are here and your mother is scared of us being here. Someone powerful orchestrated it, your childhood. I am sorry Jack, I know I don't always say things the right way and come across harsh but I don't mean to."

Finally turning his gaze to mine, he looks angry. I don't know if it is directed at me or the situation he is facing.

"You really could use a lesson in diplomacy but that's not important right now. Who do you think did this to me and why?"

"I honestly don't know Jack. Whoever it was, they must have had a good reason for hiding you until you were old enough to become a knight."

"So you think this was good! How could you possibly think that. Everyday growing up I would wish for a different life and every day I was stuck here in a loveless home."

He gets up from his chair and takes a few steps towards the garden. He is in so much pain. I don't understand, if he hated it so much here why is he hurting this much. I would think finding out there is a reason for what has happened to him should bring him a sense of comfort. His parents were awful but that is because that is not who they are. I follow him in silence. This is all connected, me coming back, Jack finding out about his past and the knights. I just need to figure out how.

"Jack do you remember anything from when you were young that seems odd? Something or someone that just doesn't fit?"

He stops and turns to me. I stand patiently while he thinks.

"Not that I can remember. I know I never had a nanny for more than a few months and I changed schools often even though we are in such a small town. They would ship me off; sometimes I would spend hours in the car driving to and from school. I didn't have any friends and spent all my time reading. When I became a teenager I told them no more and went to the local high school. I turned into a real cocky kid who was demanding and had a huge chip on my shoulder. I guess we can figure out why now."

"You cocky, I don't believe it!"

I say with mock horror. He is still cocky and a tad demanding. These are not bad traits though. I would guess they make him a very good knight. At first he looks ticked at my comment but then he gets it. He lets a small smile touch the corners of his lips. He comes over to me and as before, caresses my cheek without actually touching me.

"Thanks for being here with me. You are the reason I am not going absolutely crazy right now. I would have punched my father if you weren't there."

"I know and your welcome."

He does not move away from me keeping his hands close to my face, I can feel the heat from his palms. I wish he could touch me. What? I do, I wish he could touch me and I him. I reach up and touch his cheek. His eyes open wide with surprise. The pain is starting, I stroke his cheek and he grabs my hands. The pain is growing.

"Raine, stop you are hurting yourself."

"Jack just shut up for a minute please."

I raise myself on my toes until our faces are very close. The pain is excruciating. I carefully and slowly place my lips on his. They are so very soft and warm. He returns my advances and we are kissing. The pain is flowing through me and making my body convulse. Jack tries to push me away but he cannot I am too strong. I grab hold around his neck and pull him in closer to me. I am being ripped apart from the inside out. My body is fighting me, why is this such a bad thing? Why am I not supposed to be touching this man? It is actually very enjoyable, if I weren't in so much agony. Jack is trying his best not to touch me but only with his lips, this is funny to me. He has wanted this for so long and now it is me that is not letting go. I feel weak and realize the pain is winning I am about to pass out when it stops. The pain stops. I pull away from him, Jack immediately lets me go.

"Are you okay? Why did you do that?"

I look up at him and give a little laugh.

"I wanted to."

I go to grab for his hand and he pulls away.

"Stop it Raine. Why do you want to keep hurting yourself?"

"Jack, I think it's gone. It got to a point where I felt like I was about to die and then it stopped. I think we can touch now."

He looks at me and hesitantly touches my hand. Nothing. He links his fingers through mine and still nothing. I smile up at him.

"You really are okay? This is not hurting you?"

"Not a bit."

He leans down and wraps his arms around me in a tight embrace.

"I have been waiting to do this for so long."

I squeeze him back. I like being close to him. And would like to try kissing him again I think. I feel someone approach. I let go of him and turn to see his mother standing before us.

"You aren't like the other one that came. She was softer and glowing. You seem to be human."

I was right. I grab Jacks hand in mine we will face whatever is going to happen together. Maybe even as more than allies.

"Do you have any idea who she was?"

She looks from me to her son. She seems almost sad.

"No, she just came to me and my husband one night in our dreams. She told us if we watch over him she will grant us great fortune in life."

She turns to Jack.

"You have to understand Jack, we were struggling. They were about to foreclose on our house so we agreed. She said you would leave us one day and when that happened we were not to look for you. She said not to get attached because you were not like us, you didn't belong here but she needed you to stay safe. She guaranteed us safety in return and wealth lots of wealth.

When you finally were taken it was a relief, we didn't want that burden anymore."

"Burden? How could I have possibly been a burden to you? You were never around. I was raised by nannies and teachers. You had nothing to do with me."

"Jack you must understand, we never wanted children so when you arrived we decided to let the nannies look after you. We bought you the best of everything. That should have been enough. Besides you were never really a human boy anyway so what did it matter."

She really has no feelings whatsoever. She is crushing him with every word. What a bitch. Jack is tense beside me, I can feel he is ready to strike either with words or maybe even as a knight.
He needs to stop.

"Listen, that is enough. You have hurt him enough. Just give us the information we need and we will leave. Who was the woman who brought him?"

She turns to me and screeches.

"I told you, I don't know! She was all flowy and had colors floating all around her. She told us he was needed but had to be hidden until the time was right. He is not like the others but they can't know that. Then she floated up into the sky being carried by what looked like a rainbow. That's it!"

With that she turns on her expensive high heels and leaves us. Okay good time to faint I think. I know who she is talking about. I feel myself start to buckle but Jack catches me.

"No you don't. You are not passing out on me now."

I take a second and catch my breath. I can't face him. This is getting too strange.

"Raine, that sounds awfully familiar to me doesn't it to you?"

There is a hint of anger in his voice. All I can do is nod. He is right. We did this to him. My kind put him in this house and hid him. We destroyed his childhood. We suck.

Chapter 12

I have to keep reminding myself this is not her fault. Raine didn't do this to me but she is one of them. I saw it in her head, the same type of things my mother described. I am angry and so totally lost. They hid me here until the time was right to become a knight. I wonder why it was so important for me to become one and why they didn't want me raised like the others. I had no love growing up and the others had plenty. Why did I need to be different? I am still holding onto Raine as my mind is racing. She was about to faint again but I could not let her. She needs to stay with me and help me figure this out. She owes it to me, well not her specifically but her kind. I was right about this being a long day.

It is not even lunch time and I have discovered my past is nothing like I thought and Raine and I can now touch for some reason I am not yet understanding. When she kissed me I could tell she was in a lot of pain but she wouldn't stop. Her kiss was all wrong. There was no love in it, she did not feel the same in my arms when I hugged her either. She is beginning to like me but she is not herself yet and the girl before me is not entirely the girl I fell in love with. I have to push that to the back of my mind for now. Too much is happening all at once. I must first deal with my past and then the knights and then maybe Raine when I can have a minute to figure us out.

I lead her back up to the house and into the kitchen. I place her on a stool and sit beside her.

"Raine, I think you need to let me back in your head. You have answers and right now we need them."

"Okay."

Is all she has to say. I think better of doing it right here where anyone can walk in on us. We go back to the spare room and sit together on the floor. The sun is beating in on us and you would think this to be a romantic moment if it weren't for the fact I am about to invade her brain and try to dig up any information I can get.

"Are you ready?"

I ask her. She grabs my hands and places them inside hers.

"At least now I won't be in pain. I will try and stay open to you, if I feel you should go somewhere I will lead you."

I nod and she closes her eyes. We sit in silence our breathing in complete unison. I am there. Again in the long hall with doors on each side. They are still locked. I look from one to the next, but it is the same as before. She is not letting me enter any. I move on until I come to one where the lock looks as if it has been smashed. It is lying on the ground in a heap. I try the handle and it squeaks open for me. The room is dark and cold. I see someone in the corner rocking themselves back and forth. They look scared. I approach, the girl looks up and stares at me. She can see me.

"Jack what are you doing here? This is not a place for you. I must suffer here alone. That is my punishment."

It is Raine.

"What are you talking about? What do you need to be punished for?"

"You. I wasn't supposed to be with you. I wasn't supposed to fall in love with you. I was only supposed to watch over you and now I must be alone forever."

She continues to rock herself. She looks so small and weak. Why is this locked in her head?

"Raine, love is not something someone should be punished for. You didn't hurt anyone by being with me."

"You have no idea Jack. I hurt you. They sent you away to start again. They said you needed to be hidden from me. You are too good and important to the world and I almost ruined it all."

What she is saying makes no sense to me but before I can ask anymore I am pushed out. I focus and see Raine staring at me with big eyes. She is terrified. I go to grab her hand again and she jumps up and runs across the room. She crouches down and hides herself in the corner just like in her head. She begins to rock. I think I wrecked something in her. She looks crazy.

"Raine what are you doing?"

"Jack please leave. You need to leave. I remember. I remember everything. You have to get away from me. Now!"

I have no intention of leaving. I bend down and sit beside her. She continues to rock and mutter something to herself. I can't make out what she is saying.

"Raine I am not leaving you. You might as well tell me what is going on."

"Didn't you see it Jack. That thing in my head. It was me. When we walked into that room it all came back. I am the reason you were brought here. They wanted to keep us apart."

"But I was given to them as a baby. You would have been one as well how could this possibly have anything to do with us?"

She shakes her head back and forth violently.

"No. You are wrong. This is not the first time we have been together. I was with you before and I was your protector. You were supposed to be the leader of the knights and I screwed it all up. We fell in love and I neglected my duties, I kept you for myself and that is when Charles took over. He is not where he is meant to be and he cannot handle the power. That is why he is being infected. Only one can handle the world with no darkness. The balance is gone and to handle this he must be the purest the world has ever seen. It is you Jack."

I feel as if she has punched me in the face again. I move away from her and lean against the wall. Is she right? She believes it. It makes some sense I guess. I was not raised like the others and do not seem to conform like them. And Raine, I have been so totally drawn to her from the moment we met. Maybe this isn't the first time we have been together. My love for her has always seemed timeless but I never expected this. I look to my Raine and see she is broken. She has come apart at the seams.

"Raine, you have to get it together. I need your help. Please."

She does not respond. I have no idea what to do. I get to my feet and go to the window. This is too much. There is only one thing I know for sure. I don't want to lead the knights and I want to stay with Raine. Now both of those things seem kind of impossible. Suddenly Raine is by my side. I have no idea how she got over to me so quickly and silently.

"Jack, they are coming."

She stands protectively in front of me. I see it then. The white light is filling the room. The knights have found us. Raine turns to me one last time.

"We know now what I am doing here. I am here to help you get what is rightfully yours, I am here to put things back the way they should have been all along."

She turns back to the light just as Charles, Devon and Aaron emerge.

Chapter 13

That's it my mind is officially blown. Everything is all jumbled and flying around my head. I can't think of anything other than I did this. I screwed everything up.

The knights are standing in front of me and I can feel Jack is very close behind. I have put myself between them. They cannot have Jack, Charles must be stopped so Jack can take over. He is the rightful leader and he is the only one that can handle the job. Charles steps forward.

"Hello again Raine. Hope you are feeling better. Would you please step aside so we may collect our brother?"

Does he know? Is Charles here to take Jack and get him out of the picture so he can remain their leader? I must protect Jack. That was my job in the beginning as it is now, but before I can respond Aaron and Devon are on me. They come at me from both sides and pin me to the ground. Jack lets out a cry of pure fury and throws his light in their direction. They do not budge. I look up at my friend Aaron and see his light is completely engulfed in the murkiness of the infection. Jack's light can't penetrate it. I cannot move. I am strong; why can I not move these men off of me? I try and move Jack to send him away but cannot. I can't do anything. Jack comes flying across the room at them and suddenly stops. Charles has him by the throat.

"Jack let's stop this silliness now. She is immobilized. We have shot her with the strongest tranquilizer possible, we were not sure if it was going to work but it seems to have done the trick. If you do not come with us now I will give the order for your brothers to rip her apart right in front of your eyes."

Tranquilizer? I am a super human, more powerful than any knight but a fricken shot could be the end of me? That's just not right. I look up at Jack,

"Jack, don't do it. You need to fight them. Get away. You are too important."

Jack stares into my eyes and I see what he is going to do. I feel tears touch my eyes. He is going to give up for me. Does he not understand that I am of no importance here? He is the one that must be alive. He is the one that needs to fight so the knights can become good again. Charles is becoming more tainted with each passing second; he cannot handle the depths of this responsibility. Soon the world will be lost to a crazy man who has too much power. I can't speak. The drugs are getting to me. I feel the men slowly get off me. They each have one of my arms in their hands. They begin to pull. I scream out in pain. I can't help it. I know this is the wrong thing to do but my actions are not my own anymore. My body wants relief. I open my eyes one last time and see Jack being released by Charles. They are speaking and Jack is looking at me. He tries to smile for me but can't manage it, he turns to Charles and nods. With that I am alone. The room is still filled with sunlight and I am on the floor. I cannot move or speak. I drift off and let the drugs take their full effect.

It takes me a minute when I come to. I am on the floor in a room I do not recognize. It is dark out. I get to my feet, I am wobbly. I remember where I am. This is Jacks childhood home. I go to the washroom and splash water on my face. The day is foggy and I need to get it clear. I stare at the reflection in the mirror. I again recognize this girl. It is me, Raine. It is a wonderful feeling to feel right in your skin. But I can't let myself feel this for too long. I have a job to do.

Jack! He gave himself up to save me. I have failed him again. I remember everything from this life and the last. I was always meant to protect Jack until he was ready to fulfill his destiny. I never imagined falling in love with my charge. My kind is not supposed to feel that emotion. We are meant to be loyal and kind. We are supposed to protect and serve the greater good. I don't know how but I seem to be the exception. I fell for this man and I was punished for it. We were punished for it. I found him again, or he found me and we are repeating our past mistakes. I need to rescue him and get Charles out of the way. Jack needs to lead his kind and keep the world at peace. I need a plan.

I pace around the room for a while trying to hash how to proceed. If I simply show up in the light they are bound to be ready for me and I don't feel like being drugged again. They have figured out a way to stop me even if it is just temporarily. I have tried calling to him but he is not anywhere I can sense. He must be back in the place he was before when I couldn't reach him. There is only one other being that knows where that is other than the knights. Do I dare try and contact her? Has she been up there long enough to break her of her evil ways? They will not let me home but I may be able to get to her. I should not be here when I try. Who knows what will happen and these people although real jerks don't deserve the wrath of Lila. I grab my jacket and am about to zap myself somewhere else when there is a knock at the door. I go over and answer it. Jacks father is standing before me.

"Where is Jack?"

"He had to leave; I am on my way out to. We will not bother you again."

I try and push past him in the doorway. I don't have time for this.

"Will you please tell him....tell him that his mother and I..."

That is it, I have had enough of these two. They are strange and creepy and cared nothing for Jack.

"Listen, you are an awful person who never deserved to have a child. You were given him because he needed to be hidden from good. Do you get that? They found the two most unloving and self indulgent people they could."

He stares at me and really has no idea what I am saying to him. I still have no time for this so I leave this man to stand and stare at an empty room. He will never see Jack again and that is a good thing. He does not deserve to know him.

I rush down the stairs and out the door. As soon as I am out of sight of the house I zap myself deep into the woods. I don't really know where I am but it doesn't matter. I sit down on a grassy patch and get to work. I hesitate for a moment wondering what the ramifications are going to be bringing Lila back into this world. If she has not had enough time to embrace her goodness she will again wreak havoc on this place, but I see little other choice. I can't find Jack without her and the knights will never tell me where he is. Even if I go to them and torture each and every one. They have a code and they follow it even if it means their own deaths. I witnessed it first hand in the battle against the darkness.

I concentrate on her. I see her before me, tears streaming down her face. I feel her agony. She does not want to change who she is and the place I took her to will do just that. She will feel no more need for chaos. She will be trained to lead others and protect. I feel her as she is connected to me. We are now sisters in the fight against hate and suffering. I call her. With every fiber of my being, I call to her. Over and over I do this. For hours, I sit and silently call to Lila. My body is ready to give out. I stand and stretch. I guess it is on to plan B. I will go into the light and get Charles to tell me where Jack is, don't know how but I have to try.

"Raine, what is so important you would drive me crazy like that?"

I jump out of my skin at her voice. I even let out a little scream. What a normal girly, embarrassing thing to do. Lila looks at me and smirks. I gain my composure and finally am able to speak.

"Lila, you came. Thank you, I need your help."

"What? Why in the world would I ever help you? You ruined my life!"

So she has not been changed. She is still her, the chaos-seeking creature she always was. This is not good.

"My home has not taught you anything? You didn't feel the power of the colors?"

She paces back and forth in front of me. Looking like a caged animal but there are no bars holding her here. If she wants to she could simply disappear and I will have unleashed another monster on the world. I don't think I am very good at my job.

"Yes Raine, they have. They have been drilling well into me for too long. I am unable to do what I was created for. I am full of...peace. And that is why I am so pissed at you. I still feel like me. They did not take that away. My mind wants to do the opposite of my body. They have control of me and I hate it! This is a fate far worse than death I am sure."

Okay, so she is still herself but unable to act on any of her gut instincts. That is a twist I have not seen before. I would agree with Lila, that must be torture.

"So you will help me then, even if you don't want to?"

"I guess I have no choice do I? Now get on with it, what do you want with me?"

"It's Jack. The knights have captured him and I can't contact him. You did before and I would like you to do it again."

She pauses and looks at me rather perplexed.

"What are you talking about? The knights are good and Jack is good, why would they want to keep him prisoner, especially with the darkness gone. Isn't the world a pretty fluffy excruciatingly happy place now?"

"No Lila. Charles can't handle being leader of the knights. With the balance of good and evil gone he is being corrupted. Jack needs to lead the knights he is their only hope."

She shakes her head and raises her hand to me as if to say hold on a minute. I stand quietly and wait.

"So Charles is now evil and Jack is the only one that can save everyone, I thought that was your job?"

She is being sarcastic and mean, the old Lila through and through.

"I did too, but I had it wrong. I was supposed to be protecting Jack."

"So this whole mess is your fault. That is why they sent you back. That is why you have been forbidden to come home, you were not supposed to fall for him, but you did. You are a total screw up!"

She sounds so very delighted. I lower my head and can think of nothing to say. This is the truth, it is all my fault.

"Oh Raine, don't look so defeated. I will help you find Jack. But after that you are on your own. I don't want to do too much good all at once. They will think they are winning and I want it to be harder on them than that."

"Thank you."

Chapter 14

I can't believe it. I am again in the dark room. I hate it here. This time though I am not alone. Aaron is locked in here with me. I stare at my once-best-friend and try to make sense of it. They have all turned into something I don't recognize. They are full of power but craving more. They want to rule the world out in the open; they want to be worshipped by the ordinaries. What has happened to them? Our mission was to protect the human world but always in the shadows. They do not need to know of our presence, we are silent protectors. Their disease, or whatever it is, has taken hold of them all. Raine was right, as usual. I don't understand how I can be the difference, how I am to set it all right? They seem way too far gone for that.

"Jack, will you just hurry up and change your mind please. I would like to go home!"

Aaron is getting inpatient with my transformation. He doesn't think of it as an infection but more of a change of heart. He is to stay here with me until I give in and become like the rest of them. He said the others "agreed" almost immediately. I must have some sort of immunity to it because I feel no different, but I would think they don't feel they are any different either.

"Aaron, you might as well leave me. I can't think of any reason good enough to let the ordinaries know about us, we are not meant to be worshipped that is not what we are about."

"Why not? We have protected their kind for hundreds of years and we deserve some rewards for that. That is all we are asking for, some payment for all our good deeds and in return we will continue to protect those weak little creatures. What is so wrong with that?"

"Do you hear yourself? You are not a god! We deserve nothing other than the reward of doing our job."

I am getting pissed and need to calm down. I don't want to fight with Aaron, it is not his fault, it is Charles, if he were stronger then the others would not be like this. I think he knew. Charles knew of the power he would hold once the darkness was destroyed. He left that battle in the field against the darkness; he was not there when Raine destroyed them all. I didn't think much about it then but why did he leave? The only explanation is that he knows I am the rightful leader of the knights and he wants to make sure that never happens. As I contemplate this, I feel Aaron come up behind me. I turn just in time to see his fist flying at my head. I duck and quickly manoeuvre myself behind him. I grab his arms from the back and slowly lower him to the ground.

"Aaron stop! You don't want to do this. I am your friend remember?"

"I thought you were. I helped you with her. I protected your secrets and you stand here and say such hateful things about us! What have you turned into? It's that tramp isn't it? She has poisoned you with her lies!"

He has completely lost it. Spitting and struggling against my grip. I don't dare let him go. I think he wouldn't think twice about killing me on the spot. I can't believe this is happening.

"Aaron, calm down. Raine has nothing to do with this. You have to listen to me you are sick. Somehow Charles has infected you and is making you think this is right, but it's not. The knights are not supposed to do this. You have to believe me. Please."

I know this will not work but I must try, at this point I have nothing to lose. I am trapped in a place where no one can help me and my only other choice is to give in and become like the rest of my brothers, good creatures that are becoming badder by the second. Aaron begins to laugh in my arms. It is not his usual easy going gut laugh, more like a cackle. He sounds like Charles.

"Oh Jack. You are so naive. It is Raine that has infected you. When she came back she has slowly turned you into her puppet. She was lying you know. She did not have amnesia. She remembered everything. But it was her best explanation for why she was back, you bought right into it."

I will play along for the moment but my patience is wearing thin.

"Why would she do that Aaron? What possible reason is there for her to fake her memory loss?"

"Because she wants to destroy the knights. That is why she is here. She was sent to get rid of us. That was what she was to do the last time at the battle but she didn't because of you. Her mission was to destroy both good and evil, not just one. If you don't believe me Charles has proof, it is in the prophecy."

Okay, this throws me a bit I must admit. I release my friend and sit. My mind is racing. I know in my heart this is not the truth but there is something to this. It kind of makes sense. The knights are not needed if the darkness is gone. Why leave it out of balance?

Aaron speaks," You see it now don't you? It makes sense doesn't it?"

"Aaron shut up! Give me a minute to think."

He steps away from me and goes to the far corner of our cell. I lie on my back and close my eyes. This is not happening. Raine would never do this to me. She is here to help me become the leader of the knights not destroy us. But how was she planning on doing that? By killing Charles I imagine and once he is gone the others would be very easy to get rid of. She is telling the truth about the infection though, they are all acting completely insane but what if there is more to it than that? I must look at all the possibilities even if it hurts.

I hear it then. It is a whisper in the distance but getting closer and louder. This time I know it is not in my head. It can't be her, she is gone. I jump up and see Aaron looking scared and confused in the other corner. He hears it to. It comes at us louder then. She is here. I go to Aaron's side and wait. He goes to speak and I stop him. I have no idea if it is her or what they might want. We should remain silent until it materializes.

"Jack, come to me."

The voice is definitely hers, I see the shadow forming and her eyes looking at me. Why is she back? Raine took her away or did she? Her voice is haunting like something from my worst nightmares.

"Jack, come we don't have much time."

I am not sure what to do.

"Lila?"

"Yes, it is me, now come on Raine is waiting!"

She is working with Raine. What is going on? I need answers and Raine is the only one that has them. The knights will have to wait. I jump into the shadow's embrace and wait for her to carry me away. When we are about to leave I feel Aaron, he is on me and we are in the shadow of Lila. I hear her laugh as we are carried up and away. I am nervous and wonder if I have made the right decision for myself and my friend.

Chapter 15

I should have gone. I don't know if Jack will come with Lila but she insisted I wouldn't be able to pass into the place where they are holding him. She said only beings of the light could and since she is half made of light she can. So here I sit and wait... and wait.

The light around me finally begins to shimmer. She is back. I go over to her and wait for them to become solid. Finally they emerge, Lila and Jack and Aaron?

I run and throw my arms around him. He is alive and seems to be unhurt.

"Jack are you okay?"

He looks at me and untangles my arms from his neck. He glances over at Lila and then Aaron who is standing perfectly still like he is in shock or something. The murkiness still surrounds him.

"Why did you bring Aaron with you? What is going on?"

"I could ask you the same thing. What the hell is Lila doing back?"

Jack takes a couple steps away from me. He is pissed.

"She is here because that was the only way of getting to you. I called her and asked for her help. She is on our side. What is wrong Jack?"

Lila is standing off to the side looking bored. Aaron steps forward.

"Jack, I told you. She is working with others to plot against us. She is not here to help you; she is here to destroy our race!"

Jack looks over at his friend but does not react the way he should. He should be jumping down his throat and telling him to leave us. Instead he turns to me.

"Raine, we need to talk."

Okay then, this really doesn't seem like the time to be having a heart to heart especially with Aaron here. The knights will be on us any moment.

"Okay Jack but we should get some place safe. Charles is bound to get here any minute. Aaron you should leave. I have no idea what you are doing here and since the last time I saw you, you were trying to tear me into pieces I would prefer if you left. Now."

"No. Aaron stays."

I turn to Jack and look at him in disbelief. He was in the room wasn't he? When Aaron was trying to kill me?

"Jack, are you kidding? He is on Charles side, he needs to leave. I understand he is your friend that is why I am letting him go without disposing of him myself."

"You could though right? I mean if you wanted to you could eliminate him and all the knights, right?"

I study Jack and make sure he is not infected, I don't see any sign of it but that doesn't mean they haven't gotten to him. He is different from the others; maybe he will show no actual signs of it until it is too late. That's a comforting thought.

"Jack what are you talking about? I suppose yes, I could but what has that got to do with anything?"

Lila steps forward and grabs onto Aaron's arm.

"Okay you two, obviously you need some alone time so I will watch this one and make sure he doesn't do anything stupid and you guys go and work out your issues. Just make it fast; I want to leave this place."

With that Lila drags Aaron off into the woods far enough I imagine to where they can't see or hear us. I have no idea what is going on right now. Jack seems very upset at me. I turn to him and repress the urge to touch him. I have to keep reminding myself this is my duty. I must keep him safe and get rid of Charles. I will correct my past mistakes.

"Jack, seriously are you okay? Why are you so angry with me?"

He walks away a couple feet and turns his back to me. He speaks in a soft voice never turning.

"Aaron told me some things about you and why you are here. At first I didn't believe them but they are starting to make sense. And when I saw Lila everything fell into place."

"Jack, Aaron is not well. He has been taken over by the greed of power. You must be able to see that. Why are you questioning my loyalty to you? I love you."

I am so deeply hurt by what he is saying. He doesn't trust me. I am here only for him, saving the knights is secondary to me. That is why I guess I am not very good at my role; I put emotions and feelings before duty. He is pacing in front of me never making eye contact. He turns then and steps right in front of me looking down into my eyes.

"Love? How could you love me? You have been working with Lila all along. And you are using me to get to the knights. You want Charles dead so I can take over but why? Aaron thinks you want us all dead. That you were supposed to do it at the battle and that is why you are back, not for me but to kill my brothers."

I see it then. The smallest touch of darkness inside of him. They have gotten to him. What can I possibly do now? It will spread and he will be lost to the knights. I am too late. I reach up and caress his cheek.

"Jack please think. This is not you, they have gotten to you. I am here to help."

He grips my arm and places it back at my side.

"I will not hurt you Raine. But I will stop you. You should go home, back to where you belong and leave us. I will take Charles down myself and become the leader of the knights; you are not needed here anymore."

What the hell? I don't think so. Jack may think he is doing the right thing but his vision of the truth is warped. He needs to be away from the rest of them, isolated until I can figure out how to get it out of him.

"Jack I won't take offence to that because you are sick. But just so you know that is not how this is going to play out. Sorry."

I call to Lila then. She brings Aaron back into the small clearing; he looks upset at being man handled by a woman.

"Lila, could you please take Aaron far away from here and dump him somewhere. I don't care where but don't hurt him."

She gives me a sly smile.

"Of course. Then will I be able to leave? I really don't like it here anymore."

"Yes, I won't bother you again. Thanks for your help."

Jack steps in front of Lila blocking her way then turns to me.

"Raine what are you doing? Let Aaron go or I will have no choice but to..."

Lila interrupts,

"Raine I can dispose of this one to if you like, I have always wanted to play with him."

"Lila, watch it. Just look after Aaron for me. I can handle Jack."

"Handle me? Who do you think you are Raine? I am not under your control; you are just a little girl acting like you are frickin god or something!"

I just stare at the man before me, what an ass. I am having a great feeling of déjà vu with these two men beside me and Lila. They both feel superior and think they are in control. Why are we "girls" always underestimated? I glance over at Lila and nod in her direction. On cue in her usual Lila fashion she dramatically grabs a hold of Aaron and lets out a larger than life laugh, they disappear into the light. I don't care what she does with him. She will not hurt him because she is no longer capable of that but I do feel sorry for him a bit, who knows what she will do to him before he is released. Pushing those thoughts from my mind I realize I must act fast. Jack is going to do something stupid and I can't let that happen. Before he can react I grab him by the arm and we are gone.

Chapter 16

I can't believe the rage building inside me. I look at Raine the woman I loved completely and forever and feel nothing but hate. What is happening to me? I came back to her for answers and realized it doesn't matter what she says or does. I don't believe her anymore. She has taken me to some secluded place I don't recognize. It doesn't matter where we are, she is not going to get what she wants from me. I need to go home and be with my kind. Charles was right; we need to take control of the human world but with me in charge not him. I have to fight her, I have to get away.

Raine is sitting across from me cross legged on the floor. I am shackled to the wall of this strange place. My cuffs are made of nothing more than thin glowing string but I cannot move. They are made of her magic. This room is also made of her magic. I see no exit. It is like being back in the dark place Charles put me, but this one is full of light.

"Jack, do you need anything? Water or food?"

I turn my face from hers and ignore what she says. She has been trying to get me to talk to her for sometime but I will not give in. She is my enemy now and I was trained to never comply. Her voice is pained and soft. She seems very upset with this situation. This makes me laugh, she is the one that is doing this and yet she is sad about it. It probably is all an act, just like everything else about her. She betrayed me, lied to my face about everything. How could I fall in love with such a horrible creature? I disgust myself. She gets up when I do not respond. She seems frustrated, good.

"Jack, please talk to me. Maybe I can help you if you tell me what's going on in your head. That is why I am here, to help you."

Whatever... You can't help me.

"Fine, don't. You are here until you get better Jack. Get used to it."

With that she leaves my little cell. I am alone again. Everyone seems to really enjoy locking me up, I am getting pretty sick of it. So here I sit alone waiting for whatever is going to happen next. I am a grown man that never seems to have the ability to make my own choices; they are always taken away from me. My parents are strangers and Raine is not who I thought she was. My life is definitely taking a turn into the unknown. I want my life before Raine. When I was a knight and had brothers and fought evil. It was all so simple.

I stare off into the wall made off nothing. It is so still and quiet. As I stare the wall begins to morph into an almost crystal substance. I see my reflection. What I see is not what I expect. I see me as the monster I once was when I went to the darkness to save her. I am again deformed and gnarled. I quickly look down at myself and see that this is not the truth. I am human but the wall shows me as something else. Why am I seeing this? I concentrate on the monster in front of me and see I am in there but the two halves are struggling. I watch the battle as my face goes into convulsions. I feel none of what I am watching. The battle is an internal one. As I fight with myself I see a glow around me begin to form. This is what Raine sees I suspect. It is not the aura I would expect someone like me to have. It is brown and muddy looking. I shake my head and try to make the images go away. This is a trick she is playing on me. Trying to make me feel like the bad guy so I forgive her for what she is doing. I close my eyes tight and wish it all away. When I look again the wall is gone. I smile to myself briefly; I have won her mind games. She will not get what she wants from me and that is a very happy thought.

Chapter 17

I am out of options. What the hell am I to do with Jack? He is so far gone, he believes I am the enemy. The corruption hits them too fast for me to stop it. His transformation took longer and I gather that is because he is to be the ultimate power and was to remain good. I have him locked up like an animal and no idea where to go from here. Getting my memory back sucks.

I wish I didn't feel the way I feel for him. If I was as before I would probably just eliminate him and then go after Charles. I would destroy what remains of the knights and leave this place. My duty is clear, restore order to the knights and leave them to protect this world or get rid of them and start over with someone else in their place. My realm believed so fully in the knights and their quest in the name of pure goodness, I seemed to have screwed all that up. Love is too powerful, even my kind couldn't stop it. They tried to keep it from me and the knights. Knowing all along that this one emotion could destroy what they were trying to build. I don't think they realized that there is another emotion out there just as strong but much more destructive. It is not hate but power. That is what is surrounding the knights; I couldn't place it before and had no idea the name for it. Power. They are craving it like a drug. James wanted power and look at how he ended up. The knights should know better, they were taught better but with no one to challenge them and keep the balance in line they had their first feel for it and obviously liked it. If I really think about it the fault once again lays squarely on my shoulders. If I would have destroyed both sides the world would be safe. There wouldn't be a bunch of crazy killer knights out there ready to kill every human that doesn't submit. I let love get in the way. What a joke. I have screwed over the whole world and the guy I did it all for hates me. Can I pick 'em or what?

Okay Raine, stop it! I did this and I need to fix it. Step one: find Charles.

I look over at Jack in his cell I made him. He cannot see me but I see him. He sits there and looks so totally defeated. I can't watch him any longer. I have to let go of what I felt for him and what I feel. He was not supposed to ever be a part of my life again. I take a deep breath and begin to realize what must happen next. My pain is nothing compared to what these men will inflict on the world. The picture is clear. I will eliminate the knights of the light....all of them.

I walk slowly back into the cell and look at him. He sits on the floor and immediately turns his face from mine. I crouch next to him.

"Jack, I am going to let you go. Obviously you believe nothing I say and I see you no longer care anything for me so you can leave."

I choke out the words. He is part of the plan. I know what he will do next and it will lead me straight to the leader. I can't sense any of the knights anymore and will not be able to enter their realm undetected. But I can follow Jack and he will go straight to Charles. Then I will have but a second to do my duty and rid the world of this new and growing evil. Charles must die first, then Jack. Tears are forming but I can't let him see me cry. I turn from him and order his chains gone. They disappear instantly. I hear him jump to his feet probably ready to attack. I look back at him and see he is just staring, not at me but at the wall. I have no idea what he is looking at, it is transparent; there is nothing there.

"Do you see it?"

He yells out at me. These are the first words he has spoken and I had forgotten what a wonderful voice he has. I am caught off guard and just stare at him.

"Well do you? Do you see my reflection?"

He seems freaked.

"No, Jack there is nothing there."

I have nothing else to say, I am completely dead inside, I have to be. Jack shakes his head and turns his gaze to me.

"If I am free let me out of here! I want as far away from you as possible. And don't try and stop me, I will kill Charles just like you want and you can go."

I wish he would stop trying to boss me around. I'm really not in the mood for it right now.

"Whatever Jack, do what you want. I will leave first and then you can be on your way."

I turn to go but hesitate. There is one more thing that must be said before this is over. I walk to his side and look at him, really look at him.

"I know this means nothing to you Jack but I loved you. From past lifetimes to this one, I loved you. I will never stop loving you no matter what happens next. Nothing will ever change that.
Thank you for letting me love you Jack."

With that I turn and go. The next time we meet I will be killing him. How is that for a total absolute mind-blower!?

Chapter 18

Crazy lady has left the building. Thank god. I stand for a moment and wait. She says she is leaving but I make sure. This could be a trap. After a couple minutes I head in the direction she took. As I walk through the threshold of my cell I find myself back in the woods by my parents" house. Were we here all along? I take a cautious look around, I am alone. I can sense no one else. I stretch and figure out my next move. I push Raine from my thoughts. She is of little concern to me, Charles on the other hand is. I will go to him and demand my rightful place as the leader of my people. He will surely refuse and then it will end in bloodshed. This doesn't bother me. I am surprised at how much this doesn't disturb me. He was my mentor and friend and now I am willing to kill him without a second thought. This must be because I am right and just in my decision otherwise my conscious would totally be screaming at me. Best to get on with it.

I close my eyes and search for my brothers. They are in the light, all of them. I sense Aaron and Devon; Charles will be close to them. It takes some doing, he must have some sort of barrier surrounding him for protection, but I finally get a faint signal from him. They are in the great hall, the one I took Raine to when she needed our help. Again I have to tell myself to stop thinking of the girl, my mind continues to wander to her, it is getting very irritating. I feel my power surround me and I am off. I will soon be home.

An instant later I am standing in the entrance surrounded by all the paintings of my ancestors. They are all staring at me with tortured expressions. Why do they look like this? They have always looked down on us knights and given us their strength and encouragement. I focus on the doors in front of me. I feel the hairs on my neck stand up; I am readying for battle. Power is flowing through me. I will soon rule the knights and in turn the human world. Excitement is building, adrenaline rushing, let's do this!

I enter the room and find at least fifty knights standing at the ready. They are prepared for me. For some reason they are not intimidating in the least. I walk up to the first and grab his shoulders.

"I do not wish to harm you my friend. You are my brother, let me pass."

Without a word the knight nods his head and lets me pass. I don't know where this is coming from it just feels right. I know I am the authority and they seem to as well. This may be easier than first anticipated. I pass by many others all of which move as I go. It reminds me of the way James made his way through a crowd of his monsters. I am nothing like him of course; I am here to protect the knights from Charles' evil. I finally get to the last line before I can reach the leader. In front are my friends Aaron and Devon. They look very serious and on task. I don't think they are going to move so willingly. I take another approach.

"Aaron, I am so happy to see you my friend. You were right. Raine was trying to manipulate me, you were right about everything."

I wait for his response. He glances behind him and then turns to me.

"I am glad you see it now Jack. You are here to join us then?"

"Yes, of course. I am sorry it took me so long but I was detained for some time."

Aaron nods and seems to relax ever so slightly. I lean in to him and whisper,

"Do you think it is possible to speak to Charles in private? I would like to apologize for my actions."

"I don't know Jack. He is still suspicious of you. I don't think he would want to be alone with you."

"Understandable I guess. What if you and Devon accompany us?"

From behind my friend he finally speaks.

"Fine, Jack. Come this way."

The two knights turn and begin to walk towards the far doors. As we leave the room I remember what it was initially used for. It is the place where truth can only be spoken, I wonder when that changed.

Once we are all in the small back room of the hall, Devon closes the doors. The four of us fill up this space and there is little room to fight. I will have to make it quick and try to not hurt anyone but Charles. As I mull over my options he speaks,

"Jack, I am so glad you have finally decided to come back to us. She took you away from us for so very long."

I will play his game, for now.

"I am sorry about that Charles. I should have known better. I hate to admit it but she had great power over me."

I bow my head as if I am truly below him, a servant.

"And you're telling us that she no longer does? Are we to believe that you no longer care for her?"

"Yes you are. I have seen the truth, I was her puppet and she used me but no more. I sent her away and she will not be back."

I look behind my leader as I speak, I can't look him in the eye. He has great senses and might get what I am planning on doing next. As I look at the wall it again becomes as a mirror. The monster is staring at me again. He looks pissed. He wants out and I think that is what I will do, release him. I no longer seem to be struggling within myself; the decision has been made. I tell myself this is the right thing to do. I will save the world from his reckless leadership. Charles laughter interrupts my thoughts.

"You sent her away? You do not have the power to do such a thing! She has played you again my brother, don't you see?"

He knows nothing about the feelings of love. She loves me even now so she will do as I have asked. She can't hurt me, it is impossible for her to act against me. I no longer hold such emotions so this proves that I have played her not the other way around.

"Enough, Charles! You have no idea how truly powerful I am but you are about to find out!"

I feel the power ignite in my soul. It is unlike the pure power I used to possess, this is more absolute. It is not something I can turn off any longer; it is a part of me, completely. I flex and look at my prey. He must see the new me, this makes me smile. Fear me Charles. He gains his composure and stares me down.

"I know everything about you Jack. Who you are supposed to be and what you are supposed to do. Why do you think I have kept you away since the battle? I knew I was going to die that day and that you where to take my place. I was so happy when it was discovered you were so distraught about your girlfriend. I have been getting all the knights in line for the day you returned. I would have liked for you to follow me into greatness Jack but I know now that will never happen. Such a pity."

Charles turns his back to me and walks right thru the mirror wall where my monster self is exploding with power. I let out a cry of rage and leap after him. I am held back by the other two knights in the room.

"Jack, stop! What are you doing?"

Aaron looks confused and upset. I turn to face him and flex my hand into a fist. Light shoots out from it and knocks him to the ground I then turn to Devon and do the same.

"I am the rightful leader of us and I am here to claim my place!"

The pair looks up at me and says nothing. I turn back to the wall and am about to attempt to follow Charles when my reflection shows someone else in the room. I am stopped in my tracks by what I see. She is behind me, but just as I look like a dark beast she is my opposite. Light cascades from her hair and her eyes are as strong and pure as anything I have ever seen. The glow about her is filled with her colors and she seems to be floating on a glow that can only be described as that of love; she looks to be an honest-to-god angel. I find myself breathless at the beauty of it. I shake the image from my mind and force my gaze away from the mirror. I turn and see she is indeed in the room but she looks like herself, just Raine. I know now what the mirror is trying to tell me.

Chapter 19

"Raine, you lied to me. You said I was free of you."

Yep, I sure did. He must really think I am a dimwit if he truly thought I would just let him go. He is not making eye contact with me, he looks almost....shy?

"This is the only way I could find Charles and right the wrongs I have done. Nothing personal Jack."

There, that sounded strong and like I don't give a dam. I turn to the other two knights,

"You should go. Now!"

Aaron replies, "You have no say over what we knights of the light do. You are the one that needs to go!"

Sounding more and more like their devoted leader, ego completely out of control.

"Aaron, you need to get out of here. I get that you are under some sort of super crazy mind thingy that makes you into a complete ass but I am running out of time and patience. This is something that the big boys and girl need to deal with not the bratty kids."

I need to control myself but I can't help feeling completely helpless in this situation and this makes me a little short tempered. The pair of them in complete unison both jump. I am ready this time and dodge out of the way. They land beside me on the floor. I see the needle in Devon's hand. I bend and whisper in his ear.

"Not this time. Leave now or you will be dead with one simple thought."

He must finally get who I am and what I can do. Devon grabs a hold of Aaron and they fly through the door back into the great hall. It won't be long before the rest of them are on us. I look over the room and see Jack is gone. I swear silently to myself, he has gone after Charles while I was distracted. Without hesitation I jump through the wall and follow him.

When I emerge on the other side I am standing in a field. The training field. The wall must be a portal. I did not know the knights had such power. Standing before me are the men. They are only inches apart and both have hands glowing with the murky light. I get to them just in time to hear their final exchange. They don't seem to notice me.

"Jack you will not beat me. I am the leader and the light that flows through me is pure power. Yours is tainted with love, human ordinary love. I believe once you could have been our leader but not now."

Jacks hand clenches into a fist, Charles has no idea what he is up against.

"Enough! I am not damaged or stained with any such thing. I will rule our people and the world will bow to me not you, you stole your place and it is time to give it back!"

Just as they explode with light I dive in between them. Why? If they destroy each other my job is that much easier. But before thinking logically I think emotionally and my heart is still protecting him. I am hit with the force of light of both men. It lifts me into the air above them and seems to tear me apart at the same time it is making me collapse in on myself. I absorb what I can but it is too much. My body retches and spasms in pain. I see nothing but blackness. I try and call to my colors but they do not listen. I am alone and with everything I have I fight to stay here, alive. Minutes pass before my body is thrown back to the earth. I lay in a heap having no control over any part of myself. I hear nothing around me. Finally after much persuasion I am able to open my eyes. I see the sky above me, blue and sunny. I turn my head to look for Jack, he is not there. I turn the other way and see no one. The men are gone. I sit up and search but I am most definitely alone. Did they continue their fight somewhere else? Did they succeed in killing each other? Will someone please tell me what is going on?

"Raine are you all right?"

I jump at the sound of the voice. It is neither who I expected to answer my silent questions nor who I wanted.

"Lila, what are you doing here?"

"I felt it Raine, when they were hurting you, I felt your pleas for help. I came as soon as I figured out what was going on. Must be another one of the great powers I now possess."

She is sarcastic but seems concerned.

"I am okay I think. It took everything I had to stay in one piece. Did you see them, Jack and Charles?"

Lila shakes her head and continues to survey the grounds.

"I found only you. Did you kill them Raine?"

This question surprises me, I hadn't thought of that. Stress begins to take over and I must push it down with great effort.

"I don't know. I don't see how I could have. They were hurting me not the other way around."

"From the looks of this place, you gave quite a kickback. The ground is completely singed in both directions. Look."

I slowly get to my feet and survey the ground. There are two lines of blackened earth coming out from a centre point, which was me, going out far beyond the field. It continues into the trees, everything torn away far beyond what we can see. I fall back to my knees and feel faint. I killed him. Knowing you have to and actually doing it are two completely different things. I can't breathe. I regret everything I have done in this lifetime all in this moment. I should have stayed away, I should have kept him safe....from me. Someone's hands begin to shake me roughly.

"Raine, get it together girl. What the hell is wrong with you?"

"I did it. I did it. Jack. Jack."

Lila looks down at me with little more than morbid curiosity.

"Okay, you did it and you did it to Jack. Wasn't that the plan? Were you not supposed to dispose of the knights? It is their fault they couldn't get their shit together not yours."

She lifts me to my feet and wipes my face with the back of her hand. I can see she is getting frustrated with me. I am acting like a hysterical chick not a being of the colors, a being of power and strength. I really don't care at this moment, I want to be just a girl for a minute and mourn the boy I love.

"Lila, I need a second. I am not like you and the others I have feelings. Real feelings."

She releases me and takes a step back. She looks to the ground and then back to me.

"Raine, I am not like the others either. Before I became one of you all I felt was chaos and want and power but now it's different. I have moments of weakness; times when I think I really am becoming someone else. Like you for example. It's strange but I feel the need to be here for you, to help you. I think I care for you and it's starting to get quite annoying."

I stare at her. Lila... this creature full of hate and violence. Is she telling the truth? Does she really understand me? My home does not. They have no idea what it is to have a true human emotion. To be totally connected to someone else, to need and want someone by your side. We are independent creatures, built to help and nurture and destroy when needed. I wish I knew why I am so different. That is the question isn't it. Why?

"Lila, I care for you too. And thank you for coming to help me. I know you don't like it here."

"Whatever. Can we go now? I would like to return home."

What am I to do now? I know I am not allowed to go back yet. The job is not done. The rest of the knights are still in the light and need to be dealt with and in truth, I don't want to go back. My home has betrayed me, they let me get into this situation and feel this pain. I will never again want to be one of them.

"I will not be returning Lila. There is no place for me there."

"So you are going to stay here and mourn Jack? You are one of the most powerful beings that have ever existed and you are going to turn your back on that?"

"Yes."

Is all I can say. I sit back on the ground and close my eyes. I see him in my mind. He is smiling at me, this is where I want to be. Everyone else can get lost. I hear Lila let out a big sigh and feel her leave. She is quite a peculiar creature. I continue in my day dream when I feel someone staring down at me. I instantly feel my power come to the surface and open my eyes. Aaron is looking down at me with big vacant eyes.

"Raine? What is going on? Where are Charles and Jack?"

I jump to my feet and search the grounds for the others. There is no one. I stare at my one time friend. He looks different. His light is not cloudy any longer. The pureness he once possessed is back, but is it real?

"Aaron, are you alright? Why are you here?"

"I am fine. And I have no idea what I am doing here. I felt someone was in the field and I was hoping it was Jack. Where is he?"

"Do you remember everything that happened?"

I am still a little cautious. I can see he is back but don't trust that this is not some sort of trick. I keep my distance just in case.

"I remember speaking to you and Jack and going back into the light to find Charles. The next thing I remember is standing in the great hall with all the others and having no idea why. Do you know what's going on? Did we all get infected? Is that why none of us remember anything?"

I don't realize it but I haven't exhaled since the explosion. I let it out finally. Is it really over? I don't have to destroy the rest of the knights. I am so very relieved but so unbelievably heartbroken. I run to Aaron and throw my arms around him.

Tears stream down my face. It feels so good to be in someone's arms, they aren't his but at least they are strong and feel safe. I am a blubbering mess.

"He's gone....he's gone. I'm so sorry."

He holds me tight against him and gently rocks me in his arms. I don't think he understands anything I am saying. If he did he would be screaming at me or punching me not soothing me.

"Raine we should go. The others will be here soon and I don't think you want an audience right now."

I shake my head violently. I am not leaving. I need to stay here. This is where it happened.

"No Aaron, I won't leave. I can't."

I push away from him and run into the middle of the field. I look back at him and point to the ground. I guess I figure he should be able to read my mind or something. I look into his eyes pleading for understanding. I can't say the words. Aaron walks slowly to my side and surveys the scene. He looks out in both directions and then back at me. I am gasping for air in between my sobs. Realization seems to hit him. He takes a step back.

"Jack? Jack was here wasn't he? Did you do this?"

I look into his eyes and whisper the words, the ones I don't want to say.

"Yes, he's dead."

Aaron walks over to my side and grabs my hand. This is not the reaction I expected. I am confused.

"I just told you I killed your best friend, what's your problem? Get pissed at me! Hit me, do something!"

I push him back but he just comes at me and hugs me again. What is his deal?

"Raine, stop! Listen to me. He isn't dead. Do you hear me? Jack isn't dead!"

I do as he asks and stop. If this is a trick just to get me to calm down I am going to be more than a little ticked. I know he is wrong though. There is no way Jack survived.

"Why would you say that? You weren't here. You have no idea what happened."

"I would know if Jack wasn't here anymore. The knights are connected you know that and I can still feel his presence. His light is still burning."

"Are you sure? Are you sure it's him?"

"Yes Raine. I am sure."

I won't let myself feel hope. Not until I know.

"Where is he Aaron?"

He looks around and then closes his eyes. He is taking too long.

"Raine I don't know where he is. I think he is close. Can't you call him here, to you?"

I forgot. I have that ability and if Aaron isn't infected anymore then neither is Jack. I can call Jack to me, but what if he is gone. Will I be calling a lifeless body; do I want to see him like that? The answer is simple, yes. I need to know what happened to him regardless of what happens next.

I concentrate on Jack and almost immediately light begins to shimmer in front of me and in the middle of it is a shape. I rub the tears from my eyes but am unable to move. Aaron runs to Jack's side and picks him up. I am still unmoving. Aaron is blocking my view of Jack but I can see movement and then I hear him moan.

"He is alive. Raine, do you hear me? He is alright!"

With those words I decide it is time for me, the powerful and immortal being I am, to pass out.

Chapter 20

I feel like I have been hit by a semi. And not just once, it must have ran me over a few times. My head is pounding and every muscle in my body is limp. I focus again and see I am not in the woods anymore. Aaron is yelling in my face and holding me like a baby.

"Aaron, shut up please. I have a bit of a headache."

My buddy looks down at me and laughs. I feel as if I haven't seen him in a long time and much has happened but it was just a few minutes ago we were standing in my house and he was trying to tear Raine into pieces. That's right he is infected. I push him away and roll onto the ground.

"Get the hell off of me!"

He looks at me with surprise.

"Jack it's me, what are you doing?"

I look past him and realize I am in the training field, why am I here? I see a body a few feet away, a small body with short dark hair.....my mind explodes.

"Aaron, what have you done?"

I sloppily get to my feet and make my way to her side. Aaron is telling me something but I don't hear him. I grab her arm and pull her over yelling at her to wake. To my surprise she begins to open her eyes. She doesn't really look hurt at all. Aaron crouches by my side.

"Jack she's fine, she just fainted when she saw you were alright. You need to calm down buddy."

Raine's eyes open and she looks up at me and smiles, then goes frigid in my arms.

"Jack are you okay? Are you back?"

Everyone is acting so strange.

"Yeah I'm fine, can you please tell me what is happening?"

"You don't remember anything either?"

I look at Aaron and he shrugs his shoulders as if to say he is as clueless as me. Raine sits up and takes a moment before speaking.

"Okay guys, this is it in a nut shell. You both were infected and became obsessed with ruling the world and having everyone worship you and pretty much lost your minds. Jack, you wanted to kill Charles so you could be the boss of everyone and that's when you ended up here. You and Charles were about to kill each other and I stepped in and took the brunt of the hit. I guess I kind of shot you both out into the woods and I thought I had killed you, which is what I was supposed to do if I couldn't save you and make you the leader you were always meant to be. Then Aaron came and I saw that he is no longer infected and he told me you weren't dead and I called you here and then I guess I fainted."

She smiles at me softly and waits for a reply. Okay that's a lot to take in. I look to Aaron who still seems very lost. I guess the disease leaves you kind of blank after it is out of your system. Aaron has lost weeks, I wonder how much time I have lost? Raine gets to her feet and paces back and forth.

"What is it Raine?"

"I need to find Charles. I am going to call him here."

Raine closes her eyes and immediately Charles is in front of us. He is not moving. Aaron goes to check on our eader. A few seconds later he turns to us and slowly shakes his head. Charles didn't make it. I look to Raine but she is walking away. I decide to give her some space. Aaron comes over to me.

"Jack he needs to go into the light. He must be given the proper farewell."

"You are right, can you take him?"

"Yeah, make sure she is okay. She needs to know this isn't her fault."

Aaron is a good friend to both me and Raine. I shake his hand and he leaves with Charles' body. I wait patiently until Raine decides to come back.

"You okay?"

She looks at me and fakes a small smile.

"No."

I gently lift her hand and place it over my heart.

"It isn't your fault he is dead. You did what you needed to do."

"I know."

She is acting weird, something more is going on.

"Jack you remember what I said to you before Charles took you away? That you are the leader and you are the only one that can keep the balance needed?"

"Yes."

"Well I think now that is possible. I was listening before, listening to my home and they said it is done, the world is free of the infection. You can lead them and protect the human world and I know you will be great."

She looks so very sad. I do not understand why. If it is done and her mission was to protect me until I became leader, she has succeeded.

"Raine, what are you not saying?"

"Nothing you need to worry about. You have much to do, you need to go to your people and explain what happened to them. They must all be very confused."

"Stop it. Don't lie to me, not after everything we have been through."

She lets out a little giggle and moves in and places her arms around my waist.

"Jack don't be so dramatic. It's just work stuff, nothing you need to worry about. Really."

"Work stuff eh? Why don't I believe you?"

"Because you are paranoid. Now you go and do your job and I will go and do mine."

I feel the paranoia begin to spread.

"You are going back? Back up there? You can't!"

"I don't have a choice. I either go on my own or they take me and then I am afraid they will erase my memory again. I can't handle that, not again."

I hold her tight to me and calmly as I can, speak softly to her.

"I just got you back, tell them to let you come back to me, tell them you are loved and needed here."

The world is calm and peaceful at this moment. She looks up at me and the silence is comforting. As long as she doesn't say it, she is still here. As long as the words are not spoken, we are as we used to be... just a boy and a girl who fell in love and want to be together.

"I know you don't remember what happened the past few days and I am grateful for that. I want you to remember only this..."

She leans into me and presses her body to mine. We embrace and press our lips together; this is the deepest and most passionate kiss I think has ever occurred. It is not like the last time when she did not remember this is her, my Raine. There is so much wrapped up in this one moment, need and want, love and friendship. And sadness lots of sadness and doubt. I don't know if this is our last moment together or the start of the rest of our lives. I cannot put into words what needs to be said, what she needs to remember of me, then it comes to me.

"I hope this means something to you Raine, I loved you. From past lifetimes to this one I loved you. I will never stop loving you no matter what happens next. Nothing will ever change that.
Thank you for letting me love you Raine."

She pauses but a moment and touches my face and then she is gone. I am in the field alone, the new leader of the knights and protector of the human world. I look up into the sky and silently tell the universe that I will fulfill my duties and be the leader the world needs. I will do everything in my power to live up to what is expected of me with just one demand on my part.

Send her back to me.

Chapter 21

That was the most difficult thing I have ever done in my many lives. I left him standing there never knowing if we will be together again. I know why they want me back where I belong. Jack needs no distractions now. He is the leader of the knights of the light realm and must focus all his attention on getting them back on track and focused on their roll in all of this. I did my job.

As I ascend into my colors a feeling of absolute tranquility takes over. I feel light and at complete peace. I am greeted and enveloped by my sisters. They are all here waiting to greet me home. I search for one face in particular. She is standing at the back looking completely out of place. I glide over to her and gently and cautiously embrace my new friend. She stands motionless and waits for me to release her.

"Thank you Lila. You were such a help to me."

She lets out a small uncertain smile.

"Are you okay?"

I answer her as honestly as I can.

"Yes. I will miss him greatly and I pray one day they will let me go back and be with him, but I also understand. He is meant for greatness and I would never want to keep him from that. I know in the past I did, I kept him for myself and that was selfish of me. Jack is where he should be and I am where I belong. It hurts but I know it is right."

Lila touches my shoulder and gives it a little squeeze; and as she walks into the middle of our family and the colors that surround us, I think back on how everything has changed.

I once thought I was a crazy person bound for a mental hospital surrounded by strangers and feeling so totally alone. Now I am more loved and accepted than I could have ever imagined. I am not like the others in this place, I have felt true human emotion and would not change that for anything. I will see him again one day and when that happens it will be probably one of the most glorious days of my long eternal life.
I laugh silently to myself...

I did turn out to be a pretty great super hero after all.

Made in the USA
Charleston, SC
03 November 2011